DAY OF SALVATION

BY

PAT SIMMONS

Developmental Editor: Chandra Sparks Splond
Proofreader: Judicious Revisions LLC
Interior Design: Kimolisa/Fiverr.com
Cover Design: @designerqueen3/Fiverr.com

Praise for Pat Simmons

OMGreatness…5 Stars for Day Not Promised

My, my, my, my and MY!!! This book was so intense and emotional that I found myself interacting with the story as I read it. Pat Simmons' "Day Not Promise" had me praying, crying, speaking in tongues, lifting my hands, and rejoicing. You cannot read this novel without thinking about your salvation and those that The LORD has put in your pathways. –Reader Viv

Inspirational faith-filled demon slaying… 5 Stars for Day Not Promised

Whew, this was so inspiring with scriptures on fighting the enemy who comes to kill and destroy. But with praying intercessors, faith, and believing in God's will, anything can happen in His time. I loved how, one by one, the crew was saved. There was some tragedy, but God showed up with his angels on guard to prevent Satan's schemes. I want to be so in tune with God that I can see the enemy of darkness and be able to call on the name of Jesus to send in his army. Glory. Can't wait to read the next book. Omega and Mitchell are the Holy Ghost power couple. He truly was her hero. —Sheryl, Michigan

Timely and Sobering… 5 Stars for the Day She Prayed

Day She Prayed captures the sense of urgency we all need as Believers. It's twofold: first to work out our own salvation with fear and trembling and then to win lost souls to Christ. I was moved to feel sadness, hope, laughter, joy, tears, and gladness as

I read the book. Randall and Tally's story was so real, and just like the two of them, I feel complete after finishing. — Cameisha Barnes.

Awesome and Powerful Read… 5 Stars for Day She Prayed

I am such a fan of Pat Simmons. Her writings have truly blessed me over the years. This series has really ignited my prayer life. – Reader

Unputdownable End-Times Thriller!…5 Stars for Days Are Coming

Days Are Coming is an end-times Christian thriller. It's book three in Simmons' The Intercessors series, but it works perfectly as a standalone. I was on the edge of my seat the whole way through the book!

In a dimension beyond normal people's sight, there are demons influencing people, and there are angels fighting on behalf of God's people. Also, there are gifted people who can SEE this spiritual war and know how to intercede with prayer on behalf of the vulnerable. –Priscilla Bettis

Real Eye Opener…5 Stars for Days Are Coming

This was my book of the month for my book club. The best of the series. This book really opened my eyes. This book is powerful, and it tells you that God will is going to be done no matter what. Pat Black Pearls loves you, keep letting God you. Your books are inspiring! –Mz. Riley

DAY OF SALVATION

Chapter One

Then saith he unto his disciples, The harvest truly is plenteous,
but the laborers are few; Pray ye therefore the Lord of
the harvest, that he will send forth laborers into his harvest.
—Matthew 9:37–38

It wasn't a glamorous job, but somebody had to do it. Katherine Kincaid, one of Christ For All Church's mothers, had just concluded her morning conference call with other prayer warriors. Their sole purpose was to intercept Satan's plans to kill God's chosen, steal a person's joy, and destroy the gifts the Lord had given them.

The older woman with glossy silver hair could rival a hair color technician any day. A widow for more than ten years, she had suffered the death of her only adult child years before her husband had died. Left alone, she turned her attention to God's work as the widows did in the Bible, but in overdrive.

She closed her eyes and smothered her worn Bible to her chest. This was her lifeline. It was another day in the spiritual realm to rescue people's souls from eternal damnation. Satan's demons were well-equipped warriors who specialized in witchcraft—mental deception to take their opponents down without them knowing what happened. Depending on the situation, demons could be fierce or as subtle as a whisper to control minds and behaviors. Mother Kincaid sighed at the task.

I will not lose one soul predestined for salvation. You and the prayer warriors must bring these souls into the fold, and then the trumpet will announce my appearance, God whispered.

Jesus was coming. One scripture came to Mother Kincaid's mind: Romans 13:11— *knowing the time, that now it is high time to awake out of sleep: for now is our salvation nearer than when we believed.*

"Yes!" She couldn't grin any wider as the Lord's voice whirled by her ear with speed faster than a baseball pitcher's ninety-five-mile-per-hour fastball.

Grayson Tate and his wife

Hudson Lane

Sophia Doyle

Wyatt Sheppard

Olivia Baker

Joi Clark

Especially Amethyst Johnson

With urgency, Mother Kincaid scribbled the names, then frowned as she memorized them. "Lord, who are these souls? Where do they live? How can I find them?"

They aren't hidden, but in plain sight, God whispered. *Remember, Amethyst Johnson must be rescued.*

Mother Kincaid stood from her knees and padded across the room to glance out her bedroom window. Her heart was heavy with this assignment. "God, I need help on this."

The sun had peeped over the horizon about half an hour ago. Although her quiet St. Louis neighborhood seemed peaceful, surreal, and safe for school children to be at the bus stop at six-thirty, she didn't trust what only her eyes could see. "Show me what to pray for," she whispered and blinked. The spiritual realm became the backdrop. Three gigantic angels stood as soldiers around the children as dark beast-shaped animals seemed poised to attack but wouldn't. Not as long as God's angels kept watch.

She turned around and studied the list. God had given her names but nothing else—no ages, races, or locations.

"I might be seventy-five, but I've got internet skills." She grunted, hurried to her desk, and logged on to various social media platforms. After an hour of searching, Mother Kincaid took a break. The names were more common than she thought. This wasn't going to be easy.

She needed to call on a group of Biblically fierce intercessors for battle: Omega and Mitchell Franklin, Tally and Randall Addams, and Minister Jude Morgan and his young son Carlton. They were the superheroes in the spiritual realm. Through great faith, those intercessors knew how to break through enemy territory with the help of the Lord's army to rescue the lost and wounded.

But the minister was soon to be married. Wouldn't he opt out of fasting and praying during his honeymoon? And sisters-in-law Omega and Tally were both in the final trimester of their pregnancies, and both mommies-to-be glowed with happiness.

You don't have a say in who to pick and choose. The intercessors have been chosen for such a time as this, God thundered. *Time is not on your side.*

Chapter Two

*But sanctify the Lord God in your hearts: and be ready
always to give an answer to every man that asks you
a reason for the hope that is in you with meekness
and fear. —1 Peter 3:15*

Porsha Gilbert left the ladies' room at Christ For All Church. She immediately noticed a woman whose attire didn't seem dressed for a wedding despite the artistically ripped jeans and a tie-dye off-the-shoulder top.

Under further scrutiny, the visitor had the pretty face to rock the long braided ponytail. They appeared to be about the same age—in their thirties. She might have been a woman after Porsha's heart because she was drawn to tie-dye garments, but not today. Not now. Porsha would admire the woman's fashion statement later.

Porsha, whose career path had led her to become a traveling auditor, dared not miss the most anticipated wedding at her church. The bride, Sinclaire Oliver, was a single mother of three. God had empowered her oldest son, eleven-year-old Carlton, with a special spiritual gift as an intercessor like Porsha's sister, Tally.

Minister Jude Morgan, the groom, loved his readymade family dearly.

Their love story gave every woman hope that God had someone special for them. The ceremony was about to begin, and Porsha had to return to her seat near the front.

The woman's embarrassment made her pivot on her heels to leave after she noticed tulle and flowers delicately draped over the door frames like a window valance.

Although this was a dressy affair, Porsha didn't want the visitor to feel she wasn't welcome in God's house. *Who am I to judge someone's wardrobe?*

"Sorry. I'm at the wrong place," she said, rubbing her jeans. "I didn't mean to be a wedding crasher."

"Nonsense." Porsha smiled. God had sent her there for a reason, even if she wasn't on the wedding guest list. "People don't come to church by accident. I'm Porsha Gilbert, a member here, and you're just in time to see a wedding. We can sit in the back row and watch together." There went Porsha's opportunity for a close-up of the ceremony, but she would miss it all if she couldn't convince the woman to join her inside.

Porsha had glimpsed the processional as she ran to the restroom to remove hair from one eye before she ruined her makeup. Long lashes were beautiful but annoying and not friendly to stray hairs.

Her pregnant sister was part of the wedding party and glowed in the gown with her baby bump.

"Okay," she said, her shoulders slumping. "I'm Amethyst Johnson. Before you ask, yes, it's my February birthstone, so my Zodiac sign is Aquarius."

"Oh." Porsha lifted her brows in surprise. "I wasn't going to ask you any of that. Your name's unique, like mine. Come on."

Amethyst scanned her attire. "You're dressed up, and I feel out of place."

"We all feel out of place in this world—until we come to Christ." She took liberty by grabbing Amethyst's hand, and with a gentle tug, she opened the door to the sanctuary. Porsha allowed Amethyst to scoot into the back-row pew away from the crowd, and Porsha joined her, then spoke in a hushed tone, "See that bride and groom?"

Amethyst stared at the overhead screen with Porsha, who had left her purse and program in the front.

"She's beautiful, and the groom is very handsome." Was that awe in her voice or whimsical hope?

"Yep. I agree." Porsha folded her arms and nodded. "Sister Sinclaire Oliver is about to become Mrs. Jude Morgan. She came here scarred from life's hardships as a single mother of three."

"Three kids?" Amethyst mouthed. She sat quietly, then suddenly said, "My life is so over."

Huh? What an odd statement. Porsha placed a soft hand over Amethyst's as she stood to leave.

Weddings could be sad if you'd never been a bride. "Our lives are just beginning. I'm thirty-five. We're probably around the same age," she guessed since the woman didn't confirm.

"*Hmmph.*" Amethyst didn't look convinced. "Are you married?"

"No, but I believe God's timing is perfect…" Porsha focused on the couple at the altar, hoping Amethyst would do the same.

Before their words could be spoken, the bride and groom's expressions told their story.

Jude's voice was strong and confident. "Sinclaire Rene Oliver, I love you. You are the perfect woman for me and the mother of our children." He brought their enjoined hands to his chest and exhaled. "I take you to be my lawfully wedded wife, to have and to hold from this day forward, for better, for worse, for richer, for poorer, in sickness and in health, to love and to cherish, till death do us part, according to God's holy ordinance, and I pledge you my love, faithfulness, and protection."

Amethyst sniffed as a tear rolled down her cheek. Porsha handed her a tissue. Yeah, she was choked up too.

"Thanks."

"Breathe." The microphone picked up Tally instructing Sinclaire.

"Whew." The bride inhaled and released. "Jude, thank you for loving my children as much as I do. You have shown me what a real man of God looks like."

"Yes," Porsha whispered to herself.

"Thank you for choosing me. I, Sinclaire, take you, Jude, to be my lawfully wedded husband, to have and to hold from this day forward, for better, for worse, for richer, for poorer, in sickness and in health, to love and to cherish, till death do us part, according to God's holy ordinance, I pledge my faithfulness."

Now, it was Porsha who sniffed. She wished she was closer, but Amethyst came to church for a reason, whether she knew it or not, and Porsha couldn't leave her.

The pastor smiled. "By the power invested in me by God and the State of Missouri, I now pronounce you husband and wife. What God has joined together, let no man or woman come between you, in the name of our Lord, Jesus Christ. Brother Jude, you may now salute your wife."

Porsha's eyes teared as the groom delivered a sweet kiss, and then the two hugged as if the other was their lifeline. The gesture was endearing.

"Well, I guess I'd better go. I've been an interloper long enough."

"So soon?" Porsha mimicked a pout as applause roared throughout the sanctuary. "You sure you don't want to stay, at least for the cake? You don't have to go to the reception. You can join me on the church back patio area." She grinned. "After the vows, it's all about tasting the wedding cake for me."

"Nah. I want to sneak out before I'm noticed." She stood and seemed more uncomfortable than when she first entered the building.

Reluctantly, Porsha got to her feet. She couldn't hold the woman hostage any longer, so she escorted her out a side door. Outside, the first Saturday in May brought brilliant sunshine after a rainy week. It spotlighted Amethyst's hazel eyes, like Porsha's, but they seemed dark and empty as if a part of her was trapped in their depths.

"Maybe we can exchange numbers and stay in contact," Porsha said.

Amethyst stepped back, shaking her head as if something startled her, but it was just the two of them.

"You're welcome to come back and visit anytime. Ask for me, and I'll sit with you."

Amethyst didn't respond to Porsha's offer as she waved and walked across the parking lot. Porsha ached for the visitor. Something was going on with that woman for sure. Amethyst was hurting, and she needed Jesus but didn't know it.

Once the guest disappeared from view, Porsha hurried back into the sanctuary. The wedding party posed for pictures. Sinclaire and Minister Morgan appeared so happy, so did the young children.

Sinclaire's daughter, Claire, nicknamed "Sissy," was dressed in layers of taffeta and tulle. Jude carried her in one arm while keeping his hand linked with his new wife. Carlton stood at his mother's side, holding his baby brother's hand. Mother Kincaid said Minister Morgan hadn't blinked at the stereotype of accepting a readymade family. He welcomed it.

Porsha would not be disheartened because she had no prospects for a husband. God would send him, as He did for her sister Tally and Tally's sister-in-law Omega at the gas pump, of all places. She chuckled. That had been the beginning of the next generation of intercessors.

Once in the reception hall, Porsha waited her turn to congratulate the couple before they took their seats at the head table. She kissed her brother-in-law, Randall, who considered himself her big brother and, therefore, her protector, then rubbed Tally's bump. The couple beamed with happiness after losing their first baby.

"Where were you?" Tally whispered. "I saw some good-looking men in the audience."

"I'll tell you later," Porsha replied in a hushed tone.

The celebration was festive. Toasts were made after the delicious meal, and then the first dance was breathtaking. Mr. and Mrs. Morgan walked around the room, thanking guests for their presence before they cut the cake. Porsha was the first in line for dessert. She smiled and indulged in the white cake with a creamy filling.

Since the handsome men there seemed to have a plus-one, there was no reason for her to stay and socialize to be seen, especially when she had to return to Philly on Monday to finish her client audit at Foster and Craig Transportation.

Soon, Porsha walked to the head table to say goodbye to her family and the bride and groom.

"Hey," Tally stopped her, "when you weren't in your seat, I looked around and noticed you were in the back. Why?"

"Sis, you have the eyes of an eagle."

"You know it. Who was she?"

"*Hmmm.*" Porsha tilted her head and strained her brain to remember the woman's name. "Amethyst...I think her last name is Johnson."

Silverware clunked to China, and three pairs of eyes stared at her, including the bride and groom. Jude frowned. "What did you say her name was?"

"Amethyst. I believe God sent her here." While Porsha recalled the woman's demeanor, Randall, her brother-in-law, leaned forward. "She's on the list."

"What list?" Porsha squeezed her lips together in confusion.

"The intercessors' rescue list." Tally then explained what God had told Mother Kincaid after a morning prayer. "That woman, especially, is on high alert."

Randall pulled out his phone, and Porsha read the text as he called out the names: "So are Hudson Lane, Grayson Tate, Wyatt Sheppard, Olivia Baker, Sophia Doyle, and Joi Clark."

"Sinclaire and I fasted yesterday for them." Jude squeezed his wife's hand.

"What makes these people so special?" Porsha pinched icing from the sculptured rose off Tally's cake.

"The Lord's rounding up His chosen sheep before His return," Jude said.

Porsha's heart pumped with excitement. With all the craziness going on in this world, she was ready for Jesus to rescue her out of here.

"Randall started fasting when we got the text yesterday while I began to pray since I have to eat for two," Tally said as Randall leaned over and lovingly rubbed her stomach. "I thought we would have to go hunt these people down, but God put her in our path." Tally shook her head in disbelief. "And she just walked into the church? Did you get her number?"

"Nope. I offered mine, but she wasn't interested." Now, Porsha's heart shifted with sadness. Winning souls for Christ was the number one priority in Christian living. "Hopefully, she'll come back. Amethyst looked like she was at the end of her ropes. The wedding made her sadder."

"If she doesn't come back, we have to find her. At least we know what she looks like."

"Sorry, I dropped the ball. I didn't know. I'm glad I'm not an intercessor. It's too much pressure with that gift," she said, walking away.

I wish that all men would intercede on behalf of their brother or sister, God thundered. *What if this were your soul?*

Chapter Three

The Spirit of the Lord GOD is upon me; because the LORD hath anointed me to preach good tidings unto the meek; he hath sent me to bind up the brokenhearted, to proclaim liberty to the captives, and the opening of the prison to them that are bound. —Isaiah 61:1

Amethyst Johnson's first thought when she entered a church of all places was *Why am I here?*

This morning, she had no agenda, maybe window shopping because she couldn't afford anything or stroll through a park to which she had never been—any place where there were people so she wouldn't feel alone in this big world. She needed to mask the chaos going on in her life.

The church was not on her radar and out of her character. God had not come to her rescue during her heartache, so why should she give up her Sundays for Jesus?

Yet, when she opened the double glass doors, a rose floral scent invited her inside to relax and refresh. The aroma from the fresh flower arrangement near the closed doors lured her inside. Her first thought was a funeral, but then she realized it was a wedding. Amethyst was dressed for neither. She begged her body to leave before she was spotted. Too late.

Porsha Gilbert's inviting smile coaxed her to stay. The woman was pretty, with flawless skin and hazel eyes like hers, a refreshing aura. Porsha had strutted in heels and a flirty dress as if she hadn't a care in the world. Her friendliness sent a hidden message to Amethyst's brain to stay and indulge in the relaxation she sensed.

But it was a wedding. Didn't the couple know that a happy ending wasn't a guarantee? The vows exchanged taunted Amethyst, reminding her that things weren't alright in her world: no husband, no children, no home—forced to live with her mother again—and soon to have no transportation if she couldn't come up with the money to pay her sales tax to get license plates.

Only in Missouri were car buyers subject to this ritual.

The applause snapped her mind from drifting as the ceremony ended. A tug-of-war battled for her to leave or accept Porsha's invitation to stay for cake. The warning to leave and not come back won out despite Porsha's no-judgment-zone vibes.

Amethyst guessed they were about the same age—thirty-two—and Porsha seemed hopeful they could become friends. Amethyst didn't want to be contacted.

Church was not her thing.

I beckoned for you to come, God's voice whispered in a breeze.

Nope. She didn't believe it. Today's horoscope advised her to be weary of new people entering her life. Amethyst had to be on guard as a coat of sadness overpowered the peace she had felt inside. When thoughts of despair flooded her mind, she relaxed with her amethyst and other colorful beads to meditate. Lately, that and nothing else had been working.

She was having a bad day—no, a terrible life. The short stay in the church hadn't changed anything. Her life was crumbling. She wanted out of this world by any means necessary. Amethyst didn't care if it was by a gun, knife, overdose, hit-and-run, or suicide by police.

Life was hard. Death couldn't be any worse. Amethyst's mother wasn't on her side regarding her platonic relationship with Reggie. He seemed to be the one person who cared about her. He was her lifeline.

Mother Kincaid smiled throughout Sinclaire and Minister Morgan's wedding. Sister Lynne's heartfelt rendition of Etta James' "At Last" brought tears to the couple's eyes before they exchanged their vows.

"That wedding left this old widow breathless," she mumbled as she recalled memories of her first love, Herbert, who died too soon, in her opinion, but cancer was a terrible disease for him to suffer. She patted her chest as she entered her house and kicked off the pumps she only wore on special occasions.

Then, Mother Kincaid grew concerned and grimaced. "Amethyst Johnson had been at our church," she said in disbelief. She could have collapsed under her 170-pound weight when she was told that. Why hadn't the intercessors' spiritual antennas sounded the alarms to alert them?

Amethyst had crept inside during the ceremony, and Porsha had been clueless that Amethyst Johnson was on the Lord's most-wanted list.

God entrusted Mother Kincaid with souls' salvation.

Porsha had described Amethyst as pretty and young, but her eyes revealed unrest. The Lord brought a Scripture to her mind. As soon as she slipped into her house shoes and housedress, she reached for her Bible on the chair beside her bed. "Lord, open my eyes to understand the Scriptures You are giving me."

After taking a deep breath, she flipped through the pages until she found Isaiah sixty and began reading…

Arise, shine; for thy light is come, and the glory of the LORD is risen upon thee.

For, behold, the darkness shall cover the earth, and gross darkness the people: but the LORD shall arise upon thee, and his glory shall be seen upon thee.

And the Gentiles shall come to thy light, and kings to the brightness of thy rising.

Lift thine eyes round about, and see: all they gather together, they come to thee: thy sons shall come from far, and thy daughters shall be nursed at thy side.

She paused to meditate. The Book of Isaiah predicted Jesus' coming, and the Jews' return to Jerusalem, so Mother Kincaid strained her mind to understand.

Suddenly, she seemed to be sitting in the heavens with the Lord, looking down on earth. A dark mist surrounded it.

The earth was dead.

Not yet, God said. *Look.*

Pin-size lights flashed through the darkness until tiny slivers seemed to glow like ambers through ashes.

A few multiplied before her eyes. "What does this mean, Lord?"

You are the light of the world? A city set on a hill can not be hidden.

Matthew 5:14. Mother Kincaid had read that Scripture many times, but to see this imagery empowered her soul.

These lights are my disciples filled with My Spirit who are working in the field, searching the highways and houses, looking to rescue souls for My purposes. I'm opening your spiritual eyes because the battle is about to get intense, and you need to remember that your weapons aren't carnal but mighty through Me to the pulling down of strongholds.

It was time for Mother Kincaid to speak with the pastor about a special prayer shut-in service.

Chapter Four

And he said unto them, Go ye into all the world,
and preach the gospel to every creature. —Mark 16:15

Amethyst survived the weekend. Last Friday, she learned she would not receive the promotion for the occupational health and safety specialist position at Silo Manufacturing and Supplies. She'd purchased her car because she was in the running for the promotion and had planned to move into her own apartment with the bump in salary.

Her hopes and dreams had been shattered.

Despite that, she didn't entertain any more thoughts of self-harm or show up inside a church again.

Monday's horoscope read: *You will receive good news today.* Amethyst grinned. "Yes!" What a good way to start her work week.

Maybe the good news was her boss had reversed his wrong decision and promoted Amethyst—the more qualified candidate. She grinned, hoping that was the case. Her career was all she had to show she was successful in life.

"Why are you smiling?" her mother, Annabelle Johnson, asked, walking into Amethyst's bedroom. She hadn't planned to be her mother's roommate, but life had happened, and circumstances had changed. After a toxic three-year relationship, Amethyst had been forced to move on six months ago. Their breakup had been ugly, nasty, and irrevocable.

Life had not been kind to her. Meditation and positive thinking therapy were pulling her out of her depression.

"Because it's going to be a good day!"

"*Humph*." Annabelle eyed her attire. They were about the same height—five-five or five-six—with the same medium frame and brown skin tone. They could wear each other's clothes if they did that. Their age difference was twenty years, but they could pass as sisters. Annabelle had chopped off her long pigtails when she was old enough to leave home. Amethyst refused to cut her long braid, which some often thought was a purchased attachment.

"You look cute. Do you have plans after work again?"

Amethyst shrugged. Lately, she hadn't been coming straight home, opting to sit in a coffee shop alone and examine her shambled life—mentally, personally, and professionally. She was making good money, but not enough to repay her debt and be on her own again.

"Okay, but I would suggest you stay away from Reggie Hart. I feel he's bad news, and you don't need more drama." Annabelle didn't mince words with her only daughter. "You aren't living up to your Zodiac sign. You were born to be clever, confident, and assertive." She left the room shaking her head. Her mother's marriage was short-lived, so Annabelle knew about bad relationships.

Was anybody or anything on her side? The feeling of being unloved haunted her as she finished her makeup and headed out the door.

Amethyst didn't want to dwell on what wasn't going right in her life. After all, she would get good news today.

She arrived in the Central West End's Cortex District twenty minutes later. As she approached her building, a street vendor with a microphone had garnered some attention. Amethyst planned to walk past when something he said got her attention.

"I have good news for you today," the young man said, drawing Amethyst closer. Her heart pounded. The good news the stars promised. She was ready for it.

"Jesus died on the cross for you and me. That's good news…our slate was clean with the shedding of His blood. How many of us would love a clean slate in life?"

Trying not to hear but listening anyway, she lifted her hand only so much as not to admit she needed to hear this but again didn't want to.

Amethyst imploded, then grunted. That was not the good news she was looking for.

The man continued, "When Jesus was nailed to the cross, He claimed victory on all our sins, diseases, illnesses, and Satan. My question is, why take what's not good for you off the cross and suffer?"

Amethyst stepped back and turned to cross the street. How could Jesus have good news when there was so much bad news in the world and her life?

She kept walking. There had to be more.

By the end of the week, Porsha hadn't shaken the disappointment that Amethyst had slipped through her fingers. Porsha had returned to Cincinnati to finish an audit with a longstanding client who specially requested her for their annual audits.

"It's a shame we won't see you next year," the older gentleman said.

It was a bittersweet moment. Porsha liked the company owner and her job as a traveling CPA to conduct audits.

"My sister is having a baby, and I want to be closer to spoil my niece. I'm looking forward to babysitting duty."

Mr. Foster chuckled. "You won't if you're trying to sleep. I have five grandchildren."

Porsha said her final goodbye, and her driver appeared to take her to the airport. An hour later, Porsha boarded the plane home to St. Louis. For the past six years, she had enjoyed the freedom to roam the country, accepting audit assignments at major companies—the thrill of exploring new cities, the higher pay, and the hope of meeting someone special.

The last part was a bust, and it hadn't happened at her home church. *Lord, where is a love of my own?*

God didn't answer, but she didn't doubt that He had heard her and knew the desires of her heart.

Once she was strapped into the seat, she glanced out the window. Amethyst Johnson's face flashed before her. What was her story? Why was she on God's list?

Porsha's plane landed two hours later, and she headed to the baggage claim area. She nodded and waved at familiar airport employees, many of them TSA, whom she had come to know during her constant travels.

"Hey, pretty lady. Welcome back." The tall, dark, handsome man with a flattering mustache smiled as they passed. He wore a blue uniform, so he was an airport employee. "How was your trip this time?"

She blinked that strangers knew her travel itinerary, but she recovered with a smile. "It was good, but my last one." She grinned.

"Oh?" He raised a brow.

"Yep. I accepted a permanent job here, so the airport will only see me for leisure travel."

"That's a shame. You brighten my day every time you strut through here. His smile was brilliant.

"Really?" She welcomed his flirtation. He didn't say *walk* but *strut*, which meant he noticed her. "I've never seen you before."

"But I've seen you. Do you mind some company as you go to baggage claim?"

"*Ah*, no. But I'm making a pit stop to the ladies' room."

"I'll wait." He slipped his hands in his pockets and leaned against the wall as if he were her traveling companion.

Why did she feel giddy because a handsome man waited for her outside a women's restroom? Men flirted with her from time to time, but it was something about this man that made her want to give him the time of day.

She handled her business and reappeared. His smile welcomed her.

"I'm Grayson...Grayson Tate, by the way." He extended his hand for a shake, and it was strong.

"Nice to meet you. I'm Porsha Gilbert."

"Maybe I can buy you coffee as a parting gift."

Porsha glanced at his ring finger—no ring or trace of one—before she agreed. "I wouldn't want to take you away from your work."

"I'm off."

With her luggage by her side, they found a spot at a coffee cafe next to the check-in line. What was supposed to be a cup of coffee turned into an hour's chat. He was an aviation mechanic working out of Lambert Airport.

That impressed her. "I didn't see a wedding ring, but I must ask, are you married or have children?"

"No to both." Sadness flashed over his face, then disappeared. He asked her the same question.

She wondered about that emotion. Did that mean he was ready but hadn't met the right woman?

"Well, I'd better go." She stood to leave.

"Are we going to leave our conversation here since I don't know when our paths will cross again?"

He had to ask for her number because she wouldn't offer it. Porsha believed in making a man work for her attention and affection.

"Porsha, I would like to have your number. Maybe we can get together this weekend."

"I already have plans with my family, but I can pencil you in for next weekend," she teased him.

"Use an ink pen. It's harder to erase."

They exchanged numbers, then she took a rideshare home, unpacked, and changed her clothes. Her first stop was Tally and Randall's house. Friday night usually meant pizza, but Randall had forbidden junk food while Tally was expecting after he witnessed her bouts with nausea.

Porsha chuckled. As she was headed out the door, she received a text from Grayson. **If your weekend plans change, I'm available for dinner, a movie, or whatever you feel up to doing.**

She smiled. **What about church?**

No quick reply. She pouted. *He's not the one.*

My headspace isn't there yet.

That's fair enough. Attending church might be a major commitment if people weren't accustomed to it. She respected that, remembering what her pastor had said about witnessing to others: "Use lovingkindness to draw people to Christ as He offered to us."

Then I will pray for you, Grayson Tate.

Thank you.

When she arrived at Tally and Randall's house, they hugged.

"Okay. What gives?" Her sister folded her arms over her protruding belly.

Randall, taller than both of them, folded his arms, too. He said nothing as he lifted a brow.

Her sister got a handsome husband. Maybe if things went right, she would have that too.

"Glad to be home."

"You're glowing. Remember the glow you teased me about when I met Randall?" That earned her a kiss from her husband, and Tally smiled. "Well, you're wearing one tonight. You met someone," Tally stated. "Give me the details. Please tell me he's not in Philly. You've already accepted a job here."

"Honey," Randall said, putting his arm around his wife's shoulders, "our sister would not be beaming being separated from someone she likes."

Tally turned and kissed him. "Speaking from experience."

The two had a romantic relationship before Tally's salvation, but God pulled her away after Randall's sister, Omega, witnessed to Tally and then Tally to Porsha. Salvation spread like fire in their family, including their parents. Randall and Tally had been miserable without each other, but Tally held her ground and walked with Jesus no matter what.

Her brother-in-law, who treated Porsha as his third sister, was torn apart, and only after a miracle from God did he surrender his life to the Lord.

Maybe Grayson would come to the Lord without kicking and fighting, but easily, she hoped.

"I did meet somebody who lives here at the airport." She grinned and headed to the kitchen. "But that's all I'm going to say for now."

"Well, I hope he's a practicing Christian or surrenders to Jesus before he thinks he can date my sister," Randall mumbled as he and Tally trailed her into the kitchen.

"There's stir-fried veggies, smothered pork chops, pasta salad, and steamed broccoli," Tally said.

"Yummy." Porsha rubbed her stomach, grabbed a plate, and began to fill it with everything but the broccoli. Her sister had been craving broccoli all during her pregnancy—raw, steamed, or in soups.

"If my wife weren't expecting, we would be at tonight's shut-in prayer service at church."

"Oh yeah…" Porsha paused to give thanks for her meal and tackled the pasta first. "Anything pressing or a scheduled shut-in service?"

"God gave Mother Kincaid that list."

Porsha sighed. "Yeah. I wish I had known. I wouldn't have let Amethyst escape."

"We can't hold people hostage for Jesus. You were kind and invited her to return. That was all you were meant to do."

"Now that I'm back home, I'll be on the lookout for her, and if I see her again—"

"If you do, you'll continue to plant the seed," Randall said, massaging Tally's shoulders. "We can't make anyone surrender to the Lord." He paused and raised his hand. "I am a witness to that. If it weren't for Tally's prayers…" He choked and bowed his head. Now, it was her sister's turn to comfort her husband until he sniffed and looked up. "We would not be married today. I love this woman beyond measure."

"And I love you too." She kissed his lips and whispered, "Prayer changes the outcome of every situation."

Porsha watched the lovebirds with longing in her heart. She wanted to share her life with a man who loved her like Randall loved Tally.

Maybe, just maybe, Grayson was the one. He was charming, good-looking, and a good candidate for husband material. *Lord, please save him…for me.*

Chapter Five

For nothing is secret, that shall not be made manifest;
neither anything hid, that shall not be known and
come abroad. —Luke 8:17

"Finally." Grayson Tate pumped his fist in the air. He was moving forward with his life since being stuck in an emotional and mental state for too long. A happy place was in sight. No longer would he eat meals alone or doze on sports shows because boredom was his default source of entertainment. Maybe his three-bedroom, two-story house would feel like a home again with someone to share it instead of selling it.

Nights were the worst. He could hear whispers in the dark as if his house wasn't at peace. To look at him, he was living the bachelor life at thirty-six, and he only had two gray strands to show for life's disappointments.

The day he flirted with Porsha, the torment ceased. He was drawn to the light in her smile and eyes. She was sweet, smart…and cautious.

Grayson couldn't get her out of his head.

He connected immediately.

They could become more than friends.

She gave him something to look forward to through nightly phone calls or midday texts. While Porsha had a close relationship with her sister, Grayson's was strained with his only sibling. Since childhood, life had been nothing but a competition for their late parents' affection.

On the day they met, he and Porsha discussed the basics—age, children, and marriage. He thought about the divorce papers.

Good riddance to bad memories.

Nobody or nothing could convince him to stay in a marriage when he was no longer attracted to the woman he'd dated for three years, including the one year they'd lived together before they decided to marry. In a face-off, they said some harmful, hateful things that couldn't be unsaid, and an ultimatum was issued.

"Why are you being so mean?" his wife had asked with tears swimming in her eyes.

He wasn't falling for her reverse psychology because he had asked her the same question earlier. Her answer had been throwing an object at him. She had changed after losing the baby, and he couldn't suffer to be in the same room with her. It was too toxic for either of them to remain husband and wife.

Bad memories Grayson didn't want to delve into it. He called Porsha.

Both chatted about their day, favorite dishes, and hobbies. He noted that she enjoyed and participated in jigsaw puzzle competitions and collected key chains from cities where she worked on assignments or visited. This might explain why she had key chains from New York, Phoenix, and Cincinnati on her key fob.

Today, they had more in-depth discussions. When Grayson told her he was divorced, he was straightforward when she asked for more details about what had happened with his marriage. He had analyzed it over the months.

"I share the blame. Maybe we had a strong attraction, not the deep-rooted love that could weather the storm. We hated each other when it ended." Grayson had loved his ex-wife, or he wouldn't have married her.

"I'm sorry for both of you." No judgment was in Porsha's voice.

"Yeah. I guess we wasted each other's time."

"Nonsense. Everything that happens in our lives is a life lesson."

"What about you?" he asked while he cooked a steak and would make stir-fried vegetables to go with it. He wasn't a chef but hoped to prepare dinner for her one evening.

"I'm waiting on the right man so we can complement each other in every way."

Grayson smiled. Add intelligence to her charm. It had been a while, but he was ready to re-enter the dating game. "So, how about dinner this Friday?"

"I think I would like that."

"Yes!"

"But," Porsha said, giggling when he groaned, "how about me inviting you to church Sunday."

Grayson gritted his teeth in frustration to keep another groan from escaping. "Okay," he said with less enthusiasm.

Sunday morning, Porsha woke early and slid to her knees to pray. "Jesus, I thank You for another day and another opportunity to serve You. Lord, please let me know Your will concerning Grayson, in Jesus' name. Amen."

Porsha sighed and stood. Hoping Grayson wouldn't change his mind about attending church, she called him. "Are you still coming? I can't wait for you to meet my sister and brother-in-law."

"I can't wait to see you and them. I hope this is a new beginning," he said.

"Me too." She ended the call, danced happily, then began her morning regime before dressing and leaving for church. On the way, she called Tally. "Hey. Grayson's coming."

"Grayson?" Tally paused.

"Yeah, the guy that I've been seeing—"

Suddenly, Randall took the phone. "Hey, sis. Tally isn't feeling well this morning, so we're staying in, but we want to meet this Grayson guy. Bring him by after church. Let me pray for you before you go: Lord, in the name of Jesus, use my sister-in-law for Your glory. Let her draw the lost to You, in Jesus' name. Amen."

"Amen." Wasn't God already using her to win a soul? Porsha thought as she arrived at Christ For All Church.

The parking lot was packed because it was Family and Friends Sunday. Porsha found a space and texted Grayson. **Are you here yet?**

Seconds later, he responded, **No. Not far away.**

Attendance almost doubled for this once-a-year service. She got out and headed toward the entrance, greeting the saints, then located two available seats. She knelt and prayed, then asked a person to hold the seats while she walked to the foyer and joined other saints waiting for their visitors to arrive.

Finally, she saw him. Grayson crossed the parking lot in a confident stride. The dark suit was made for his height and build. When he opened the door, their eyes locked.

"Hi." He towered over her.

"I'm so glad you came." Porsha was so giddy that she grabbed his hand and guided him to their seats.

Grayson wasn't shy. He stood when she did and clapped to the rhythm of the songs. During the sermon, he seemed relaxed as he followed the Scriptures on the overhead monitors.

This was the first time she had taken a chance on a man outside the church to entertain an attraction. Porsha's heart swelled with happiness.

Pastor Rodney seemed deliberate in his message to visitors. "God gives us grace every day, whether others do or not. At your lowest moment, the Lord is there. When you are at a high point in your life, Jesus is celebrating with you. All He asks for in return is…" He paused and folded his arms, scanning the sanctuary to ensure that he held everyone's attention.

Grayson leaned forward. Porsha held her breath, watching him.

"You. God wants you to spend some time with Him. Talk to Him. In Isaiah sixty-five, verse twenty-four, the Lord says, *'And it shall come to pass, that before they call, I will answer; and while they are yet speaking, I will hear.'* That is the most important Scripture to remember today when you leave here…"

Grayson bobbed his head—a promising sign and bad timing to empty her bladder. In all the excitement, she hadn't used the restroom when she'd entered church as was customary.

"I'll be right back," she said, leaning over and tapping him.

He nodded without breaking his concentration from Pastor Rodney. Excellent.

In record time, she finished and then exited the ladies' room. Was that Amethyst—again? Porsha blinked and called her name in a whisper.

The woman entered the sanctuary without responding, and Porsha hurried behind her. It was as if Amethyst had vanished in the crowd. Porsha huffed, disappointed that she had let her get away again. She had turned to walk back to her seat where Grayson was waiting for her when she spied Amethyst in the back row.

Porsha smiled. "Pardon me," she said a few times, stepping over people to get to Amethyst. The woman looked up at her in surprise as Porsha scooted an opening beside her with her hips.

"It's good to see you again. I'm glad you came back," Porsha said, then craned her neck to the other side to check on Grayson, who seemed content. Good.

"And I don't know why." Amethyst shrugged. "At least it's not a wedding this time."

Does the woman ever smile? Porsha wondered. Didn't matter. She was determined to get Amethyst's contact information.

Porsha sat there waiting for Amethyst to say an amen, disagree, or ask a question. She remained silent until Pastor Rodney ended his sermon and asked the congregation to stand.

"This is the time set aside in our service to minister to your needs. If you need prayer, the ministers are waiting at the altar to pray with you. If you want salvation, repent and consent to the water baptism in Jesus' name, and leave today with a fresh start with God…"

"That's my cue," Amethyst said, nudging Porsha out of the way.

"Amen!" Porsha angled her body so Amethyst could step into the aisle and walk to the altar. Amethyst did the opposite and turned to the door to leave.

"Wait. Don't you want prayer?" Porsha asked, dumbfounded.

"Prayer cannot rewind my past. I don't know if I'll come back again. I don't feel a connection to God or this church." She shrugged and walked out into the foyer.

Porsha refused to let her escape God's blessings so easily this time, so she trailed Amethyst. "Maybe not today, but hopefully, you'll feel God's presence because He loves you. If you don't want to walk to the altar, I can get a minister to come and pray for you," Porsha said desperately. *God, help me here!*

"Nah. That's not necessary." Amethyst walked outside.

Come on, work with me. Inside the sanctuary was a man who came to church willingly. Outside was a woman on God's list who kept showing up unknowingly and unwilling to stay. "Amethyst, if you're looking for a friend, maybe we can exchange numbers to at least do lunch."

Holding her breath, Porsha could see *no* forming on this woman's lips, but Amethyst hesitated, and Porsha prayed.

"Tell you what, nothing in my life is making sense, and I don't need to complicate it, adding people in the mix. My horoscope today says three times a charm, so if we run into each other again, a friendship might be meant to be, and we'll do lunch." She headed to the parking lot with her hand in the air, waving goodbye.

If a man wants friends, he must show himself friendly, Porsha recalled Proverbs 18:24. This woman did not want to be her friend. Porsha pivoted on her heels and hurried back inside to Grayson. She prayed Amethyst hadn't messed up her chance to see the start of Grayson's salvation journey.

She returned to her seat, almost out of breath. He offered her a smile.

"I thought you'd deserted me."

"Nope. I saw someone I knew. Sorry about that." She lowered her voice. "Did you enjoy the service?"

"I did. I thought about getting prayer, but…"

But? Porsha held her breath. Grayson shrugged without explaining what changed his mind.

The pastor gave the benediction, and minutes later, Porsha watched Mother Kincaid heading her way, and she made the introductions.

"I want you to meet Grayson, my guest today. This is Mother Kincaid. If you want to pray, she has God on speed dial."

Shaking her head, Mother Kincaid seemed to study Grayson. "Grayson. What's your last name?"

"Tate," he said.

"Welcome. Glad you are here." She nodded suspiciously. "I'm inviting myself over to the Addamses' house for dinner. Tally's sister wasn't up to coming to church. She's pregnant. When she called this morning to tell me, it was a good thing I had gotten up early to start a pot of greens to take over and add to their main course. Please join us."

Porsha touched Grayson's arm and looked at him. "Yes, my sister and brother-in-law would love to meet you." She had forgotten Randall told her to stop by with Grayson.

Mother Kincaid smiled and tugged Porsha's arm away from Grayson.

He frowned.

As Porsha reached for his hand, Mother Kincaid grabbed it and gently squeezed it.

"We would love to get to know you."

"Maybe another time." He smiled at Porsha. "I'll talk to you later." Grayson began to walk away, and Porsha was about to escort him out, but Mother Kincaid's grip on her made her immovable.

Porsha masked her irritation at the elderly woman. "Mother Kincaid, why would you stop me from walking my guest out? I hope you didn't run Grayson away."

"If you have his number, then we can reach him. His soul is important. Grab your things. Sister Tally and Brother Randall are expecting us."

"Okay." *What just happened?* Confusion swirled in Porsha's head as she walked to her car on autopilot. This day was not going as she'd hoped.

Grayson thought about prayer but didn't act on it.

Mother Kincaid acted strange.

Amethyst showed up but didn't want to be there.

The more Porsha thought about it, Mother Kincaid was rude when she pulled Porsha away from Grayson as if he were the demon's handyman.

Grayson seemed wounded and unsure if he should return.

As she slipped in her car, she huffed. "Lord, show me what is going on."

Chapter Six

For God so loved the world, that he gave his only
begotten Son, that whosoever believes in him should
not perish, but have everlasting life. —John 3:16

Porsha was in trouble. She sensed it when Mother Kincaid opened the door to the Addamses' home. How had she gotten there so fast? God must have given the church mother a path of green lights to beat Porsha to her sister's house.

Mother Kincaid's demeanor had also changed. Unlike her harsh behavior earlier, she hugged Porsha warmly and genuinely.

Tally sat at the table, picking at her food. Randall was beside her, scooping up collard greens and coaxing her to eat.

Porsha kissed her sister and then her brother-in-law.

"Fix a plate. There's enough for all of us, and let's talk," Mother Kincaid said calmly. Besides the greens, there were baked chicken, corn muffins, and a pasta dish.

Talk about what? Porsha mouthed as if her parents were about to grill her on dating protocol. She washed her hands in the kitchen sink, then fixed her plate and sat to bless her food.

All eyes were on her as she ate. "What? Somebody tell me what's going on."

Randall reached for his phone on his belt clip, tapped it, and then showed her the screen. She recognized Amethyst Johnson's name from Mother Kincaid's salvation list, which God had given her.

Hudson Lane

Sophia Doyle
Wyatt Sheppard
Olivia Baker
Joi Clark

Porsha's jaw froze. "And Grayson Tate?" She blinked, then sucked in her breath as she read the last part. "And his wife?" She met their eyes and dropped her fork on her plate. "Is this a prophecy that I could be his wife and God's saving him for me?" Happiness was beginning to bloom in her heart.

They shook their head before Randall said, "We believe his wife isn't you because he already has one."

"But he's not married," Porsha defended him.

"Dating Rule 101: Did you ask him?" Tally squinted. She looked ticked.

"Of course! He said he was divorced." This could not be happening as her stomach began to rebel dinner. The corn muffins did nothing to coat her stomach as the collard greens churned inside. Anchoring her elbows on the table, Porsha rested her head in both hands.

"Well, clearly, that's not what God is saying," Mother Kincaid said gently. "God is calling this unnamed woman his wife. He has a wife. We don't know who she is."

"How could red flags not flash?" Tally demanded. "There's an expiration date on these souls' salvation. That's two souls that slipped between your fingers. Saints have been fasting and praying for these people, and you—"

Randall rested his hand on his wife's arm. "It's okay, babe."

Porsha's eyes watered. She and her older sister seldom argued, but Porsha had been snapped at a few times since Tally had been expecting. "Don't scold me! I'm not a child. My mind has been so focused on Amethyst that the other names seemed to fade. What are the odds of me crossing paths with two of them? And Amethyst was there today."

They gasped in chorus.

Tally covered her mouth in shock.

Porsha shook her head. "Before you ask, I tried to get her number and suggested she get prayer, but Amethyst is not friendly." Her mind switched back to Grayson, and her shoulders slumped. *"Grayson and his wife…*he's married? That means he lied to me."

Grayson texted her as if he knew they were discussing him. Porsha panicked. "I'm not a homewrecker, adulteress, fornicator, or any of those things that shouldn't be named among the saints. We cannot be friends." She folded her arms.

"Of course you're not!" Randall fumed. "We know that, but you can't cut him off. His soul's redemption depends on us witnessing to him. You may not have Amethyst's ear, but you have his."

"But I'm not an intercessor."

"You can't opt out of your responsibility as a saint of God. We all have to pray, witness, and be an intercessor for those in bondage," Mother Kincaid said and patted Porsha's hand.

Porsha sighed. She was falling for a married man. Nausea settled in her stomach. "Okay. How do I respond to Grayson?"

"Suggest a double date, and I'll take it from there," Randall said.

"Date? I'm not doing it." Porsha jutted her chin. "I had hoped to find that special love like what you and Tally have."

Tally looped her fingers through her husband's. "But you witnessed the heartache we suffered for our love."

Randall leaned over and kissed his wife's cheek. "If it weren't for my baby following God's guidance, I would not be here today married to the woman I've loved since we met. I'd be in perpetual torment in hell. Be obedient, sis, and you will be blessed. Guaranteed."

"Right." Porsha exhaled. "I'm going intercede for Grayson and the wife he's not claiming."

She looked at her phone and replied, **Still at my sister's house. They are eager to meet you. Can we double-date on**

Friday night? She deleted *double-date* and typed, **Let's do dinner with them on Friday.** Porsha showed them her reply, they nodded, and she hit send.

Mother Kincaid hugged her. "Until Friday, be careful in your conversation with him while encouraging him to seek God and read his Bible."

"Yes, ma'am."

"And memorize the rest of those names! These souls are closer to us than what we think," Mother Kincaid said.

She soon kissed everyone goodbye. This was not the work assignment Porsha was expecting. Accepting a permanent job at home was. Suddenly, she craved an out-of-town assignment.

Porsha repented. Mother Kincaid told her that God's business was every Christian's business to intercede on everyone's behalf. No exceptions.

***

Amethyst didn't know why she was so irritable. Church was supposed to make her happy. It had failed. The tarot cards gave her more hope.

Lies, a voice whispered.

She had snapped at her mother and almost gotten evicted from the apartment.

"What is wrong with you?" Annabelle demanded with a fist on her waist.

Shaking her head, Amethyst's signature single braid was unraveling like her life. "I don't know." Amethyst's moodiness frustrated her. What was wrong with her? "Sorry, Mom. I've got a lot of things on my mind."

Her mother sat on the bed's edge, anchoring an elbow on a knee. "Such as?"

Amethyst sighed and shut her eyes. "Nothing has been going in my favor for the past year. My relationship busted, my hope for a job promotion dashed, and I feel alone."

"You have me."

"Yeah, but I have no real friends, and my horoscope told me a few weeks ago to be leery of new people who want to be my friend."

"Well," Annabelle said, shrugging, "astrology is a perfect science. You'd better listen. Any word about any luck coming your way?"

"Nope. I've read ahead a whole week. No mention of anything good about to happen. Only Reggie seems to care."

Annabelle grunted. "I don't trust that he's genuinely concerned about you."

"He's been there for me when I…" Amethyst paused. One self-help book told her to let go of the past. She had to move past trauma and disappointment to go forward. "Mom, I *need* someone to be concerned about me. I feel like darkness is gripping me, squeezing the life out of me." She still had the gun her mother didn't know about. Reggie gave it to her and said she might need it for protection one day after she left her husband.

I care about you, God whispered.

Blinking, Amethyst wasn't sure even God cared.

Prove me, God challenged.

Chapter Seven

*Behold, all souls are mine; as the soul of the father,
so also the soul of the son is mine: the soul that sins,
it shall die.* —Ezekiel 18:4

A dream woke her at about two in the morning, the night before Porsha was about to start her new position at the tech company in the Central West End.

A raven or a squirrel had found prey for food and was feasting. Porsha rolled over, shuddering at the thought of the poor animal. She felt a finger nudging her in the back.

Get up and pray, God whispered.

For a squirrel or whatever the animal was in her dream? Porsha snuggled deeper into her satin pillow.

That prey is a soul that will die unless you pray, God whispered.

Drowsy, Porsha slid to her knees. As she prayed, the vision became clearer. She was too late. It appeared that the soul was already dead, and what she thought was a squirrel in her dream was a beast. More horrified than frightened, Porsha prayed fervently until there was movement.

Though wounded, there were signs of life. The beast struggled to kill it, but the prey broke away—injured but free. Porsha exhaled. The soul had escaped.

Porsha felt her heart pumping, and tears streamed down her cheeks. That person—man or woman—was about to die. "Lord, let that person recover and never be caught in that situation again."

She climbed back in bed, but sleep didn't return quickly, as she thought about what it would have been like if she had ignored God's voice. *Was that Grayson's soul?* she wondered.

Hours later, the alarm woke her. She stretched, sluggish from a restless night. Not the way she wanted to start her first day on the job.

Porsha tossed her covers back and stepped out of bed. Instead of the carpet meeting the soles of her feet, her feet began to sink on uneven ground. The colorful furnishings of her bedroom had turned into a war zone, like an old black-and-white movie.

The stench of death was powerful and suffocating, like burning sulfur. Porsha heard growling and hissing, which made her shiver.

She came face-to-face with an animal covered in alligator scales. It stood taller than a bear with claws. Bodies were on the ground everywhere—women, children, and men.

Suddenly, as if Porsha had been spotted, an animal raced toward her at an unbelievable speed. She couldn't outrun it. "Jesus!" she screamed to the top of her lungs.

A ball of fire with the shape of a hand circled Porsha and pushed her behind it to form a shield.

The air was still, and the noise stopped. Peeping over the fire, she saw the creature bow.

My people will face this today, tomorrow, and to the end of time. Now, go out into the highways and save my people, God thundered.

Panting for air, Porsha found herself back in her bedroom. How was she supposed to continue? The day would be interesting, as Porsha would have to work in the spiritual realm, looking for souls to rescue and be mentally and physically at the top of her game on her new job to prove why she commanded the top salary as the new senior internal auditor for the tech company.

She showered, dressed, and ate without thinking. As she headed out the door, Grayson texted, **I wish you good luck on your first day at the new job. We're celebrating this weekend.**

Porsha hoped that he and his wife would work out their differences. **Remember dinner with my sister and brother-in-law, and blessings got me this position, not luck.**

Oops. Sorry, I have to remember the right phrases to say to you. Forgive me. :)

Forgiven.

There was no future for them, and the Lord was the person Grayson needed to impress. Still, Porsha felt sad that Grayson wasn't meant for her. She slipped the phone into her purse, slid behind the wheel of her car, and headed to her new adventure, counting down the days until Grayson was exposed for better or worse like the marriage vows he'd professed to the wife he no longer claimed.

On Tuesday, Amethyst enjoyed leftovers for lunch in the campus-like setting described as the Cortex in the Central West End of St. Louis. At least six businesses shared the open courtyard for lunch, meetings, or lounging. It was Amethyst's hangout every chance she got to think or daydream unbothered.

She had spoken to Reggie Monday night when he'd called to check on her.

"Hey. What's going on? You don't sound right."

"A little bummed. It doesn't seem like I can catch a break with anything." Amethyst told him about not having enough money for her sales tax to get the license plate for her car, which wasn't brand new but pre-owned.

Reggie was a good listener and offered to help without her asking. "Tell me how much money you need. Let me work on it, and I'll get back to you tomorrow."

Amethyst sniffed. Reggie always came to her rescue. She didn't care what her mother said. He was a good person.

So today, she waited for his call. He always made her forget about her troubles. Amethyst grinned when his name flashed on her phone.

"Hey. You got the money. I just sent it to your account."

"Thank you so much." She closed her eyes, choked with emotions. "You're keeping me from losing my car."

"Nonsense. I wasn't going to let that happen." Reggie chuckled.

"But fourteen hundred dollars is a lot of money. I have to pay you back."

Reggie exaggerated a sigh. "How about you set an amount and pay it back over a year or two? It doesn't matter to me."

He was kind and generous. As an account manager for a Fortune 100 company, he earned an impressive salary and lived large—he had a house, a car, and clothes. His wife and children didn't go without. He denied himself nothing when it came to material things.

They chatted and laughed as she dipped her fry into ketchup. A familiar face appeared at her table.

"Amethyst?" Porsha waited for an invitation to join her, ignoring that Amethyst was on the phone.

"Reggie, I'll call you back, and thanks." She ended the call with his "no problem" tag.

Porsha grinned at her. "You look happy. I've never seen you smile. Girl, you glow, and your eyes twinkle. Is Reggie your boyfriend?"

He wasn't, and Amethyst didn't want to share her private business with a stranger. But it was hard for her to be rude to a woman who consistently offered her a smile. Amethyst wasn't always this moody or unpleasant, but after her marriage crumbled, she just wasn't happy. She switched the subject. "Do you work at one of these buildings in the Cortex?"

Porsha nodded and took the seat across from her. She opened her bag and displayed a sub sandwich from the neighboring food strip. After blessing her food, she took a bite while Amethyst waited for her to answer.

"Today is my first day at Microsoft as the senior internal auditor. I've been a traveling CPA, so I'm excited about being home close to family." She smiled. "Do you have family?"

Amethyst shook her head. "Just Mom and me."

"Oh." Porsha was quiet as she took another bite. Amethyst could tell she was thinking. "I would like to invite you back to Christ For All Church, where members our ages have formed a bond. We're like family. I hope you will return and get to know us and…Jesus."

That was Amethyst's cue to end lunch early. She was okay with not being a religious person. She stood to leave.

"*Awww*. I was hoping you would keep me company." Porsha feigned a pout and stopped her from retreating.

"Sorry. My lunch is over."

"Amethyst, do you mind if I pray for you?" Porsha stopped eating.

"What?" Amethyst heard herself say sure instead of screaming no. "Don't make a scene."

"Understood." Porsha closed her eyes and bowed her head.

"Lord Jesus, protect Amethyst's mind, body, and soul. Lead her on Your path when, at times, she might feel like giving up. Jesus, I ask this because of the power in Your name. Amen."

When Porsha finished, Amethyst's eyes watered. She couldn't describe what she felt. "Thanks."

She walked away without looking back. How dare Porsha pray as if she was peering through her soul. One thing was certain: Amethyst would change her lunch schedule and location.

Chapter Eight

But if ye will not do so, behold, ye have sinned against
the Lord: and be sure your sin will find you out.
—Numbers 32:23

G rayson was nervous Friday evening. Last weekend had been perfect—until he met Mother Kincaid at Porsha's church. She was friendly enough but seemed weary of him. Did that mean she disapproved, and Porsha would follow her advice?

He sighed.

Hopefully, he would meet Porsha's sister and brother-in-law's approval. Grayson couldn't strike out on making a good impression because he liked Porsha.

As he shaved, his ex-wife's face flashed in his mind. Grayson never wanted another relationship that wasn't built on love, or otherwise, his marriage would have lasted. True, he had cared for her, but they weren't in love when they started sleeping together—not smart—then she became pregnant. Grayson didn't feel trapped, but he accepted they were about to become parents and asked her to marry him.

His ex had the nerve to walk away from their marriage as if Grayson had been the problem after she lost their baby. It didn't help that his half-brother snooped around his wife, casting doubt in Grayson's mind that they could have been more than friendly in-laws. He was relieved when she packed up and left. Grayson hadn't put up a fight for her to stay. Once she moved out, his emotions bounced from depression and irritability. He blamed her for that, too.

What I have joined together, let no man separate, God whispered.

"Never again," he murmured, disgusted that he had allowed himself to get into that situation. Of course, his brother made him feel like a failure, especially when his wife served him with divorce papers.

Grayson sighed. Three years of his life were wasted.

He was moving on.

No memory lane.

No looking back.

When he walked out the door thirty minutes later, he grinned as his heart pumped with excitement. He was a free man.

He arrived at Beyond Sweet in the Central West End on Delmar. Grayson had never heard of it, but Porsha said it was her sister's favorite eating place.

Grayson strolled into the restaurant and looked around. Porsha stood from a table and waved him over as a buffed man stood, too.

The man wasn't smiling.

Porsha's eyes weren't sparkling.

And Grayson already knew it would be a long night to win them over.

When he approached, the man smiled and gave him a firm handshake. "I'm Randall Addams. Nice to meet you. This is my wife, Tally." She remained seated, rubbing her protruding belly. She favored Porsha, but both were beauties.

Their smiles seemed genuine, but something was off.

"I'm glad you could make it," Porsha said, scooting farther away in the booth than he would have wanted. After all, it was a double date.

Randall folded his arms and gave him a pointed stare. "Grayson, tell us about your wife."

Grayson blinked. That wasn't the conversation starter he had expected. "No wife. I'm divorced and have the papers to prove it." He glanced at Porsha to make sure she believed him.

"That's not what the Lord says," Randall countered.

Porsha watched as shock flashed on Grayson's face. She admired Randall's no-nonsense approach when it came to anyone's salvation. Although her brother-in-law remained easygoing, in the past, he probably would have feasted on dinner and then launched a surprise attack.

"I'm clueless about what you're talking about. I'm no longer married," Grayson explained.

"God doesn't lie." Porsha didn't hide her pain.

"You put my sister in an awkward situation to sin against God," Tally said.

Grayson exhaled and bowed his head. "Our marriage ended long before she filed for divorce. Porsha, I'm not a messy person. I would never hide that from you. I never cheated on my wife while I was married."

"But you were about to if you started dating Porsha," Randall argued. He wasn't giving Grayson any slack.

Porsha felt sorry for him and wanted to comfort him. That wasn't her right. She felt his eyes on her, but she ignored him.

"I wasn't trying to deceive you. I am not married." Grayson raised his voice, then apologized.

"Check those papers when you get home," Tally said.

"Although I don't need to, I will prove I'm not a liar or cheat."

Randall tapped his finger on the table. "This dinner is more than our objection about dating Porsha, but to inform you that God has you on a list."

"Huh?" Grayson frowned and seemed exhausted.

"Your soul and others' are in danger. You need to get your house in order."

"What? Are you telling me I'm about to die?" Grayson's voice was filled with alarm. He looked from Randall to Tally to Porsha.

"No one knows the day nor the hour, but I do know if you leave it up to the devil, you will die without Christ. It's our job to make sure that doesn't happen," Randall paused. "We've got your back."

Seemingly skeptical, Grayson folded his arms and leaned back. "And supposedly where did this list come from?"

"Mother Kincaid," Porsha whispered.

"The older woman from your church?" He shifted in his seat and grunted. "That explains why she responded to me the way she did."

Randall reached for his phone. "Look at this. It will be up to you to believe it's heaven-sent. After a morning prayer, God told Mother Kincaid the following souls were important to Him for salvation." He tapped on his messages and showed Grayson the phone screen. "As you can see, your name is at the top of the list. 'Grayson Tate and his wife…and especially—'"

"Amethyst Johnson," Grayson said along with Randall. His eyes bucked, and he grasped for air before swallowing.

"Do you know her?" Porsha exchanged shock glances with her sister.

"Yes, but that can't…can't be right," Grayson stuttered. "Amethyst is no longer my wife. I have the divorce decree."

Porsha couldn't believe how susceptible she had become because she couldn't look past the attraction.

Shock and disbelief registered on Grayson's face as he stared at Randall's screen. "Why would God say, *especially Amee?*"

Did his question mean Grayson still cared for his wife? "Grayson, Amethyst—or Amee as you call her—is in danger. We can't fight a spiritual battle until we put on God's spiritual armor, which comes with receiving His spirit. Amethyst seems troubled."

"Have you met her?" Grayson lifted a suspicious brow as if she was part of a conspiracy.

Porsha nodded. "Yes, she was at church the same Sunday you came."

"*Hmmm*," was Grayson's response.

Randall asked, "What's stopping you from committing your life to Christ?"

"First off, I need to check my divorce papers as soon as I get home, and this thing with Amee... I don't know what to do about that situation."

"God can help you restore your relationship with your wife. He is the one orchestrating the delay in your divorce," Randall said.

"That's not the only relationship that sets me off. It's my brother—half-brother—Reggie." He gritted his teeth and balled his fists.

The anger he harbored was apparent.

Wait. *Reggie?* Amethyst had been all smiles while she was on the phone with him. Porsha had thought the woman was speaking with her boyfriend. This situation was getting messier by the minute.

"Babe, let me out," Tally said. "I have to go to the bathroom."

She scooted until Randall helped her stand. Porsha took that as an opportunity to go with her. "Excuse me, Grayson. I'm praying for you and your wife to reconcile. It's the right thing to do, Grayson," Porsha said as he stood to let her out of the booth.

He did the same. As they were on their way, Porsha whispered, "Perfect timing."

"What?"

Porsha looked over her shoulder back at the table. Grayson was watching her. "Reggie keeps in contact with his sister-in-law, and I got the vibes that there may be some attraction between them when I heard Amethyst talking to him."

Tally moved her lips from side to side, processing that tidbit as she entered the stall. She reappeared minutes later to wash her hands, then faced Porsha. "That's a deadly combination. Maybe that's why the Lord said, *especially Amethyst*. I don't know."

Tally shrugged. "At least you work in the same area where she does. With this knowledge, you can tweak your witness with her."

"I hope so. I didn't tell you this," she said, leaning against the counter until she had Tally's attention, "but the night before my first day on the job, the Lord woke me and planted me on the battlefield with demons that could kill from their fiery eye sockets."

"*Whew*." Tally dried her hands, then looped her arm through Porsha's. "Sis, I don't know what this is all about, but you need to keep your spiritual eyes open. I wonder if that's connected to Amethyst."

When they returned to the table, Grayson was gone, and Randall was perusing the menu, smacking his lips.

Chapter Nine

*For we wrestle not against flesh and blood, but against
principalities, against powers, against the rulers of the darkness
of this world, against spiritual wickedness in high places.*
—Ephesians 6:12

Am I still married? The horror that raced through Grayson made him so weak at the knees that he groaned.

No wonder Porsha and her family initially gave him a guarded reception. He thought about Porsha. Grayson could tell he had hurt her, but he would never, ever do what he was accused of—stepping out on his wife or any woman he was dating.

Even while he and Amethyst were separated and then divorced—or so he thought—Grayson had no interest in talking to a woman. Porsha had been an exception. "And I see how that turned out." He was disgusted with himself for being put in that situation and seen in a negative light.

He thought the copy in his possession was the final divorce decree. The story his attorney told him was the judge signed on the wrong line, making the papers in his possession void, then he went on vacation. After his vacation, Judge Doane was out for a sudden medical leave. There had been one delay after another in finalizing their divorce. The setbacks had been ridiculous. Now, a new judge was reviewing the divorce before signing off on it.

Why did God single him out and reveal his marital status with Amee?

Why did God have his wife's name on the list with "especially" before her name?

Although it was Sunday, he did not intend to attend church, not at Christ For All Church anyway. Amethyst had walked out last year before Christmas. He had a hunch that Reggie was coaxing her.

He sat on the edge of his bed, holding his head in his hands. Grayson's eyes were closed. What a mess.

Amethyst accused him of being emotionally detached after they lost the baby. "I married you because I loved you and you were pregnant!" he screamed to his empty bedroom.

He wanted to close the chapter with her. After they married, the court hadn't filed the paperwork for her name change. Since his wife was experiencing morning sickness, she had planned to take care of it as soon as she felt better.

That should have been a sign.

Rehashing old wounds wasn't how he planned to spend his Sunday.

Grayson wanted to call or text Porsha to plead his innocence for no other reason than to clean up his image with her, but her body language and Randall's warning to leave before the ladies returned from the restroom closed the chapter on contacting her ever again.

"I'm praying for you and your wife to reconcile," Porsha had said.

No one was praying for them when their marriage showed signs of trouble.

How in the world did that seem like the right thing to do? he wondered. Amethyst hated him, and his feelings were numb concerning her.

The only number he was allowed to call was Porsha's brother-in-law, Randall, who offered to befriend him to show him the path to Christ.

Why would Grayson want to follow Christ when it was the Lord who had his life in limbo with a woman who hated him? Grayson would instead go in the opposite direction. Randall wouldn't hear from him again.

Two days later, Porsha had recovered from her disappointment with Grayson. He had work to do on his marriage. She needed to keep her mind off him and the plunder she'd made because she had not memorized God's salvation list, as she had begun to call it. With purse and keys in hand, Porsha was walking out the door when Tally called.

"Hey, sis. Can you stop at the store and grab three bags of ice? I forgot them when I placed my grocery delivery order."

Memorial Day was the unofficial kickoff to summer, and Porsha's brother-in-law and sister were hosting a barbecue.

"Yep." Porsha slipped behind the wheel of her car. Tally lived about fifteen minutes away, perfect for the couple needing an emergency babysitter. Porsha grinned at the thought, wondering who the little princess would resemble. They already knew the baby would be a girl.

While en route to the grocery store, she reflected on the repeat vision God had revealed the night before she started her new job. Why was God showing her a rerun?

When she wasn't traveling to a client's site, she didn't miss a Sunday service, Bible study, shut-in prayer, or any event that was church related. Despite the practicing Christian résumé, Porsha wasn't an intercessor.

She parked, entered the store with a cart, and headed to the ice bag bins. The express lane was long with customers like her who had a few things. Porsha opted for the regular checkout where she was two shoppers away from the cashier.

"Hi, honey. Did you find everything?" An older woman with the most beautiful fuchsia lipstick smiled at her. Moments later, she gave Porsha her total.

"Do you need any help, ma'am?" the teenager asked with a soft-spoken voice and kind eyes as he bagged her items. He was a handsome, thin, and tall young man, inches above her five-foot-six. The dark brown, thick curls on his head begged for a haircut.

Porsha was about to decline until she glanced at his name badge: Hudson. She almost dropped her wallet. Was that his first or last name? Porsha gnawed on her lipstick, thinking of a way to find out. If so, this was the third person God had put in her path. "Why, yes. Thank you. I like your name. It's unique, like mine."

"Thanks."

"Is it your first or last name?"

He chuckled. "My mom gave me a last name as a first name…"

Please don't leave me hanging. "What's your last name?"

"Lane. Hudson Lane," he mumbled as he lifted her bags and waited for her to take the lead out of the store.

Nervous, she had no idea what to say.

Open your mouth, and I will give you the words, God whispered.

"Did you know God has a purpose for you?" Porsha repeated what God told her.

Hudson laughed.

Porsha stopped at the crosswalk and faced him. "What's funny?"

"God." He shook his head and looked both ways before they proceeded to walk across the parking lot from the store entrance. "I don't even know if there is a God the way people like my parents say *God said, God did, God…God.* God doesn't even punish hypocrites and people lying to Him." His expression was a mix of disappointment and disgust.

"You can be the one to prove them wrong by following Christ for yourself," she said as she neared her red Jeep and unlocked the hatchback.

"How?" Hudson stared at her.

Porsha waited for God to answer the how. The Lord didn't, so she scrambled for the right words to draw Hudson, something she had yet to accomplish with Amethyst. "I'd like to invite you to my sister's house today for a barbecue. There will be plenty of food and fun. There are even teenagers there who can show you how they are walking with the Lord."

He was quiet.

"What else do you have planned today?"

Hudson shrugged. "I was going to catch the bus to one of my friends' houses to hang out."

In the blink of an eye, in the middle of the parking lot, Porsha saw grotesque, giant beasts riding on horseback like warriors, kicking up a dust storm in their path.

One reached to scoop up Hudson, and Porsha reached for his other arm, but God halted her movement.

You wrestle not with flesh and blood, but your weapons of warfare are not carnal, but mighty through Me to the pulling down of strongholds, God whispered. *Pray in My name!*

"Lord, in the mighty name of Jesus, I rebuke the hands of the enemy and ask You to send angels to protect Hudson from the forces that want to destroy him," she prayed, not realizing she said it aloud until the teenager cast her a bewildered look. "At the name of Jesus, demons tremble. I command them to retreat, in Jesus' name. Amen."

The beasts halted their reins immediately and bowed.

Porsha exhaled as she felt God's overpowering presence, which caused the demons to retreat.

"I never heard a prayer like that before, as if it was really for me." He didn't hide his awestruck expression.

I had never prayed like that before and saw the result of prayers answered that speedily, Porsha admitted to herself. "I can give you their address, or if you need a ride, I can come back and get you." She was not about to let Hudson Lane slip through her fingers.

"Okay." He shrugged. "I'm off now. I need to clock out."

"I'll wait for you." Porsha closed the hatch after Hudson adjusted the bags. "Should you call your parents and let them know where you're going?"

"Nah. They never ask where I've been."

Porsha wondered what was wrong with his parents not being concerned about the welfare of their child, even though he was a teenager.

"You should be afraid of offering rides to strangers, but I ain't going to rob or hurt you or anything. Just sayin'." He stepped back, turned around, and jogged back inside the store. Porsha sat in her car and called Tally.

"I'm so out of my element," Porsha said when her sister answered. "You're not going to believe this."

"What? That you're not almost here?"

"Well, yeah, that, too, but—"

"Girl," Tally cut her off.

"I met another person on the list."

"What?" Tally shrieked. "Who?"

"Hudson Lane. He's a teenager who works at the store not far from you. I invited him to the barbecue, and he's coming."

"Hallelujah! We'll be ready. See you when you get here." As she ended the call, she yelled in the background to her guests, which included church members, "God revealed another person on the salvation list."

Now Porsha wondered, what was Hudson's story?

Chapter Ten

But now thus saith the Lord that created thee, O Jacob,
and he that formed thee, O Israel, Fear not: for I have redeemed
thee, I have called thee by thy name; thou art mine.
—Isaiah 43:1

Hudson was treated like a celebrity when he entered the backyard of a two-story home with a large wrap-around deck. Although his birthday had passed, it felt like his surprise birthday party.

One he'd never had.

His parents, Byron and Kendra Lane, thought money could be better spent buying him things. This had been the norm since he could remember.

His head was spinning from the introductions.

"Hudson, unless you have allergies, I'll fix you a plate," Tally, Porsha's sister, said. She was pretty, even though she was pregnant.

Their mother, Cynthia Gilbert, looked older than Hudson's mom and was pretty too.

"The teenagers are playing cornhole, knockerball, and other games," Porsha said.

"Knockerball?" Hudson grinned. He had only played it once at a school picnic. He had climbed inside the chamber of an inflatable bubble and played soccer, tag, and other games. "Cool." Hudson was ready to jump in where he could fit in.

"You might want to eat first," Tally said.

"Yeah. The food does smell good." Hudson had plenty of company as small children and adults came to his table and welcomed him.

Home. Hudson couldn't explain why he felt so comfortable.

An elderly lady who introduced herself as Mother Kincaid sat beside him and smiled while he ate. "You sure do enjoy your food. Good to see hearty appetites." Her wise eyes twinkled.

"Yes, ma'am." Hudson gulped his soda can, then wiped his mouth. "Are you Porsha's grandma?"

She glanced away and chuckled. "Everyone calls me Mother Kincaid because I'm up in age. It's a sign of respect, like addressing adults as Miss or Mister. Understand?" She peered at him. "I'm glad *Miss* Porsha brought you as our guest."

"Yes, ma'am." Hudson sat straighter. He was big on taking hints.

"We've been praying for you, young man," Mother Kincaid said softly.

"Huh? But you don't even know me."

"Doesn't matter, Hudson Lane. God knew you before you were born."

Hudson frowned. "Po—I mean Miss Porsha prayed for me too. Is that something all of you do?"

She nodded. "As Christians, it's our priority to always pray for one another. That's what our Bible teaches us."

"Oh." Hudson hoped a sermon wasn't coming because he would have to bear it. He'd heard more people quote the Bible, then acted like they didn't even believe it.

Mother Kincaid became quiet but doted on him with food, napkins, and anything else like he was her grandson. Hudson liked it here.

Two brothers raced up to the table, out of breath. They made him wish he had a brother—younger or older, it didn't matter. It wasn't all that being an only child.

"I'm Carlton, and this is my brother, Harry. We're both eleven. How old are you?" he asked, clearly the leader.

"So you're twins?" Their features were strong, but they weren't identical. When they shook their heads, Hudson didn't ask questions, so he answered them. "I'm sixteen."

Hudson couldn't believe how comfortable he felt. *I belong here.*

Tally's husband, Randall, approached the table and grinned. "Hudson, you definitely belong here."

Huh? Did the man hear his thoughts? Hudson blinked.

"We would love for you to visit us any time at our home and church, where we mentor young men and women who don't have fathers in the home."

"Oh, I have a dad and mom, but we don't have many friends."

"Well, you have a lot of us now." Randall waved over a tall guy who Carlton and Harry called Dad. "Minister Jude Morgan, you met Hudson earlier, but I want you to talk to him about our mentoring program."

"Sure." The minister nodded and straddled the bench to face Hudson. Neither one of his sons looked like him. He bumped fists with Hudson and seemed cool. "I would like to include you in our group activities. How do you feel about coming to our church on Sunday and meeting more young people?"

Church was not Hudson's thing after witnessing his parents' hypocrisy. They never said anything good about churches, people in them, preachers, or God. Shouldn't he be the same way and decline? Most times, Hudson worked on Sunday mornings, but not next week.

He liked these people. His parents would find something wrong with them. "Yeah, okay."

"Do you need a ride?" Minister Morgan asked when he told him the name of the church and where it was located.

"Nah. I can catch the bus. I live on Plum Tree Lane."

An older teenager walked by with a pile of food on his plate, then backtracked to the table. "Plum Tree Lane? Hey, man. I'm

Bobby. You might not remember me from earlier, but I stay around the corner on Apple Blossom Court. I can give you a lift. No brother of ours is catching the bus when we're going the same way."

Wow. Free rides and free food. "O-okay."

Hours later, Porsha's mother clapped and announced it was time for the clean-up committee to take over.

"Everyone," Mother Kincaid added.

Bobby tapped Hudson on the shoulder. "That means you too. Come on. Let's collect the games."

Hudson followed orders. It was a team effort. Some collected the trash, and others packed up the food. Porsha and a few others were in the kitchen, while Tally rested in a lawn chair.

The sun was setting as guests thanked the host. For the first time since he'd arrived, his mother texted him. **Everything okay, son?**

Yep. On my way home. Hanging out with some new friends.

She texted back, **Okay.** No questions were asked about his whereabouts. Was that the norm? His father said as long as Hudson stayed out of trouble and jail, he was a good kid.

Porsha seemed to have disappeared once they arrived, but now she was walking toward him with her purse, jingling her car keys. "Have a good time?"

"Yep. Thank you, Miss Porsha, for inviting me," he said, then turned to her sister and brother-in-law. "Thank you for all the food and fun."

"Before you leave, Hudson, please join the teenagers and children in the circle for prayer," Mother Kincaid said.

The older woman said it so nicely that saying, *I'm good* would be rude, so he didn't.

"Minister Morgan, please lead us in a word of prayer," Mother Kincaid called and waved him over, then bowed her head.

Hudson followed others but kept his eyes open.

"Father, in the mighty name of Jesus, we thank You for the cross where You took our sins away. Every sin. Protect our children from every plot the devil attempts against them and give those who don't have Your power, power to overcome this world, in Jesus' name. Amen."

Hudson mumbled, "Amen," along with the others.

"We have your back, Hudson," Minister Morgan said.

"Thanks. Nice prayer." Hudson followed Bobby to his car, an older, blue, shiny Dodge Charger with a clean interior. His playlist included Christian rap and a cappella songs.

"I'm glad we met today," Bobby said as he roared his engine and glanced in his rearview mirror. "I'm glad Sister Porsha invited you."

"Me too." Sister Porsha, Hudson noted, not Miss Porsha.

"We need to get together and play ball or go out with some of the brothers from church. How are your grades?" Bobby asked out of nowhere.

"They're alright. I'm passing."

"That won't do, bro. As Black males, we need to excel, and our church backs us up."

"You almost sound like a parent." Hudson studied him. He wasn't like his circle of friends, who preferred getting in trouble for excitement over boredom. Hudson was the youngest of his friends and the only one with a job. He wanted to save for a car.

Bobby laughed. "I hope not, but Christ For All Church invests in their youth—community services, jobs, and education. They raise money for college scholarships, and all graduating seniors get money. There's a team of people at church whose job is to find us money for college, and the church supports college students with care packages each month."

That was a lot. Speechless, Hudson listened until Bobby became quiet. "Your church does all that for its youths?"

"Why not? It's more than the 'children are our future' slogan. They help us in every way. I'm sure some of us would have been in jail or in gangs or be teenage parents, but honestly, they teach us to impress God rather than them with our faithfulness. I'm going to miss them when I go away to college next year."

For some reason, Hudson was going to miss him too. Soon, Hudson pointed to his house. "The white brick ranch there."

Bobby pulled to the curb and asked for his phone. "Here's my number, bro." He tapped it in. "You don't have to wait until Sunday to reach out. Mind if I pray for you?"

"Again?" Hudson groaned, then opened the door and stepped out. Before shutting it, he said, "I'm good."

He heard his parents arguing before he reached the porch. His parents needed the prayers, not him.

And that's what I called you to do, God whispered, *pray*.

***

God answered two of Porsha's prayers on Sunday. Her soul screamed "Hallelujah" when she saw Hudson sitting with Bobby, and Hudson appeared to enjoy the service. Grayson came after Randall sent him a personal invite. Porsha kept her distance from him, knowing that he was married. He sat in the back.

Pastor Rodney led a congregational song, "My Soul Says Yes," then preached Romans 6:23, *"For the wages of sin is death, but the gift of God is eternal life through Jesus Christ our Lord."*

"Payday is coming. Don't think you can do whatever you want to anybody, and nobody will notice. God is keeping the record, and your judgment will be based on whether you accepted the gift." He paused. "It's a no-brainer. Who turns down gifts? No excuses will be accepted for not taking the best gift of a lifetime," he continued with examples until he closed his Bible.

"So," Pastor Rodney paused, "will you accept God's gift of eternal life with Him or eternal damnation where there is not a parole system? You go to hell, and you're stuck. My dear brothers and sisters, the choice is yours. Repent today. God's ready to cancel your debt. This is your time. Dig deep within yourself and tell God that you're sorry. If you feel compelled, come to the altar for prayer, and then get your spiritual sins washed away."

Porsha heard Hudson whisper to Bobby.

"I think I'm going down to the altar, man." Hudson stood and walked in that direction.

She smiled. One down, six more to go. Porsha scanned the rear of the sanctuary where Grayson sat next to Brother Kennedy, who was a little older than Grayson. Randall had handpicked brothers in the church to befriend Grayson to ensure he stayed away from Porsha and introduced him to men with compatible personalities.

Judging from Grayson's expressions, he didn't appear compelled to surrender. His eyes darted as if he was looking for an escape route.

Porsha wondered if Amethyst was hiding in the back.

Pastor Rodney pulled her wandering mind back to the present. "Praise God for the souls who have come. But there is still one who is holding out. God knows who it is, and so do you. If you think you have no sins, I am sorry to inform you that the day your mother brought you into this world, sin was on you before a diaper. It's in the bloodline. Baptism cleanses the bloodline."

After no movement, the pastor closed with prayer and waited for baptismal candidates to change their clothes.

One by one, the candidates stepped into the water. Each time, the pair of ministers lifted their hands, they said, "My dear brother and sister, upon the confession of your faith and the confidence we have in the blessed Word of God concerning His death, burial, and grand resurrection, we now indeed baptize you for the remission of your sins in the mighty name of Jesus, the only name under heaven that has the power to save us. Amen."

The roars of the congregation were more deafening than those of fans in the stadium at a game as people were submerged, buried in water, and resurfaced with the help of the ministers.

When Hudson, the last candidate, stepped into the water, the atmosphere shifted in the sanctuary.

"My dear brother, Hudson Lane…" Minister Jude Morgan said the candidate's name to alert the congregation that he was one on God's list for whom church members had been fervently praying.

Those who weren't already standing got to their feet. Porsha jumped in place, clapping wildly.

"God has redeemed you and rescued you from the jaws of death," he continued. "It is because of God's mercy that I baptize you in the mighty name of Jesus Christ for the remission of your sins. Because of the confession of your faith, you are about to become a new creature in Jesus. May you serve God until the end."

A couple pushed through the crowd as Hudson was about to be submerged. "Wait. Hold it right there." A woman pointed. The organist and singers paused. Everyone turned toward them.

"Mom, Dad!" Hudson waved, grinning from ear to ear.

"Stop, son. We overheard you talking about coming to this church on the phone. It seemed like it took us forever to get here, but we're here now. Do you know what you're doing?" his father asked.

Porsha couldn't believe it. Now, they wanted to act like concerned parents?

"Yes. I'm about to be set free from sin and hope to be a light to show you what a practicing Christian looks like." Hudson nodded to Minister Morgan. "I'm good. Let's do it."

His parents' protests were drowned out with cheers.

Porsha was in awe. She had never seen someone stop a baptism before. Only weddings on television or social media were sometimes interrupted. She didn't know what was happening, but God did.

Seemingly unconcerned about their protests, Pastor Rodney waved for his parents to approach the glass wall enclosing the pool as Hudson reappeared.

"Hallelujah," Hudson shouted repeatedly while pumping his fists. Then he turned and looked at his parents. "Mom, Dad, I feel different. Jesus is real."

"The Lord Jesus Christ is ready to fill you with His Spirit," Pastor Rodney said to Hudson.

"I want it!" Hudson said, wiping tears out of his eyes as Minister Morgan guided him to the stairs to climb out of the pool.

"We forbid it. You are not a consenting adult to this nonsense," his father demanded.

A hush came over the sanctuary as they watched the unprecedented action.

Remaining calm, Pastor Rodney defused the situation. "Mr. and Mrs. Lane, I believe God's will overruled yours. Why don't you have a seat? Hudson will come out that door, and I suspect soon."

Mrs. Lane huffed and stomped her foot.

While deacons attempted to placate the couple's complaints, Pastor Rodney instructed the saints to pray.

Hudson returned with a glow about twenty minutes later. "I got it!" He leaped in the air for joy. "I got it!" Hudson worshipped with his hands lifted and tears streaming down his cheeks. The teenager praised God, conversing in heavenly tongues.

"What happened?" His mother squinted when her son panted for air.

"It's hard to explain, but I received the Holy Ghost. I heard the voice of God speaking to me in a foreign language." He grinned. "You've got to receive this, Mom. Jesus is real, but you and Dad have to repent first." The anointing was heavy on Hudson as he approached and embraced them.

His parents screamed out in agony as Porsha and others saw the outlines of demons tugging unknowingly with the Lanes' spirits to keep from surrendering.

"Release them, in the name of Jesus!" Hudson said with an authority that came from God.

The demons obeyed, and his parents dropped to their knees, weeping and repenting. Their emotions were raw. The power of the Holy Ghost emboldened Hudson, so the demons obeyed.

Jesus' presence was overpowering, and everyone bowed their heads in submission. Where was Grayson? Where was Amethyst? They both needed to be there to surrender and make the intercessors' jobs easier.

There's nothing easy about being one of my disciples, God whispered. *The hard work is just beginning.*

Chapter Eleven

It had been a few weeks since Amethyst had seen Porsha. That had been strategic. Her daily horoscopes warned her to avoid conflicts, people with bad vibes, and sharing plans with strangers. Since she resisted the urge to return to the church, Amethyst had also changed her lunchtime to avoid Porsha.

Within that time, things had changed for Amethyst, thanks to Reggie. He looked out for her.

Amethyst was in a happy place and decided to enjoy the mid-June sunshine in the Cortex area for the last time before the brutal heat and humidity punished St. Louisans. The shaded trees, neat landscape, and the birds in flight relaxed her.

She glanced up and saw trouble heading her way. Nothing was going to kill her joy. Not today, especially when her horoscope said, *Happiness is yours. Take it with you wherever you go.*

Porsha's flowing white skirt bounced with every strut she took, and her smile glowed as she carried her food bag to the table. What was her story anyway? Wasn't she married with a family, boyfriend, or close friends, so she wouldn't have to try so hard to be her friend?

"Hi, Amethyst. Want some company?" It wasn't a question as she took the chair across from her. "I missed seeing you." She seemed disappointed.

That's because I've been avoiding you. Amethyst dared not voice that. It sounded rude to her ears, but somehow, she hadn't been herself since she'd lost her baby. She was constantly agitated and preferred to be alone. The psychic said she was stronger by herself because others were jealous of her aura.

Porsha made herself comfortable and bowed her head to say grace. There had always been something about the woman's presence that made Amethyst uncomfortable. Maybe it was her aura. Amethyst always felt a tug-of-war with Porsha that she couldn't explain.

"Amen." She looked up and asked. "Have you been sick?"

"Nope." Amethyst took a sip from her straw and curled her lips into a smile. She couldn't be happier. "I have some good news."

Porsha wiggled in her chair and leaned forward, ready for the scoop. The excitement in her eyes made Amethyst chuckle.

"Today is my last day on the job!" She exhaled. Amethyst had been employed with Silo Manufacturing and Supplies for four years as a safety tech. It wasn't a glamorous job but an important one, she thought.

"Congratulations, Amethyst. How exciting to start somewhere new, but it's a bummer for you and me." Porsha pouted. "I had hoped we could become friends."

"I don't have too many friends."

"Which is why we should get together and find common interests." She had a gung-ho spirit.

Amethyst didn't want to commit, so she stalled for an answer.

Porsha must have sensed her hesitation and changed the subject. "So, what's your background?" She acted like she had all the time in the world instead of an allotted time for lunch.

"Well, I attended the University of Missouri at Columbia."

"Oh, MIZZOU. That's a great school. I had friends who went there."

The university was the state's largest of four public universities. "It is. I majored in health sciences and couldn't find a job. I took one as an adjuster for workers' compensation claims. After about five years, I decided I would rather do something proactive to prevent employees from getting injured on the job." Amethyst couldn't believe she'd rambled.

"I admire your passion for helping people."

"Thanks. I changed careers and trained to become an occupational health and safety technician for Silo." She pointed to the sandstone three-story building near the corner. "I've done good work, saved the company money by citing workplace violations before employees got injured."

"That's rewarding."

"Yeah, and I applied for a specialist position and was a top candidate but didn't get the job." Amethyst wouldn't forgive her boss, telling her he chose someone with better skills.

Her horoscope had warned her to be on guard for bad vibes, and the person Amethyst helped train got the position. Coming on the heels of her divorce, it was not a good time for another blow.

"I'm sorry." Porsha reached across the table and patted her hand. The gesture was warm and comforting—a foreign emotion. But Amethyst was still leery of strangers.

"Yeah. Thanks." Amethyst recovered and removed her hand. "I'm moving on. On Monday, I start a new job as an occupational safety specialist for a major company, making more money." She was not about to tell Porsha where, or the woman might follow her there.

"Well, congratulations." Porsha stood to wrap up the remains of her sandwich and collect her trash. "See, we just had lunch and got to know each other more. I wish you would take my number so we can chat again."

Amethyst watched as Porsha walked away. She hadn't planned to chatter like that. Besides Reggie, no one knew how hurt she was to get passed up for that promotion. Her mother told her to stop whining about the job and do something instead.

But things were looking up. Reggie had lent her money to pay the sales tax for her car and referred her for the job she'd accepted.

Luck was on her side, and Reggie said they had to celebrate. Amethyst stood and threw her trash away. She was too happy to be sad as she walked back to the company to do absolutely nothing for the next few hours.

Porsha drove home Friday night after work and cried in defeat. Amethyst's good news was not good for God's mission. "Lord, send help because I've fasted and prayed for Amethyst, Grayson, and others on the list, and nothing. I've witnessed to her with lovingkindness. I planted the seed. Let someone else water it…" Flustered, Porsha had no more words to add.

She didn't know how long she had been in prayer. When she had said her last Amen and sniffed, she sat quietly on the floor by her bed and drew her knees to her chest. Porsha checked her phone and noted she had missed three messages from her brother-in-law and two from her mother.

Panic pricked her heart as she called Randall first. "What's going on?"

"Where have you been? Your sister is in labor, and we're on our way to the hospital."

"Already?" She leaped from the floor and searched for her sandals and purse. "I thought she had a couple of weeks."

"Yeah, well, Little Miss Addams is ready now."

"I'll meet you at the hospital. I guess that's why Mom called me."

"Yep." Randall ended the call, and Porsha decided to change into comfy clothes in case of a long wait. She smiled, dismissing her pity party from earlier.

"I may have lost this battle, but we're gaining another little soldier in the Lord."

The battle was already won, God whispered.

In record time, Porsha raced to the hospital's family waiting room. "Did she have the baby?" Her heart pounded with excitement.

Her mother, Cynthia, stood and hugged her. "Not yet, sweetie. This is Tally's first one, so it can be a while."

"I ordered takeout for us," her father said.

Porsha blinked and scanned the crowded room. There were a lot of "us," including Randall's parents and his youngest sister, Delta.

Since Omega was also expecting, she and her husband, Mitchell, thought it best they wait it out at home so Omega could rest. A few close friends from church, including Mother Kincaid, who had appointed herself the Gilbert sisters' godmother, and newlyweds Minister Morgan and Sinclaire were also there.

Porsha worked the room, hugging and speaking to everyone before she took the open seat next to Mother Kincaid. The church mother wasn't a faultfinder but serious about God's assignment. Porsha hoped she wouldn't ask her about Amethyst.

Everyone was in a chatty, upbeat mood to keep Randall calm whenever he appeared in the room to give an update, which amounted to "not yet."

Not many people knew that Tally had miscarried their first child, and Randall hadn't known about the pregnancy until after they had broken up. That worry had been in the back of the couple's minds.

Minutes later, Randall came back to the room and sat down. "Tally said I'm making her nervous and kicked me out for now."

His parents laughed, and Mrs. Addams shook her head. "Good for her. If something changes, the nurse will come and get you."

"I still don't like it." Randall huffed.

Some church members joked with him and then teased the newlyweds who were cozy in the corner. Sinclaire blushed while Minister Morgan grinned. With a protective arm around Sinclaire's shoulder, he relaxed and changed the subject to take the spotlight off himself and his wife. "The Lord sure knew how to pick the souls on the list," he began as Porsha's stomach sank. "That young man is winning souls!"

"Yes! Every Sunday, Hudson brings more friends and neighbors to church, and some are surrendering," Mother Kincaid said. "We have to keep praying for the others. Has anyone seen Grayson Tate in church lately?"

"I've spotted him coming late and leaving early before the altar call," Randall said.

Mother Kincaid *tsk*ed. "He's running. But his salvation is paramount." She turned to Porsha. "Anything to report on Amethyst?"

Gritting her teeth, Porsha glanced away, then stuffed her hands under her bottom as if they were cold. "Well, I saw her today. Nothing has changed with her attitude, but it was her last day on the job." She expected no mercy because the intercessors were prayer warriors on steroids, and it was all hands on deck when it came to winning souls. "Sorry."

Randall stood and scooted another saint out of the way to play big brother, and his gesture comforted her. "God knows how to reach her, sis. The responsibility isn't solely on one person."

Minister Morgan added, "There are seventeen of us on the intercessors team. God will put one of us on the trail. Just keep praying,"

"Right. Why couldn't all of them be easy like Brother Hudson?" she asked.

Mother Kincaid patted her leg. "None of us come to Jesus the same way. Some will follow Jesus after some miraculous event in their lives, others will come when they hit rock bottom, and only the Lord can pull them out."

The hours dragged on until almost everyone was dozing, including Porsha, until Randall burst through the door crying and yelling, "She's here! My little princess is here!" He wiped his eyes. "Valeria's so beautiful, like her mother."

Not surprisingly, Tally had loved that name since they were children after hearing it in a cartoon.

As everyone congratulated him, her mother asked, "What is little Valeria's middle name?"

Randall smiled at Porsha. "Valeria Porsha Addams."

Now it was Porsha's turn to boo-hoo. Tears of joy. "Thank you."

Maybe, one day she would have a family of her own and return the favor with a daughter having Tally as her middle name.

Chapter Twelve

What man of you, having a hundred sheep,
if he loses one of them, doth not leave the ninety-nine in
the wilderness and go after that which is lost until he finds it?
And when he has found it, he lays it on his shoulders, rejoicing.
—Luke 15:4–5

Jude Morgan rolled over in bed, cuddled his wife of seventy-seven days, and smiled. He drifted back to sleep.

Get up and pray! God thundered.

Since the sheep know their shepherd's voice, Jude stirred and groaned. Now? It had nothing to do with him being married. When the Lord woke him as a single man in the middle of the night, he asked the same thing. But he and Sinclaire had spent hours at the hospital with Tally and Randall, then church on Sunday. Both of them had to work in the morning.

Groaning, he untangled his arms from under Sinclaire and rolled out of bed. Instead of his bedroom serving as his prayer room, Jude had constructed a makeshift prayer room in his finished basement.

He stood, yawned, grabbed his robe, shoved his feet into his slippers, then quietly hurried downstairs to his prayer room. God didn't like to wait.

Once he was behind the frosted glass pane bi-fold door, he fell to his knees.

He bowed his head, closed his eyes, and waited. "Speak, Lord."

Satan has dispatched his demons to the battlefield. Pray to overcome, not faint, or yield to temptation because I am with you, God whispered.

That's all Jude needed. "Jesus," he yelled at the top of his lungs, knowing the foam padding on the walls muffled his voice. "I know our weapons aren't carnal but mighty through You to the pulling down of the demons' strongholds. Your name is so mighty that demons tremble. We stand on Your Word, and demons know their end. Satan, you will not shake our faith. Jesus has made us battle ready…"

Jude prayed hard, entering the spiritual realm where angels stood at attention at the Lord's throne, waiting for God's command. Heavenly tongues filled Jude's mouth as he felt a weight shift beside him. He didn't know the object until he heard his wife's sweet voice as she joined him in prayer. "Satan, you are the father of lies, but we stand on God's truth, which is His Word…" Sinclaire declared.

Jude wanted to smile at the helpmate God had given him but couldn't as his spiritual eyes opened to see the war waged against the saints on earth. Demons snatched up the souls of men, women, and children and tossed them into a pit where thick, black smoke bellowed. As Jude called on the name of Jesus, angels were dispatched to rescue them from their grips. Sinclaire entered the throne. She fought beside him until they were exhausted.

Spiritual warfare was draining. Jude stood and helped Sinclaire to her feet. He kissed her forehead. "Did I wake you up?"

She smiled and shook her head. "The Lord did."

He squeezed her tight and then attempted to open the door. It appeared stuck until he saw a body lying on his side.

"Carlton," Sinclaire called softly, but Jude shooed her.

Jude leaned over and scooped his adopted son in his arms, then heaped him over his shoulder, wrapped his arm around Sinclaire's waist, and headed back upstairs.

They took Carlton to his bedroom, and Jude slipped him under the covers, then checked on Tyler Jr., who was named after his biological father but called TJ, who was sound asleep.

"I thank God for my wife being willing to pray alongside me," Jude said as they returned to their bedroom.

She brushed a soft kiss against his lips. "A family that prays together stays together, right? I wouldn't want to miss the presence of God's glory like that. Whew!" Yawning, she spied the time. "But we only have a few hours before our alarm goes off."

"Trust me, from experience, God will multiply our sleep time." They slipped back under the covers and closed their eyes.

When they woke, he and Sinclaire were refreshed as if they had gotten eight hours. In the kitchen, Jude helped prepare a quick breakfast for their three children. It was the first day of summer camp for Carlton, TJ, and Sissy. All three were excited to see Harry, Carlton's half-brother, whom most thought was his twin.

Once Jude kissed each family member goodbye, he was headed out the door when Carlton stopped him.

"Dad, you forgot to pray for us," his eleven-year-old son said.

Jude returned to the table and joined hands. "Lord, as we go our separate ways, bless and protect our family. Let us return home safely and remember to tell someone about Jesus."

"In Jesus' name!" shouted Sissy, two years younger than Carlton.

"Amen," they said in unison, and Jude was out the door.

"How can a man not be happy with a family God gave him?" He grinned while driving to the aerospace company near his home. He had been strategic when he purchased his house as a bachelor. It was in a safe neighborhood—except for a shooting at his home a year ago. Despite that incident, his robust neighborhood watch association made sure curb appeal was meticulous in keeping their property value competitive.

Jude strolled into work minutes later and was about to head to the employee kitchen to put away leftovers when he realized he didn't have his wallet. He called Sinclaire.

"Hey, babe. Are you still at home?"

"I was about to walk out the door with your wallet."

He chuckled. "I love this woman."

"And I love this man. See you in a few." He ended the call, then heard voices and felt a presence. He glanced over his shoulder. No one was there. This happened for about ten minutes.

He shook it off, and seconds later, Emerson Carey strolled into the kitchen with a woman.

Pivoting on his heels, Jude's spirit alerted him to be on guard as his eyes met hers.

"Hey, Jude, I want you to meet our new employee, Amethyst Johnson."

Amethyst Johnson. Finally, they meet. Jude thought about suspects who evade authorities on The Ten Most Wanted List. Amethyst had been playing a game of hide-and-seek with the intercessors. She might have run from Porsha, but she couldn't dodge him on the job. Jude would make sure of it. Behind Amethyst, dark witch-like figures followed her. Instead of shaking her hand, Jude grinned. "Welcome aboard. It's nice to meet you."

The woman had no idea how much he had waited for this opportunity to be a witness. Where Porsha had planted the seed—or tried to—Jude would attempt to water it.

She blinked. "You look familiar." Amethyst stared at him, and he refused to be pulled into the depths of her eyes. Amethyst was into some dark stuff, which controlled her emotions.

"I think I was at your wedding." She smiled. It appeared genuine—not the stand-offish woman Porsha described. Then she began to gush about the ceremony as a light seemed to flicker in her eyes. "She was beautiful, and you have three children, right?"

"Yes, we do." Sinclaire glided in the room. TJ raced to him as if he hadn't just seen him at home. "Hello." She nodded at Amethyst and introduced herself and then the children.

"I'm Amethyst Johnson. I was at your wedding, and it was beautiful."

Emerson's phone rang, and he stepped away to talk. Carlton stepped forward when Jude saw the dark figures whispering in Amethyst's ear.

"Release her!" Carlton ordered with spiritual authority.

"She belongs to us!" The demons sounded like a manipulated AI experiment.

"It is written in the Word that all souls belong to God," Jude said, focusing on the demons. "What are your names?"

"Zoarx, Mole, and Sarx."

"In the name of Jesus, I rebuke the stronghold on Amethyst. Release her," Jude commanded in the spirit.

"She will die," one of them said.

"Amethyst will live. Jesus has preserved her soul from the beginning of time, and Christ died on the cross so as not to lose one of them," Carlton said with a power that illuminated the room, which oddly enough was empty of employees as if God had barricaded them inside during the battle.

When the demons realized they weren't overcome with fear, they flew out of the room.

Amethyst immediately blinked. "I feel dizzy."

They helped her to a chair.

Sinclaire asked, "Are you okay?"

"I guess I blacked out." Amethyst nodded. "I don't know what happened. I haven't been sleeping well."

Sinclaire turned to her husband, and he read her concerned expression, knowing this woman was on the devil's hit list, but in Jesus' name, Satan couldn't have her.

Amethyst had to catch her breath.

Her head was spinning.

She was suddenly exhausted, blinking at her audience—three children and the parents. "I'm embarrassed. That's never happened to me."

Jude squatted in front of her. "We prayed for you to have a good day. I'm an engineer in the non-destructive department on the fourth floor, so reach out to me."

"Thanks." She nodded as his wife handed her a glass of water, then faced Jude.

"Here, babe." She gave him a wallet, which he stuffed in his back pocket. They shared a quick peck on the lips. "Come on, children. Let's get you to summer camp."

"It was nice meeting you," Amethyst said, trying to catch her breath.

As they turned to leave, their oldest son stopped and faced her again. He was so handsome and good-mannered. She sometimes wondered if the baby she had lost had been a boy or a girl.

"Miss Amethyst, your baby is okay. You would have had a boy named Braydon."

"How…how did you know I lost a baby?" Amethyst frowned. The psychic said she was pregnant, and the toxic relationship she was in would cause her to lose it, and she'd hated Grayson ever since then.

"God showed me," Carlton said. "He would have looked like his daddy."

Amethyst grunted and took her time standing as Emerson returned, apologizing for leaving her stranded.

"Well, it was interesting meeting you all," she added, then mumbled, "I guess."

She began to walk away on shaky legs. She chanced a glance over her shoulder at the family. Carlton waved the most enthusiastically. Despite their distance, he mouthed something she shouldn't have been able to hear, but the air carried the child's words.

"God has two more babies for you if you return to your husband."

That was eerie. How did he know she was divorced? And no way in this world was she getting back with Grayson Tate. Reggie and the psychic both said that wasn't a good idea.

Nope. She shook off the conversation and regrouped to wow her coworkers on day one.

It is My will that you and Grayson remain married, God whispered.

"It ain't mine," she mumbled and followed Emerson as he made more introductions.

The remainder of her shift was uneventful, but she stayed away from the floor where Jude worked. His son was creepier than the psychic on Amethyst's first visit, yet she believed him.

The day ended on a good note. Her coworkers were friendly and welcoming. She returned to her mother's place, craving privacy to process what had happened at work.

After eating dinner with her mom, Amethyst retired to her bedroom, and Reggie called to check on her. "Hey. How was your first day?"

His positive energy inspired her to smile. "So far, so good. I love the pay, people, and the atmosphere."

"I hear a *but* coming."

Amethyst strained her brain as she rocked her head from side to side. Reggie didn't know she had stepped foot in a random church while a wedding was in progress, then ran into the newlyweds at her new job. And their son left her in a confused state about her miscarriage and predictions of more babies to come. It didn't make sense. Were the stars misaligned?

The nonsense wasn't worth discussing and upsetting Reggie. He was very protective of Amethyst. Reggie came to the house she shared with Grayson and helped her pack her things while

Grayson fumed. His brother—half-brother, as Grayson always clarified—wasn't concerned. Her former husband's lack of emotions caused her to leave. She wanted him to beg her to stay, show that he cared. In the end, Grayson didn't.

Amethyst was almost in perfect harmony, so she wanted to keep the peace. "You know I'm selective of my circle, so I'm feeling people out. If anyone gives me any problems, I can tell my big brother, and you'll get them." She chuckled.

"I hope I'm more than a big brother to you," Reggie said. His tender voice wrapped her in a cocoon of safety.

"You are." He was her best friend, confidant, and more. Amethyst smiled when she heard giggles in the background. "What are your babies doing?" Kiya was three, and Victor was six years old.

"I'm taking them for snow cones. You want to come? I'll treat you to celebrate your first day on the job."

"Thanks, but I'm tired. I need to get some rest." That was true. Plus, his wife, Jessica, hadn't cared for Amethyst since she'd started dating Grayson, but she tolerated her. Once Amethyst overheard Jessica say, "It's something about her that I don't like…"

What did that mean?

Of course, her brother-in-law defended her. "My big brother picked a winner, and he had better treat her right."

When Amethyst and Grayson had problems, only Reggie seemed sympathetic and took her side. To this day, friends were hard to come by, and Amethyst didn't trust them.

But she trusted Reggie completely.

Chapter Thirteen

*"I have planted, Apollos watered, but God gave the increase.
So then neither is he that plants anything, neither he that waters;
but God that giveth the increase. Now he that plants and he that
waters are one: and every man shall receive his reward according
to his own labor."* —1 Corinthians 3:6–8

Jude phoned Mother Kincaid on his way home from work that evening. After the customary greeting, he gave her the startling but good news. "You'll never believe who's a new hire at my company." He didn't give her a chance to guess. "Amethyst Johnson works in my building."

"Hallelujah! Thank You, Jesus!" Mother Kincaid laughed as she praised God until she said goodbye so she could worship Him.

Grinning, his next call was to Porsha, and he told her the latest.

"Unbelievable. Are you kidding me? Wow. I don't know if I'm relieved that God answered my prayers to send help or disappointed that I couldn't get the job done to bring her to Christ."

"Witnessing to a person's soul takes a team effort, like a village," Jude tried to assure her. "I had to stand down as Carlton took leadership to pray for her and order the demons that were torturing her to leave." Jude was proud of his son and how he had yielded to the spiritual gift God had given him.

"At least we all know where she works. She has access to me, and I plan to pray and give her encouraging words when I see her around, even if I have to go to the floor where she works. I sense she is tormented."

Porsha sighed. "Yes. Thanks, Minister Morgan, for letting me know."

"Comfort her soul, Lord," Jude prayed for her after they ended the call.

Minutes later, he drove into his garage. The kitchen door opened, and Carlton and the other children peeped their heads out, greeting him with smiles and excitement. Jude would never get enough of their hero worship.

He kissed his wife and children, washed his hands, then helped prepare dinner. Even the children set the table with plates and silverware.

At the dinner table, Carlton talked nonstop about Ms. Amethyst while stuffing his mouth with pasta.

Jude corrected him. "Use the manners your mom taught you."

Wiping his mouth, Carlton apologized. "Dad, the devil doesn't like Ms. Amethyst, but I see angels behind her and the devil's army in front of her." He twisted his lips in concern.

"That's why the Lord God has commanded the intercessors to fast and pray without ceasing on this assignment. We have to pray for her soul, no matter what the devil's strategy is to take her down," Jude said.

"Okay, Dad. Harry is praying too." He grinned and slid peas into his mouth.

Carlton and his half-brother were as close as two brothers could be. The unfortunate death of their biological father put the two boys together, and they have been inseparable ever since.

Since Harry carried their biological father's last name, Wakefield, Carlton wanted that name too. Jude couldn't deny him that birthright, so they changed Carlton's surname to Wakefield when they married. His siblings' last names were changed from Sinclaire's maiden name, Oliver, to Morgan.

After a day at summer camp, the children were ready for bed when they finished their meal. Jude and Sinclaire took advantage of their quiet time to cuddle up and listen to music and each other's heartbeats.

Soon, they yawned and headed for their bedroom. As Jude laid his head on his pillow and closed his eyes, God showed him Amethyst and the devils following her step by step like bodyguards. They had a stronghold on the woman.

Go to work early every morning and begin to pray around her desk, chair, and the perimeter of her workspace, God whispered.

So the battlefield was coming to Jude's job, and he had to be on double duty—for his job and the Lord to watch and pray for Amethyst.

The devil was going down.

Grayson's world was shattered. He thought his marriage was over on paper, but the dissolution was in limbo. Supposedly, his estranged wife was in danger. What had she gotten herself into?

Feeling helpless, Grayson went through the motions of attending church, looking for answers about what to do. He wished he could talk to Amee. She made sure they couldn't have direct contact, cutting all ties with him until their court date. His options were to communicate through their attorneys, call her job, or call her mother.

He learned Amethyst had blocked his number when he called her about a clause in the divorce decree. Grayson was hot after that, adding fire to their disdain.

Despite the arguments, hateful words, and rejection on both sides, Grayson suddenly cared when he learned she was in trouble almost a month ago.

Church came to mind, but he didn't see how that was the solution. During the times he had attended service, Grayson felt uncomfortable and ready to leave, but his feet wouldn't move, so he was stuck in quicksand.

Grayson sat home bored after work and rubbed his head between his hands. His phone rang—a welcome distraction.

Reggie's wife. What did Jessica want? He answered, not having a problem with her, just her husband.

He liked Jessica. She was a good mother to her two children and always nice to Grayson. She never got between her husband and Grayson's disagreements. He couldn't say the same thing about Reggie when he and Amethyst had a war of words.

"Hi, Grayson. I hate to bother you. Reggie and the children have been gone from the house for a while. I was wondering if they're over there."

"Sorry. I haven't seen them." If Reggie had brought his children to Grayson's house, his half-brother would not have stayed long because of their strained relationship.

He was about to end the call when Jessica stopped him. "Do you think he's having an affair?"

"Whoa." Grayson blinked. Reggie boasted about his money and family. "How would I know?"

"He calls Amethyst a lot." She sighed. "I will kill him, Grayson, and if your ex gets in my way, she'll get hurt too." Jessica ended the call.

Blinking, Grayson sat straighter and replayed the conversation. Was Reggie having an affair—with Amethyst? He needed a minute to wrap his mind around that possibility. What if what Jessica said was true? Grayson hoped Amethyst would not be involved.

Emotions whirled in his head. Reggie needed to focus on his family.

When Grayson asked Reggie why he was at his home to help Amethyst move, he replied, "To keep you from doing something stupid. Face it, bro, she's leaving you and doesn't want you to stop her."

Grayson couldn't stop the laughter from rolling in his stomach. "Stop her? She is free to go if that's what she wants to do."

"That's what she wants," Reggie said without Amethyst saying a word. She just kept packing.

Grayson fumed and wanted to retaliate, and he couldn't punch his wife—or his brother. As a child, Grayson was reprimanded for fighting his younger brother instead of protecting him. There was never any love lost between them as teenagers, and as adults, they were cordial and tolerated each other. Grayson never knew hate could be so strong until he stared down Reggie, who dared him to try anything with a smirk.

Questions remained, and Grayson had no right to demand answers.

Did Amethyst have an affair with his brother while they were married? Was Jessica crazy enough to carry out her threat? She was quiet, unassuming, and devoted to her husband and family.

That night, Grayson didn't get any sleep. He teetered on dismissing Jessica's concern and calling Reggie to see if he was home. The next morning, he wished he knew the outcome of Reggie's whereabouts.

If he called Reggie, his brother would only bait him. Growing concerned about being in the know, Grayson called Amethyst on her job the first chance he got a break. He was surprised she no longer worked there. Now, he was troubled.

His coworkers noticed his distraction all day.

"Lord, I don't know what to do," he mumbled as he left work Thursday evening. He drove home in a daze.

Pray, God whispered.

Hadn't he done that in his marriage? But to be honest, Grayson went through the motions with little sincerity. He was fed up with the arguments and drama between them. "Will it make a difference now? I don't know how." Grayson was ashamed to admit that to God, but it was true. They had just been words.

Randall had told him that Amethyst was in trouble—something about a spiritual battle. Grayson cursed and pounded his steering wheel. "What does that mean?" The only way to keep Amethyst safe was to keep her close, but how could he do that?

When he pulled into his driveway, Grayson decided to end the turmoil and call Amethyst's mother since Amethyst lived with her now. He debated whether to leave a message or call back as the phone rang. He was ready to disconnect when she answered.

"Well, well, well. Grayson Tate. My daughter's ex. How are you?" She didn't hide her sarcasm.

"Hi, Miss Annabelle. How are you?" Grayson remained polite. "I'm calling to check on Amethyst."

Silence. "She's fine and happy. You're divorced now, so Amee is no longer your concern."

That's what I thought too. Grayson measured his next words. "I know things didn't go right between Amethyst and me, and I blame myself and your daughter for our troubles, but I would like us to be at least polite."

"Now? After all this time, you two haven't talked." She chuckled.

"No, ma'am." Grayson swallowed. Although Miss Annabelle didn't interfere in their marriage, she sided with Amethyst about anything. Whatever she told her mom made Grayson the villain. "Is Amee at home?"

"She isn't."

Whether she was truthful or not, Grayson wouldn't challenge her. "Okay. Sorry to bother you. Will you ask her to call me, please?"

"I'll do that. Take care."

Grayson felt lost, resting his head on the steering wheel. What should he do?

Call Randall, God whispered.

Why? He was connected to the woman who caught his eye. No, he would have to figure out something else.

Chapter Fourteen

Amethyst woke exhausted. Had she been beaten up in her sleep? The fear of someone or something clawing had made her scream. It was too real. Amethyst heard the piercing sound in her ear. She punched and kicked out of darkness toward a sliver of light she could never reach.

Groaning, Amethyst sat up in bed, gagging and panting for clean, fresh air to rid herself of the pungent smell of rotting or burning flesh, an odor she would never forget after citing a cook for a safety violation that resulted in third-degree burns for an employee.

She had experienced a nightmare of nightmares and was relieved when she opened her eyes to see she was in the safety of the second bedroom in her mother's apartment. The curtains swayed from the cool air blowing from the floor vents. The room was inviting with recently vacuumed beige carpet and white wood bedroom furniture.

Safe.

For the third time in a row, spirits were angry and tortured her all night.

Drowsy, Amethyst stepped out of bed to get ready for work. Standing in front of the bathroom mirror, she noticed her face seemed twisted. Her hair, which she had wrapped the night before, was loose from its scarf, and wild strands pointed in every direction. The crazed look scared her at first glance.

She stretched, and her body ached from exertion.

If it weren't the first week on the new job, Amethyst would have called in sick and climbed back in bed for some rest. She couldn't.

Thanks to Reggie, she got what she wanted—a new job and the plates for her car.

An envelope arrived from her divorce attorney a few days ago. Something seemed off, so Amethyst hadn't bothered to open it.

Nothing had seemed normal since the first day she'd met Jude and his family. His son Carlton's details about her baby made Amethyst believe he had seen him alive. But her baby had died after only a few months inside her belly, so that was a lie. Amethyst thought she heard a child's cry in her dream. She shivered and banished that thought.

Amethyst put extra effort into her morning routine because she looked tired. She showered, dressed, and then walked into the kitchen for coffee.

Her mother turned from the window, looking refreshed. Annabelle had gotten a good night's rest.

"Morning, Mom." She kissed her cheek.

"It's going to be a great day." She grinned like she had the winning lottery ticket. "I checked our horoscopes. Mine says, 'You're attractive and enthusiastic. Compliments are coming your way.'" She grinned and pivoted on her heels as if modeling a new outfit.

"And mine?" Amethyst poured a cup of coffee and closed her eyes to take a sip while her mother found Amethyst's horoscope again.

"Today is a good day to nurture your ambition," her mother added. "You're unstoppable."

Who says? Amethyst thought. Those dark figures visiting her at night seemed to have another message.

Jude was certain Amethyst had been avoiding him all week, so on Friday morning, when he arrived at work, he asked Emerson, her supervisor, which cubicle was hers since there were four lined up against the opposite wall.

"Over there with the bouquet on her desk."

Flowers? Who would send her flowers? Had Grayson reached out? he wondered.

At Amethyst's desk, Jude began to pray silently. From her chair to the floor where she rested her feet—the walls, the top of the desk, and the atmosphere around it. He prayed until he heard voices coming from the elevator. Jude took the back stairwell, not wanting Amethyst to see him and spook her—or worse, accuse him of stalking or harassment.

"Lord, protect her while she's here from the forces of evil, in Jesus' name. Amen."

He didn't see anything in the spiritual realm, but his spirit felt the presence of opposition, although God had commanded him the night before to get up and pray.

This time, Sinclaire didn't follow him. She was sound asleep, but Carlton found his way downstairs and entered the prayer room with Jude. They prayed until all their strength was gone.

Carlton dozed off, and Jude lifted him and put him back in bed, then got under the covers with his wife and asked God to give him renewed energy for the day.

As expected, he didn't see Amethyst by the time he left work for the weekend.

It was prayer time at Christ For All Church. Intercessors were expected to attend the all-night prayer shut-in service, but the new mommies and daddies were the exception.

Sissy and TJ spent the night with Tally and Randall to play with the baby.

Carlton and his brother Harry would not be denied prayer time with God.

On his knees, Jude pleaded for Amethyst and the others' souls, and Satan seemed to taunt him.

"I'll never let her go!"

"You have no choice, in Jesus' name," Jude boldly stated, and he wasn't the only one in the sanctuary talking back to the devil as God directed them.

On Saturday evening, after resting from the all-night prayer, Carlton and his siblings gave a recap of their first week at summer camp at the dinner table.

"Guess what, Mom and Dad?" Carlton's face beamed excitedly.

"What, son?" Jude smiled at Sinclaire. She knew how much he loved being called Dad or Daddy. They had also discussed having one or two children together in the future.

"There's a girl there named Sophia Doyle."

I'm coming for the children, God whispered.

Jude's heart pounded. He hadn't thought that those on the list could be children.

"She's in my group and nine years old like me, Daddy." Sissy was proud.

Unlike Carlton, the Lord hadn't manifested the gift of intercessory in Sissy or TJ. Time would tell if Sissy would follow their lead and learn how to witness to other children effectively.

As if Carlton knew her thoughts, he said, "Harry and I have been praying for her, but we can't talk to her because the older boys can't play with the younger girls."

Jude nodded. "God will make a way. After dinner, we'll let Mother Kincaid know."

Sinclaire called on the speakerphone, and Jude repeated what their children said. Sissy and TJ were about to go to their rooms and play when Mother Kincaid stopped them.

"No one is exempt from doing God's work. Sissy, I need you to listen to God's voice and say and do whatever Jesus tells you, okay?" Her voice was gentle.

Sissy nodded as if Mother Kincaid could see her.

"What do you say?" Sinclaire prompted their daughter to respond.

"Yes, Mother Kincaid. I will. Can I go now?" Sissy looked from Jude to Sinclaire.

"Yes, child. Mother Kincaid loves you." She paused, then continued. "Is Carlton still there?"

"Yes, ma'am." Carlton sat straighter.

"I'm glad the camp counselors are monitoring the children, but she's on the list and must be witnessed delicately in a way for her to understand to save her soul and those of her family and others."

"Okay," Carlton said and stood to leave. "I'm going to call Harry and tell him what you said."

Jude, his wife, and the church mother prayed, especially for those on the list. "I see these souls could be anywhere—on my job, church, or summer camp."

"Yes. So where are Wyatt Sheppard, Olivia Baker, and Joi Clark hiding? We can't let our guards down now."

That was two adults and two children, although Hudson Lane was a teenager. The remaining three could be either/or.

You haven't rescued Sophia yet, Satan taunted.

But we will, in Jesus' name, Jude's spirit roared back.

Chapter Fifteen

Porsha sat in church on Sunday, battling self-doubt since Minister Morgan told her Amethyst was working in his building. Did Amethyst open up to her because she thought they would never see each other again?

Meditate on these things. Whatsoever is true, honest, pure, lovely, of good report. I have given you a good report with Hudson, God whispered and comforted her self-doubt about the effectiveness of her witness.

Yes, Hudson Lane thrived inside and outside the congregation. Today, his parents repented and made the decision to return to God. They had made a one-eighty from barging into the church to stop Hudson's salvation journey to wanting to take that same walk as their son.

He believed God for his parents to return to God with sincere hearts, and they did. Like a sponge, he was bringing classmates and neighbors to church. Some returned, and others didn't.

The important thing was the teenager was evangelizing for the Lord.

Apparently, Carlton and his half-brother Harry had been assigned to draw the little girl Sophia to Christ.

"Praise God for that."

She stood and swayed to the song. Porsha thought about Grayson. When he came, he hid in the back but was in plain view of the intercessors. She prayed harder for him because Grayson never left his seat and walked down the aisle to the altar in response to Pastor Rodney's invitation to repent and reconcile with God.

Amethyst, on the other hand, was more of a challenge. Her hiding place was always on the other side, in the corner, always late, then leaving early. That one Porsha had to search out.

As Pastor Rodney walked to the podium to deliver the sermon, Porsha glanced over her shoulder. Yep. Just as she thought. Amethyst was in one corner, Grayson in the other, and the church was their boxing ring.

Lord, they are both here—again. What are You going to do to draw them? she wondered.

It is My will they are not consumed, God whispered.

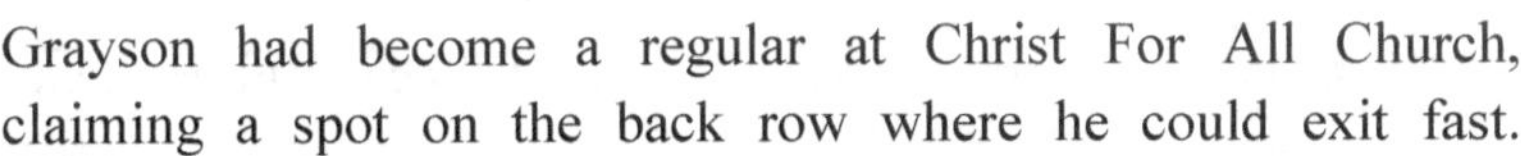

Grayson had become a regular at Christ For All Church, claiming a spot on the back row where he could exit fast. Showing up had to account for something, he guessed.

According to Randall, God claimed Amethyst as his wife. That was so far from the truth.

I am not a man that I should lie. God's words lashed out at him.

Fear gripped Grayson. He sat motionless despite the energy surrounding him.

What did God want from him? The pastor had almost persuaded Grayson through his sermons to surrender his will and control of his life, but it wasn't that easy.

Salvation was the comeback for people who had hit rock bottom in life. Divorce wasn't the worst thing that could happen to a person.

It is when it's not really what you want, his mind told him.

Too late now.

"There's still time for you to make a one-eighty in your life!" Pastor Rodney screamed into the microphone as if he was talking directly to Grayson. His mind had drifted, and he hadn't realized the man was preaching.

"As long as you have breath in your body, there is hope for your situation to change, but the devil doesn't want you to know that. Stop letting the devil beat you up. John ten verse ten says, *'The thief comes to steal, kill, and destroy. I have come that they might have life and that they might have it more abundantly.'* Know your enemy and know its mission."

Kill. Jessica's words replayed in his head about killing Amethyst if she was having an affair with Reggie.

Reggie would get hurt if he had an affair with Amethyst. Grayson shook his head to dismiss the thought. He squinted, then blinked. Was that Amethyst? It couldn't be. The woman was shaped like his ex-wife, but she looked lifeless, dark, and almost like a zombie, not the glowing, vibrant woman he had married.

What had happened to her in six months?

Yes, she was angry when she left but still beautiful. His heart cried for her.

What had worn her to the core? Grayson stood to go to her, but his feet wouldn't obey his command to move.

God thundered, *Save yourself before you save others.*

Inwardly protesting, Grayson's steps took him to the altar as the pastor encouraged people to come. Heavy emotions overpowered Grayson and tears flowed freely. Once he stood before a minister, he lifted his arms to God. "I want to be saved." The words spilled from his mouth. "I want to believe that Jesus can forgive me. I want to fight the devil."

"Brother, your salvation is sure when Jesus died on the cross for you," the minister said. "The Bible says to repent and be baptized in the name of Jesus for the remission of your sins. Have you repented?"

Grayson admitted his life was out of control and repented on the spot. *Lord, I'm sorry for making a mess out of my life. I'm sorry for the people I hurt for not investing in my marriage.* The sins rolled through his mind. The word *yes* escaped his mouth as the strength in his legs gave out, and his knees hit the floor; he couldn't stop bowing in the Lord's presence.

Next, he met a minister who introduced himself as Jude. He helped Grayson to his feet and guided him to a small dressing room.

"You're about to become a new creature in Christ. Your life will belong to Jesus, and His blessings can't be compared to what you think you can provide for yourself." Once he entered a single dressing room, the door closed behind him, and he took a deep breath. Realization hit him that he, Grayson Tate, was doing this.

"Change into one of those white T-shirts and pants, and I'll see you in the pool," Jude said from the other side of the door.

Grayson did as instructed before he changed his mind, but something told him he couldn't go back to the life that he had been living.

Two men were standing on either side when he opened the dressing room door. They were also dressed in white, clapping and cheering him on. Hyped, Grayson was ready. They introduced themselves, but their names didn't stick as he followed to an entrance that led to the pool.

On the other side, a woman stood dressed in a white gown and swim cap, ready to descend.

Jude, the minister from earlier, and another man awaited them.

Was that Amethyst? he wondered, but she was shorter and thicker, not the woman he'd spied across the sanctuary.

He stepped into the water and crossed his arms over his chest as Jude instructed.

"Grayson Tate and Brianna..." Jude began.

Grayson didn't recall giving this man his name—or maybe he did—but was disappointed it wasn't Amethyst.

"My dear brother and sister, upon the confession of your faith and the confidence we have in the blessed Word of God concerning the Lord's death, burial, and grand resurrection, we now indeed baptize you in the only name under heaven by which any of us can be saved, Jesus Christ, for the remission of your sins, and Acts two verse thirty-eight says you shall receive the gift of the Holy Ghost."

The minister had a firm grip on the collar of Grayson's T-shirt when he submerged him. For a moment, it seemed like Grayson was trapped in a case, and a hinge was loosened so that he felt he could float. Grayson re-emerged from the water like a rocket was fired.

He couldn't explain what happened next, but Grayson did not feel like the same Grayson Tate who had stepped into that pool. He had been set free of every burden that had him nailed inside the coffin.

"I'm free!" he shouted, and everything else that came out of his mouth was the Voice of God.

Now, you can serve Me, God whispered.

Chapter Sixteen

For we wrestle not against flesh and blood,
but against principalities, against powers, against the rulers
of the darkness of this world, against spiritual wickedness
in high places. —Ephesians 6:12

Tears streamed from Porsha's eyes as she witnessed Grayson's baptism. She swallowed back the emotion. "You have a chance now," she whispered. One down, and his other half to go.

Knowing who Grayson Tate was, the saints roared in praise as they worshiped God for His mercy. Porsha was no exception—until she felt a tap on her shoulder. Annoyed that someone wasn't in accord with the Spirit of God, she opened her eyes to see the culprit.

The saints praised God as more candidates stepped into the pool for their baptisms. Porsha squinted through the crowd, standing throughout the sanctuary, and God allowed her to zoom in on Amethyst, who seemed unaffected by the movement of the Lord's Spirit.

Porsha began to pray. This could be the day of salvation for Amethyst and Grayson. Porsha took off in Amethyst's direction.

Carlton and his brother Harry cut off her path. They beat her to Amethyst. Carlton smiled. Amethyst didn't. That's when Porsha noticed a dark, human-shaped, giant-size figure hovering over her.

"Don't touch her!" Mother Kincaid's voice said from behind Porsha.

The boys froze, as did Porsha.

"So you see it too?" Porsha asked.

Mother Kincaid nodded as her nostrils flared. "Prepare for battle. The devil is on our turf—holy ground."

"Should I go and get Mother Lynn and—"

"No. You are here for such a time as this. This is our fight."

"In the name of Jesus, release her now!" Mother Kincaid said and grabbed Porsha. "You have to intercede on Amethyst's behalf, or she will die in darkness."

With a boldness that Porsha didn't know she possessed, she stood before Amethyst, whose eyes were glossed over. She snarled like an animal and became aggressive, spewing curse words at no one.

"In the mighty name of Jesus, you have no authority over her!" Porsha stayed focused on the dark form. "The Word of God says every soul is God's."

"She's mine!" It didn't sound human.

Amethyst continued to growl and hiss.

Jump in as my backup anytime, Mother Kincaid, Porsha wanted to plead as the older saint prayed silently. Porsha yielded her spiritual sword and began to quote the Word of God, "We are overcomers because Jesus has overcome this world. The Lord rebukes you. The Power of His Holy Ghost resists you."

"If Adam and Eve could be beguiled, Amethyst is weaker," the thing said with a roar coming out of Amethyst's mouth.

By now, others had joined in prayer, but Porsha was still taking the lead in the spiritual battle, repeating the words God gave her until the force of heavenly tongues pushed forth.

The adversary was formidable, but Porsha refused to back down. Amethyst's soul depended on it. Grayson depended on it, and the Lord demanded it.

Porsha was no longer in control as the Holy Ghost's presence strengthened her. Loud, angry, commanding heavenly tongues flowed from her mouth, causing the dark form to retreat.

We will be back.

Multiple figures split from one dark form and flew away from around Amethyst. She shook violently until she collapsed on the pew.

Amethyst appeared drugged and disoriented.

"We can't let those demons return and possess her," Mother Kincaid said.

Next, worshipers surrounded Amethyst, shouting hallelujahs and singing, "Victory Is Mine."

"Porsha," Mother Kincaid said, "when those demons come back, Amethyst needs to be washed clean and her temple filled with the Holy Ghost, so there won't be room for Satan's demons to stay."

"I know." Porsha gnawed on her lips. She had worked feverishly to befriend Amethyst to draw her to Christ.

Taking a seat next to Amethyst, Porsha softly asked her as Carlton sat on the other side of Amethyst. "Do you know what happened to you?"

Rubbing her forehead, she shook her head. "No. I must be dying or something."

"Amethyst, Jesus wants to save you. For some reason, demons have targeted, latched on to, and overpowered your weakness, but the Word of God will set you free if you just come to Him. Will you surrender today and take charge of your life?"

"I think I'm feeling better now." Amethyst seemed to recover, but she didn't say yes.

"It's praying time," Mother Kincaid said to the group that had formed around them. "God sent Amethyst to us, and she needs us. Her life depends on our prayers."

Many bowed their heads and whispered their petitions to God.

Amethyst faced Carlton. "Did you really see my baby?"

He bobbed his head and grinned widely. "Yes."

"How?"

Porsha watched as Carlton had Amethyst's attention. She prayed he could minister to her.

"God showed me, Ms. Amethyst. You had a boy and a little girl too. She looks like you. Jesus wants to show you things, but the Bible says we can't serve two masters. We either hate one and love the other, so you have to choose whether you will love God or the devil who has you deceived through horoscopes and psychics."

What? Porsha blinked. Indeed, God had revealed something to Carlton, which would explain the spirits tormenting her. "Amen, Brother Carlton. So now, Amethyst, the choice is yours. Stay in your lifestyle, or walk away, repent of your sins, and be baptized in Jesus' name and let the Lord Himself breathe the Holy Ghost into you."

Amethyst looked from Porsha to Carlton, who grinned widely, encouraging her to say yes.

"Yes," Amethyst whispered, not sounding convincing, then she repeated with more determination.

***

"Today was a good day," Mother Kincaid said after Amethyst left, relaxing on the front pew of the near-empty sanctuary.

"Yes, it was Mother," Pastor Rodney said in passing as he headed toward the exit.

She turned to Porsha. "You did a great job leading the spiritual battle as Jesus directed you."

Porsha shivered. "Thank you. I didn't know if I was ready for that. I hate scary movies, and those creatures of darkness were images my mind will never forget. But God..." Porsha didn't hide the look of relief as she fumbled with her manicured fingernails.

Mother Kincaid smiled and patted the young woman's lap. "God doesn't want us fearful when it comes to His battle.

Remember the passage in the Old Testament where the Lord reduced the army's size so they wouldn't boast in victory but give honor to God?"

"You're referring to Judges seven and two: *'The Lord said unto Gideon, The people with thee are too many for me to give the Midianites into their hands, lest Israel vaunt themselves against me, saying, Mine own hand hath saved me.'* He cut that number by the way soldiers drank water from the river," Minister Morgan said.

"There was a reason God had you on the front line, Sister Porsha, to strengthen your faith in Him."

Porsha leaned over and hugged Mother Kincaid. "You have so much wisdom and see things clearly. I never thought of it that way."

"Yes, but our mission remains incomplete between the two. The Lord said Grayson Tate and his wife, especially Amethyst Johnson." Mother Kincaid looked away from the few people who remained with her, including Minister Morgan and his family.

Minister Morgan cleared his throat. "They're not in sync. Maybe that's what happened in their marriage. Lack of unity. They were baptized in Jesus' name on the same day but missed each other in the pool and prayer room. They are still disconnected."

"God may be strengthening them separately to put them back together to become a Holy Ghost power couple. Grayson had left minutes earlier rejoicing at the same time as God filled Amethyst with heavenly tongues while she was still in the baptismal pool," Jude said. "Even if Grayson was still here, God kept them separate for His purpose."

Shaking her head, Porsha *hmmph*ed. "When it comes to Amethyst, all I encountered were missed opportunities."

Mother Kincaid didn't want Porsha to become discouraged or let her guard down. "Despite the win, the couple is still our assignment. You met Amethyst first. Hopefully, she'll warm to you now. Then you met her husband, and we know his attraction to you was God's doing—not for romantic purposes but for spiritual gain."

"Okay, so what now? I don't want to be a distraction."

Jude nodded. "You won't be. I've got access to Grayson—he gave me his number, and Amethyst, who now works in my building."

"I can't believe Amethyst finally gave me her number."

Mother Kincaid started a round of high-fives, laughing.

"Plus, she likes my son." Jude rubbed the curls on top of Carlton's head.

"Carlton?" Mother Kincaid lifted a brow. "How are things going with Sophia Doyle at summer camp?"

"She and Sissy have become friends. I've tried to tell Sissy what to say to her." Carlton grinned.

"I don't wanna say it. Sounds stupid." Sissy scrunched her nose.

"God will whisper in your ear what He wants you to say." Mother Kincaid smiled, wanting to reassure the child it was okay.

As they decided to go out to dinner, Mother Kincaid silently prayed for Sissy to become bold for the Lord. It was critical to God's plan that everyone on His list accept His salvation, and Mother Kincaid didn't know how long they had left to do that.

Chapter Seventeen

*I must work the works of him that sent Me while
it is day: the night comes when no man can work.*
—John 9:4

Why did everything start to make sense to Amethyst? From the nightmares to forgetting to check her horoscope. Then, she couldn't find her beads as comforting as a sip of hot tea.

"Yes, I want to be baptized, but it's going to take a minute for me to list all my sins."

Porsha smiled. "No need. God already has your list, and He nailed your past, present, and future sins to the cross."

"Hi, sweetie. I'm Mother Kincaid." The woman had the kindest eyes. "All you have to do is be sorry." She smiled. "Sorry for your thoughts, actions, and offenses you've committed against God."

The more the woman spoke, the more Amethyst felt convicted as the Lord flashed one scenario after another before her until she found herself crying.

Porsha rubbed her back. "Come on. Once God washes your temple clear, His Word says he will fill you with His Spirit to help you from purposely sinning against Him again."

Amethyst stood and sniffed. She turned to the young boy. "Will you tell me more about this baby?"

"That's all I know." He shook his head. "God will show you more."

Hopeful, Amethyst smiled, took a deep breath, and stood. If Jesus had good times for her besides this newfound, unexplainable peace, Amethyst craved it.

A group of women followed her, singing, "Take me to the water, take me to the water to be baptized. In the name of Jesus…"

The voices were soothing, and the words comforting. Maybe after today, her life would turn around.

Inside a small room, a woman handed her a white gown and swim cap and pointed to a private dressing stall behind a beige curtain. "Today is the beginning of a new life for you." The same middle-aged woman released a praise, chuckled, and added, "One thing about Jesus' salvation is He will remember our sins no more, so after today, don't you let anybody remind you of what you did and said yesterday and beyond."

"Yes, ma'am." That sounded good to Amethyst as she changed her clothes and stepped out of the dressing room. She followed the woman to the top of the pool. Amethyst spied a man waiting for her as he reached to take her hand.

She swallowed, and with each step into the water, Amethyst questioned her decision. Was this really necessary? Despite the doubt, she felt she was meant to do this.

Come to Me, God whispered.

A smile tugged on Amethyst's lips. The Lord was talking to her. Yep. She was going through with this.

"Have you repented?" the minister asked. He was shorter than Amethyst.

Would he be able to keep her from drowning? "Yes. Everything that I could remember."

He smiled. "God will take care of the rest. Cross your arms over your chest."

She did and closed her eyes as she began to shake uncontrollably and fear struck her. She was ready to make a run for it when she opened her eyes and blinked.

An angel stood in the pool with her and the minister. His sword was drawn, and she saw dark figures try to get her.

Surprisingly, she wasn't afraid. Amethyst felt safe.

"Ready?" the minister asked.

"Most definitely."

With a strong fist, he gripped the back of her gown. "My dear sister, Amethyst, upon the confession of your faith and our confidence in the blessed Word of God, concerning His death, burial, and grand resurrection, I now indeed baptize you in the name above every name. Every knee shall bow, and every tongue confess that Jesus Christ is Lord. So, in the name of Jesus, I baptize you for the remission of your sins, and God says in the second chapter of Acts that you shall receive the Holy Ghost. Receive it, sis."

Amethyst was submerged underwater, and the same angel seemed to guard her.

When Amethyst resurfaced, the angel reached out his hand, which looked like a raging fire, and touched her lips, releasing an explosion of words she'd never heard. Amethyst felt different as she cried and shouted, but the words that came out of her mouth weren't hers.

Wow, she thought but couldn't say. She couldn't remember getting out of the pool or redressing. Porsha and others were clapping, congratulating her, and cheering her on. Whatever she experienced must have been a good thing.

Before walking out of the church, Amethyst exchanged phone numbers with Porsha. For the first time in a long time, she felt different, carefree, and genuinely happy. More importantly, Amethyst felt the presence of angels as her bodyguards escorting her to the car.

Hours later, when she woke up, Amethyst glanced around the room. It wasn't her bedroom. She noted monitors, and then her mother's face came into view.

"You scared me." Annabelle patted her chest. Her eyes were puffy from crying.

"What happened? Why am I in the hospital?"

"A wrong-way driver crashed into you. The police said there was no way you should be alive from the looks of your car. It's totaled."

Crash?

Totaled?

Survived.

Thankful came to mind. Amazingly, Amethyst wasn't stressed about her new car and the money Reggie loaned her to pay her sales tax. He would understand and be glad that she was alright.

Now, she understood the saying, *Angels watching over me.*

Free. That's the way Grayson felt. No cares, worries, or burdens too great to wear him down. When he got home from church, he prayed some more to hear God's heavenly language and feel His presence.

This was good news he wished he could share with his parents. Both were deceased. His remaining relative was Reggie, and his half-brother was never excited about anything good in Grayson's life, even when he professed his love for Amethyst or announced they were expecting a baby.

Everything with his brother was a competition.

I have given you someone to pray for, God whispered.

"Right." Without knowing what to pray for concerning Reggie, God filled Grayson's being and spoke as his emotions welled up. Grayson remembered their good times as children and the bad times as they grew older and apart. He asked God to fix what was broken between them and save Reggie's family before his wife made good on her threat to kill her husband and possibly harm Amethyst.

Following an emotional prayer, Grayson stood and wiped tears from his eyes. It had been a while since the last time he cried over broken relationships and released the pain and guilt.

Once composed, he found his Bible, which had gathered dust on the shelf among his stacks of books. He opened it and became comfortable on the sofa. It was Sunday afternoon, and watching sports was his routine, but he craved God more than entertainment.

He thought about Amethyst. Grayson saw her today at church, and questions filled his mind. Why didn't she look like herself?

Was she a member?

And a question he didn't want to wonder: Did she have an affair with Reggie? Only Amethyst and God had those answers.

After reading for about an hour, Grayson closed his Bible as thoughts of Amethyst nagged at him. Grayson called Miss Annabelle, hoping to speak with Amethyst. If not, he would leave a message for her to call him.

"Grayson, I can't talk to you right now," Annabelle answered with panic. "Amethyst has been in a car accident, and I'm on my way to the hospital now."

"What? Which hospital?" His thoughts were jumbled. His heart pumping, Grayson grabbed his car keys while waiting for her to tell him.

"Barnes-Jewish."

"I'll meet you there," he said as Annabelle ended the call. Despite their rocky past, Grayson still cared about what happened to Amethyst.

As he drove, his mind replayed the happy times he and Amethyst shared. Divorce shouldn't have been an option, but it had happened, and now a revised copy was in the mail. Grayson prayed, asking God to keep him from getting a ticket for driving over the limit to arrive safely. "Please let Amethyst be okay, in Jesus' name. Amen."

Entering Barnes-Jewish Hospital's ER, visitors were subject to high-security prison measures to enter the waiting room. The State of Missouri had designated it as a level one trauma facility that treated car crash, stabbing, and shooting victims, plus sprains and everything in between that wasn't life-threatening. What kind of condition was Amethyst in? His heart dropped at the thought of her possible fate. "Jesus, please don't let her die without me telling her I'm sorry. Please."

After passing the security check, he hurried to the nurses' station. "I'm here to see Amethyst." Then he paused, doubting she would have used his surname. "Johnson."

"And you are?"

"Her husband." Grayson gripped the counter.

"Technically, her ex," Annabelle said, clearly not knowing they were still married, as she walked up behind him, "but since he's here, Grayson can see her. She's drowsy from the pain medicine."

"Thank you so much, Miss Annabelle." Grayson startled her with a tight hug.

The nurse activated the double doors to open. "Ms. Johnson is in bay ten."

Grayson measured his steps, praying that Amethyst would recover from whatever happened to her.   Was this the danger Randall had mentioned? He peeped through the curtains and stared. A bruise marred her face, and her hair was in disarray, but she looked at peace. Not the troubled person he had seen earlier at church or a mangled body doctors were trying to keep alive. Grayson exhaled and gave thanks.

Was she in pain? He couldn't tell. "Amee," he said softly, walking closer. "Are you okay?"

She opened those beautiful hazel eyes that had attracted him from day one. Their color seemed to darken whenever she was upset at him, which was annoying. Amethyst stared, then blinked.

Upon closer inspection, he noticed glass fragments in her hair. His heart ached.

"Grayson, what are you doing here?" she asked in a weak voice instead of snapping at him, her trademark whenever they had to talk to each other after they separated.

"I called your mom to get a message to you, and she told me you were in an accident and here, so I came."

She was quiet as she searched his face. She pursed her lips as if she was about to say something but stopped. "Thanks for visiting. I should be discharged tonight once all the results come back from the labs and X-rays to make sure I don't have any broken bones, stool in my urine, and other stuff."

"Your mom says your car was totaled. I can wait and take you back to your mom's."

Quiet—again. Weak from her injuries, she didn't have the strength to argue, so he took this moment to tell her he was sorry.

"Amethyst, I want to apologize for everything I said or didn't say during our marriage that made you want to leave me."

She mustered a smile. "I forgive you. I'm sorry, too."

Grayson blinked. Why was this so easy between them now? He held her hand, and she didn't withdraw it.

"I'll be fine." Amethyst squeezed his hand, then closed her eyes and dismissed him.

Chapter Eighteen

I will give you a new heart and put a new spirit within you;
I will remove your heart of stone and give you a heart of flesh.
And I will put My Spirit within you and cause you to walk in
My statutes and to observe My ordinances carefully.
—Ezekiel 36:26–27

Amethyst's day flashed before her eyes as she lay in the dark, small room. Her mind wandered as she listened to voices on the other side of the curtains: nurses' chatter, patients' groans or screams of agony, and officers giving unruly visitors orders. She felt the squeeze on her upper arm, then realized it was a blood pressure cup. The beeping sound made her turn her head, but the movement was too painful. Why was she in the emergency room?

The last time she was in the emergency room… A tear fell. That night had been the beginning of the end of her life with Grayson. She couldn't call it a marriage. They had only been husband and wife for four months, and the lifetime she thought they would have fizzled.

"No sad memories again!"

She was still processing today's events. Something about that church seemed to lure her in every Sunday, and she had been able to resist the temptation of surrendering—until earlier.

Today's experience was perplexing and hard to explain. It felt like her soul was being ripped from her body, and she had no power to fight for it. Then she heard God speak. The voice was as real as her mother's, but she didn't understand the words.

But God did something to her that she couldn't explain. *Set free.* Amethyst knew her worries, fears, and burdens were gone.

Gone.

When she walked out of the church, Amethyst felt the presence of angels, even though she couldn't see them. Just like she didn't remember seeing a wrong-way driver coming at her, only a flash of light.

In all her thirty-two years, she had never been in a car accident, not even a fender bender. Today was the first time she had seen Grayson Tate since their court appearance six months ago. Her heart softened for him because Grayson had come. *He had come*, her mind repeated.

Grayson seemed as concerned about her as the day they'd learned she had miscarried. The moment was touching until she recalled his rejection, their arguments, and her isolation.

Because of her mental angst, Amethyst had planned to carry the grudge against him to the grave. Reggie told her she wasn't wrong for her feelings. After receiving God's gift, she forgave Grayson. A clean slate gave her civility before she closed her eyes. Her salvation experience changed everything, and she desperately wanted to pray, scream, and clap for joy.

Her body halted the celebration as she succumbed to sleep.

Amethyst's eyes strained at the wall clock when she woke again to register the time. It was four-something in the morning. She had been there all night! The lights were off, the curtains were drawn, and she wasn't alone. It wasn't an angel. She recognized Grayson's light snoring. She smiled. Funny how she remembered that.

While they were married, Amethyst thought it was cute and not an obnoxious, loud, or deep, penetrating sound.

Where was her mother? She closed her eyes without an answer to fight her back pain.

Suddenly, someone flickered the lights on, startling Amethyst. She blinked and focused on the young Indian-descent doctor who approached her bed more chipper than she felt.

"Ms. Johnson, your X-rays, scans, and lab tests are okay. Apply ice to the bruises on your face and shoulder, and the cuts on your face are minimal and will heal in time. There is no reason to keep you here. It's unbelievable that you had not one broken bone. You are a lucky woman to be alive. The officer told paramedics that whoever was in the car you were driving was dead, but you," he said, shaking his head, "walked away with minimum cuts and bruises. Your neck and back might be sore for a few days, so I'll prescribe medicine for pain. Do you have any allergies?"

Was the accident that bad? she wondered before answering, "No, I don't think so."

"Yes. Sulfa. She breaks out in hives," Grayson said from his perch in the corner behind her, reminding Amethyst of his presence. Why was he still there?

"And you are a family member?" The doctor lifted a brow.

"I'm her husband." Grayson sounded too confident.

Their divorce papers said otherwise. "Ex," she corrected.

"I see." The doctor resumed the outpatient instructions. "Do you have any questions?"

"When can I go back to work?" Amethyst shifted in the bed and cringed.

"What kind of work do you do?"

"I'm an occupational health and safety specialist in the aerospace industry. On any given day, my routine could be squatting, bending, walking, or sitting at a desk to file a report." She never had a problem with any of that.

"If you can get a good night's sleep and tolerate sitting, you can return tomorrow on light duty. But it would be best to let your body rest for a few days. I can write you a three-day sick excuse."

"I'll be fine." Amethyst groaned.

"What's wrong?" Grayson stood from his chair.

"I just realized I no longer have a car. If I can't use Mom's, I'll have to take public transit."

"I'll take you, Amee." Grayson gave her a tentative smile.

"Thanks, but I don't want to inconvenience you. I'll figure it out."

The doctor looked from Grayson to Amethyst, then left the room.

"I see you've changed jobs," Grayson said without waiting for her response. "Although you didn't say the name of your new company, if it's aerospace, it has to be close to the airport where I work, remember? But it doesn't matter where you are. I'll pick you up in the morning and drop you off, then come back and pick you up and take you home."

"That sounds like doing a lot for someone you owe nothing to." It was, and Amethyst wasn't sure what to make out of it as another realization hit. "Oh no, I had just paid the sales tax for my license. At least my premiums were paid." She gnawed on her lips. "I'm sure they'll give me a rental. Grayson, thank you for trying to accommodate me. Things were never this easy for us. I'm not the same woman who signed those divorce papers—"

"We're still married, even though you never changed your maiden name. The judge signed on the wrong line and is out. A new judge has to sign it. Didn't you get a letter?"

Amethyst didn't want to hear this. She did get mail from her attorney but hadn't bothered to open it. She was quiet as Grayson's words sunk in. How could they still be married? Neither one of them wanted to be husband and wife anymore. "Our attorneys will work it out. Anyway, I gave my life to Christ yesterday. What's done between us is done. We don't have any child…" She paused when she recalled what Carlton had said about seeing her baby who died—a son—and then two more, including a little girl. She wished God would tell her that or show her what Carlton saw.

"I'm a changed man, too. I repented and was baptized in water at a church called Christ For All, and I received the gift of the Holy Spirit."

"You did?" She tried to scoot up. He gently helped her when she grimaced, then stacked pillows behind her back. "Me too. I was at church, and I can't believe what happened."

"I thought I saw you—"

The nurse reappeared with the discharge papers for Amethyst to sign, unhooked the IV, and unfastened the blood pressure cuff around her arm.

"Thank you. Where are my clothes?"

"Miss Annabelle dropped off clothes in case she didn't make it back." Grayson lifted a plastic bag. What she had worn to church was cut up. She guessed for them to examine her.

Her mother was acting oddly. Although she wasn't a fan of her ex, she gave him many liberties.

That is my doing, God whispered.

Why?

God didn't answer.

Amethyst sighed. "Thanks. Do you have something I can tie my hair up? It has glass from the crash in it."

"Yes. Let me see if I can find a surgical cap to hold all your hair," the nurse said, then began to open cabinets.

"I'll step out." Grayson left the room.

Exhaling, Amethyst was glad he respected her privacy. When she reached for her top, she cried out in pain.

"You alright?" Panic filled Grayson's voice on the other side of the curtain.

"Yeah. Sore from laying here."

"Okay." He didn't hide his relief.

Her mother had sent an oversized T-shirt she sometimes wore to bed and a loose skirt. She slid her feet into the sandals she had worn to church and was set. "Ready."

The nurse pulled the curtain back. "Do you need a wheelchair?" the nurse asked.

"No, I'm good." Amethyst smiled to hide an ache. The doctor was right. She would call her supervisor and take off for the next three days.

"I'll keep her steady," Grayson offered.

Amethyst rolled her eyes. They were past the pampering stage she'd received after losing the baby. It didn't take long for him to say, "Get over it," and to dismiss her tears as overemotional. Each day, she resented him more and more because he didn't grieve the way she did.

She walked into the hall, and Grayson extended his arm, which she reluctantly accepted as they strolled through the maze to the waiting room, then out the door to the parking lot.

"Thank you," she said softly as he helped her into the passenger seat. She clicked her seatbelt and waited for him to slide behind the wheel.

She took a deep breath. When was the last time she had taken the reins as his queen in this seat? That's what he called her when they were happy.

Grayson smiled. "Ready?"

"Yes. Do you remember the way to my mom's apartment?"

"I think so." He took off.

Amethyst closed her eyes, thankful for the ride and the silence between them, which could build a stone wall in the past. Now, the grudge was gone. God did that. "Tell me about your salvation experience on Sunday. I wonder if it was the same as mine."

Although she was okay with the silence, this was one topic she was ready to jump into. Amethyst opened her eyes and studied him.

Grayson's tired face came to life with a glow rivaling the sunrise, and he grinned. "It was powerful. I felt small compared to God. Once I acknowledged my sins, I hurried to the altar, crying like a baby. I couldn't stop as I surrendered to Christ. Angels were in the pool. To experience God's power when He spoke through me in a heavenly language was overwhelming, scary, then comforting that God had saved me." Grayson turned to Amethyst. "What about you?"

She sighed. "There are some similarities, but..." she said, frowning, "I don't know how to explain a tug-of-war feeling while people around me prayed. Suddenly, I was released from a stronghold as if someone dropped the other end of a rope. I repented, was baptized, too, and heard a heavenly language come out of my mouth. I knew I was no longer part of this realm—if that makes sense."

Grayson nodded. "It does because, at that moment, nothing in this world was more important than being with God."

"Right!" Amethyst moved too quickly and felt pain. Thank God for the medicine. "When I left church, God's presence was with me. The next thing I knew, I was driving on the highway, singing words to a song I didn't know I was listening to. A car was coming toward me, and I screamed *Jesus*. I woke up looking into my mother's face. Her eyes were puffy."

Before they knew it, Grayson pulled in front of her mother's apartment building. "Thanks again for the ride."

Grayson rested his hand over hers. "Let me know if you need anything. Since we were at the hospital all night and most of the early morning, I took off work today. Call me if you need anything—when you're ready to return to work or get a rental car. I'm available. It wouldn't hurt if you unblocked me so I can check on you." He looked hopeful.

Taking pity on him, Amethyst took her phone and unblocked his number as he watched, then she stepped out of his car, wondering why Grayson was being so nice to her.

Because I changed his heart and yours too, God whispered.

Chapter Nineteen

*I must work the works of him that sent me while
it is day: the night comes when no man can work.*
—John 9:4

Amethyst rolled over with a groan. She forced her brain to remember more details of what happened. The clock read two-thirty. It was Monday afternoon.

She was still sore and drowsy, so she lay there. Amethyst hated taking medicine because, most of the time, it made her nauseous. When her phone alerted her of a text, she reached for it and wished she hadn't after experiencing a sharp pain.

You up? Hungry? I can bring you breakfast or lunch or dinner. Remember, I'll be on standby for you.

Wow. Really? Amethyst didn't know what to make of this new version of her ex-husband. She glanced at the envelope from her divorce attorney. Was it true what Grayson had said that they were still married? She wanted to know but didn't.

She spied the Bible she'd received at church yesterday and other belongings someone had retrieved from her wrecked car. Her life was at a crossroads, for sure.

Pray about it, God whispered.

Instead, she closed her eyes and drifted back to sleep.

Amethyst woke again when her mother walked in with a bed tray containing a sandwich, fruit, and a side salad. "Amee, it's time to eat." Annabelle sat on the side of the bed. "I'm so glad you're okay." Her eyes watered, and she sniffed and mumbled, "My only child."

"Thanks, Mom." They exchanged a soft hug.

"When you're up, I can rewash your hair. A lot of glass came out the first time, but there's probably more tangled in it."

Amethyst vaguely remembered coming home from the hospital and resting her neck on the tub. She had drifted off as her mother washed her hair. "Yes, please. Thank you."

They chatted while Amethyst ate, then her mother left when her phone rang. After the usual pleasantries, Grayson asked, "Are you in pain?"

"Some, along with the aches." She began to ramble.

"What's the matter? I can hear it in your voice."

"My car is totaled. I need a replacement, and I have to pay Reggie back." The problems kept flashing in her mind. Since Grayson was quiet, she assumed he was fuming because he hated his brother helping her.

"Amethyst, I have no right to ask, and you don't have to answer, but why did Reggie lend you money?"

"To pay my sales tax to get my car license plates. Reggie said it was no rush to pay him back."

"Thank you for telling me. How much? If you let me, I'll give him the money so you can start fresh."

His offer, although she didn't plan to accept, was touching. "I'll be okay."

Grayson sighed. "If you need me, I'm here."

"I'll remember." With nothing else to discuss, they said their goodbyes.

That evening, her mother shampooed her hair again, and more glass fell out. This time, she could sit and allow her mother to blow dry and braid her hair like she used to when Amethyst was a little girl.

At dinner, she took her meds and soon climbed back into bed. She didn't want to think about Reggie, the money he'd loaned her, or Grayson's offer to clear her debt. She drifted off to sleep.

From Monday morning to evening, the buzz at Jude's company centered around the "new girl." He was shocked to learn that Amethyst was involved in a horrific wrong-way driver car crash where the other driver was killed.

Images of the mangled car flooded the newscasts. Jude and his family grieved for the loss of life and prayed for the family and survivors.

Amethyst's boss, Emerson Carey, spread the word while strolling out of the first-floor kitchen, leaving Jude speechless.

"Yeah, when I listened to the news this morning, the names were released from the accident. My heart dropped." Emerson patted his chest. "I called the emergency contact number in her file and spoke with her mother…"

Jude tuned the man out as he rambled on about the crash details. He already knew some from watching the newscast the previous night, but he had no clue that someone he knew was involved—and a new Christian convert. His mind was on Satan's attempt to take Amethyst out. It wouldn't be appropriate to ask Emerson for her mother's number since Amethyst didn't work in his department.

"Her mother said she wasn't seriously injured—a few cuts and bruises—but a lot of soreness from the impact. Amethyst is resting and will be back before the end of the week. I told Miss Johnson to tell Amethyst to take her time to heal and keep me posted." Emerson frowned. "Can you believe that she survived that crash?"

"Actually, I can. The Lord is a Protector," Jude said as Emerson headed toward the stairs, and Jude made a beeline to the men's restroom. He checked to make sure he was alone, then lifted his hands in praise that Amethyst's life had been spared. God had saved her hours before a pending death trap.

His spirit boasted in heavenly tongues, then quieted seconds before the door opened. Jude turned on the water, washed his hands as if he had used the facilities, and left.

Once in his office, Jude sent a group text to some intercessors.

Hallelujah! The devil thought he had our new sister Amethyst. Jesus said no. She was involved in that wrong-way driver fatal crash on Sunday. She walked away.

The text responses came in rapid fire.

Praise God!

Thank You, Jesus!

Amen. I heard about that accident.

#TeamJesus 1 Satan 0.

Throughout the day, Jude's mind drifted to Amethyst and the what-ifs she hadn't decided to submit to Jesus yesterday. What if she wasn't persuaded to follow Jesus? What if her soul had been lost in eternity forever? What if…

Sinclaire called him late afternoon, and he answered with a smile. "Hey, babe."

"I can't get my mind off of Amethyst. I know I'll see you at home soon, but I had to ask: It's not a coincidence she and Grayson surrendered yesterday, is it?"

"I don't think so. God is strategic with our lives. We don't know the big picture." He spied the time. "Babe, I love you, but I need to finish things here to get home to my wife."

"Okay." She chuckled. "I can't wait to see my husband. Bye."

Jude stopped not far from home to get a bouquet for Sinclaire, then called her. "Hey, babe. I'm at the store. Do we need anything?"

"Nope. Just my handsome husband. I'm about to heat yesterday's leftovers."

When he got home, Jude kissed and hugged his family after giving Sinclaire flowers, then told his sons, "Carlton and TJ, when you love your wife, bring her tokens of love."

Carlton twisted his lips. "You mean gifts, Dad?"

Jude and Sinclaire chuckled as Jude rubbed the curls in his hair. "Yes, son. Gifts."

"Wash your hands and set the table." Sinclaire turned toward the kitchen. Jude stopped her and pressed a kiss on her lips. "You know one thing I love about being married to you?"

She glowed, waiting for his answer.

"I had always hoped to come home and enjoy dinner with my family. Thank you for giving me that." They shared a kiss until the children's excited chatter drew closer.

At the table, Jude gave thanks for their meal, then the children told them about their day at camp.

"Dad," Carlton said, "Harry and I need help to talk to Sophia about Jesus. All Sissy wants to do is play."

Sissy frowned at her brother. "Mommy, Daddy, playing with my friend is okay."

Smiling at his cute daughter, who would grow up to be a beauty like her mother, he said, "Yes, but we want to share Jesus with our friends because He wants everyone to go to heaven."

"Okay." She bobbed her head and resumed eating.

Dinner was enjoyable, and the children helped clean the kitchen before playing. At bedtime, Carlton asked his question again, serious about the mission God gave them.

"I tell you what, I'll pick you up one day this week at camp, and we'll pray that God will open the door for us," Jude suggested.

"Thanks." Carlton hugged his parents and left for his room.

"*Whew*. It's good that the Lord only gave us seven people to find and witness to them because it's not easy to tell someone you need to surrender to God." Sinclaire slipped her fingers through his as they retreated to their bedroom, which he had remodeled once they were married. It included a lounging area with a large bay window overlooking the backyard. A neighborhood park was nearby.

As they stretched out to watch a movie, Sinclaire asked, "How can we play matchmaker for Amethyst and Grayson?" She grinned.

"Babe, I think this is deeper than a love connection. That will come, but somehow, there is more to their story that God hasn't revealed to us yet."

"More?" Sinclaire shivered. "I don't like the dark spirits that didn't want to release her at church yesterday. She wasn't even a new saint for twenty-four hours, and the devil was ready to take her out." Sinclaire snuggled closer.

"The devil is testing to see how deep her spiritual seed is planted—whether she will toss the Word of God to the side, be choked by outside forces so she can't witness for Jesus, or cultivated on good soil to yield fruit thirty, sixty, or a hundredfold."

"Sounds like you're talking about the sower in Matthew four."

"The Lord just gave me that, and something tells me that I might have to do some early morning praying for her so that she can yield a lot of fruit."

Souls are depending on her to rescue them, God whispered.

Yep, it's going to be one of those nights, Jude thought but didn't share with his wife, who had other plans as she turned off the light.

Chapter Twenty

It was another night. Amethyst sensed she wasn't alone in her bedroom, and fear began to creep up her bed like the sheet covering her.

Pray, Amethyst, pray. They are coming for your soul but are too late, God whispered. *I have My intercessors praying for you.*

"Jesus, help me!" Amethyst screamed. Opening her eyes, she was outnumbered. Demons. They were real. Their claws were as long as fangs in an ill-shaped opening for a mouth.

She couldn't move, no matter how much she tried to break through the paralysis. Yet, with her own eyes, Amethyst witnessed her spirit stand at attention, ready for battle like David had been to fight the giant Goliath. Then a strong wind wrapped around her like an arm of God and pushed Amethyst behind Him to protect her from harm.

A fierce battle ensued. The more she prayed, the more demons were beaten down, and they made sounds of agony.

Read My Word in Exodus 17:12–14, God whispered.

Suddenly, Amethyst could move her arms, legs, and entire body, so she stood, walked to the desk in her bedroom, and opened her Bible to the passage God had given her.

Moses' hands were heavy, and they took a stone and put it under him, and he sat thereon, and Aaron and Hur stayed up his hands, the one on the one side, and the other on the other side; and his hands were steady until the going down of the sun. Joshua discomfited Amalek and his people with the edge of the sword. And the Lord said unto Moses, Write this for a memorial in a book, and rehearse it in the ears of Joshua: for I will utterly put out the remembrance of Amalek from under heaven.

Was this a Moses battle, and her prayers were like lifting the hand of God to win the battle? Amethyst didn't fully understand the correlation, but one thing was certain: calling on Jesus's name was a battle cry. She shouted the name of Jesus.

Her mother burst into the bedroom. "Girl, what is wrong with you with all this carrying on? Some of us have to get up and go to work in the morning."

"Sorry, Mom. I guess I had a nightmare, and I was praying."

Annabelle huffed and adjusted the hair wrap on her head. "I'm sure God can hear you just fine if you whisper." She turned around and left the room, slamming the door behind her.

Closing her eyes, Amethyst prayed softly, "Lord, let my mother experience Your salvation as I did, in Jesus' name. Amen."

She thinks you're a fool. Stop praying in her house if you don't want to upset her.

Amethyst gave it some thought. She hadn't had a chance to share her salvation experience with her mother, but she had to pray. That's what Mother Kincaid and Porsha did at church, and their prayers helped set Amethyst free. Nope. That wasn't God talking to her.

"I'm going to keep praying!" Amethyst was determined to stay close to God.

She stood and walked into the bathroom for a cup of water. When she returned to the bedroom, she saw faces outside her window, clawing to get inside. One face looked like the last psychic Amethyst had visited. She heard the woman whisper, "Come back to me."

Amethyst saw an army of angels coming to rescue her. They were bigger and appeared stronger than the grisly figures snarling at her. Instead of the battle inside her room, the conflict happened outside her window.

Swiftly, she wasn't in her room anymore but in a place where she heard echoes of screams, yells, and groans. Amethyst gasped for air. A repulsive odor made her pinch her nose, but the sickening smell of something burnt seeped inside her nostrils. The acrid smell made her nauseous in this damp, dark space. She had never smelled anything like it—hair, meat, plastic, or maybe melting skin. Where was she?

Amethyst prayed for an escape until she was exhausted. She inhaled and exhaled until a sweet fragrance filled her lungs. Amethyst peeked an eye open and recognized familiar surroundings.

Her mother was not happy when she stormed into Amethyst's bedroom for the second time. "If you make that much noise every night, you can't stay here. Somebody from some church dropped off flowers and food. Maybe you can go stay with them. I'll be glad when you go back to work!"

The church? People from Christ For All Church knew what happened and thought about her. Amethyst smiled that someone cared—besides Grayson, of course. She opened her mouth to apologize, then closed it and nodded.

She blamed it on the pain medicine that she thought she wouldn't need until her body began to feel like she hadn't been someone's punching bag. The doctor had been right that she needed rest. Maybe the nightmares would cease after she was weaned off the medicine so she could return to work on Thursday.

The next morning, her mother entered the bedroom, dividing the curtains to invite the light in and slamming things to wake her. "It's not a good feeling to be disturbed while resting, is it?" She smirked. "While you were sleeping like a baby last night, a news reporter called and wanted to interview you today. I left his number on the refrigerator."

"Thanks, Mom. Hopefully, I won't disturb you tonight since I've taken all my medicine."

"Good." Annabelle walked out of the room. She returned with a big bouquet.

"They're beautiful." Amethyst sniffed and slid the card out of the small envelope. *We love you, Sister Amethyst. The saints are praying for a speedy recovery in Jesus' name. Amen.*

God said the intercessors were praying for her. What she saw and experienced last night and every night that she had been on that medicine was real.

Amethyst had to get out of this room and this apartment. All she sensed was bad vibes.

What have I gotten myself into? Seeing the last psychic she had visited outside her window was creepy. She threw the covers back and stepped out of bed with minimum pain.

The following day, with a heartier appetite, Amethyst prepared herself pancakes and sausage patties since her mother had returned to work after taking off a couple of days to nurse Amethyst back to health. There were covered dishes in the refrigerator, which Amethyst knew her mother didn't cook, and a fruit basket from her job was on the counter.

She called her supervisor to thank the company and verify her return on Thursday.

"If you need more time, let us know," Emerson said. "We are all amazed you're alive."

"Me too." Amethyst smiled. "See you on Thursday."

Grayson texted as she ended the call with her boss. **Daily wellness check. How are you?**

Getting better. Thank you for checking on me. Amethyst felt loved by his attention.

A call from the local television station stopped her from typing more. She answered. "Ms. Johnson, I'm Craig Russell from KMKS-TV News Channel Seven. Do you have time for me to interview you today about the accident?"

"Sure." Amethyst agreed on a time that he could come to the apartment.

She checked her appearance in the mirror. The bruised side of her face was still swollen, so she would have to ice it.

Amethyst prayed as loud as she wanted with the apartment quiet, then opened her Bible.

When the TV crew arrived, they set up a tripod, then put a microphone on her.

Testify of Me, God whispered.

"Amethyst, have you seen the photos?" Craig Russell asked.

"No. I've been resting, and my mom didn't want to discuss it, so I didn't ask." When he showed her, Amethyst blinked, and her jaw dropped. Tears streamed down her cheeks.

"Yeah. Amazingly, you survived."

"The other driver?" she asked.

"Oh, you didn't know?" Craig looked surprised. "She died at the scene."

Amethyst was quiet as she reflected on someone's death. No one told her, and she hadn't thought to ask—or maybe they did tell her, and she couldn't remember. Amethyst assumed God had spared both of their lives. "That could have been me. On Sunday, I walked into a church with no plans to make a change. However, the power of God's redemption was so strong, I surrendered to Christ. I repented and was baptized. I walked out of that church with angel escorts."

Craig seemed uncomfortable as he steered the conversation back to the accident, and Amethyst hijacked it back to God to testify of His mercy as the Lord had told her.

"I'm sorry that woman lost her life, but that would have been two fatalities if God hadn't spared mine." Becoming overwhelmed with grief for the other woman's family, Amethyst ended the interview, and they thanked her and left.

Why hadn't Amethyst asked about the other driver? Maybe because she was too busy sleeping and fighting demons in another realm. What was Amethyst's purpose for being alive?

Your assignment will be great as you battle the forces of evil, God didn't whisper.

Day three, and Grayson hadn't gotten Amethyst out of his mind since he'd dropped her off at her mother's place. He tried to give her space to rest, but she hadn't made one request of him, even when he had followed up on the first day with a text.

Despite their harsh words and outward hostility toward the end of their separation, God showed him how much he still loved her through this crisis and had allowed pettiness to divide and conquer them.

Also heavy on his mind was the trouble Amethyst was in. "What kind?" he asked. On his way from work, Grayson pounded the steering wheel and glanced to his left at the car, waiting at the light with him. "I'm going to protect her at all costs."

The passenger in the other car gave him a curious expression as the driver took off.

Grayson proceeded, his thoughts still on Amethyst as he drove to the home they had shared briefly for three years.

That evening, he tapped Amethyst's mom's number for an update. "Hi, Miss Annabelle. I'm calling to check on Amethyst. Is she okay? Do either of you need anything?"

Her mother grunted. "People from her church have been dropping off food and flowers. Who knows what else is in those boxes? I didn't even know she was going to a church."

Me either, at first. Now, we both are. Grayson withheld his thoughts. "Is she up for some company?"

"Ask her. She's sitting right here."

"Hello," Amethyst answered. Her voice had gotten stronger since Monday.

"How are you feeling?"

"Getting better. I'm still sore and bored doing nothing. Today, I got out of bed and cooked breakfast while Mom was at work. I can't wait to go back to work myself."

Amethyst never was one to stay in bed. He could have dropped off breakfast on his way to the airport before his shift started. Grayson smiled, listening to her chatter. "Are you accepting visitors? Your mom said people from the church have brought things by."

"They have overwhelmed me with love, and even my new employer sent a fruit basket." She was quiet, then said, "Reggie is stopping by with Kiya and Victor. Your niece and nephew give the best hugs. Reggie said they were upset when they heard I was in the accident."

Now, Grayson remained silent. He wouldn't speak without thinking when it came to his brother. Reggie's purpose in life seemed to *be* to make him look bad. Instead, he prayed, *Lord, what should I do or say because Amethyst is clueless about Jessica's intentions against her if Reggie is up to no good and trying to pull Amethyst into his game.* When he repented, Grayson's animosity toward his younger brother was nailed on the cross, so Reggie could no longer bait him to act out of his new Christian character. *Help me, God.*

Pray, God whispered.

Grayson did before responding. "I won't overwhelm you. Enjoy your visit, and I'll be praying for you."

"Thank you." Amethyst's voice softened, "It's nice to hear you say that. Bye."

That night, Grayson slid on the floor at his bedside and prayed that the Lord would keep Amethyst safe and save his brother and sister-in-law so no harm would come to anyone. "And please change Amethyst's heart toward me, in Jesus' name. Amen."

Trust Me, God said when Grayson finished and spied the letter from his attorney, advising that a new judge needed to sign the divorce papers. The divorce wasn't happening. Grayson would do everything in his power to win Amethyst's love back.

Chapter Twenty-one

The Wednesday night before Amethyst returned to work, she woke panting for breath and sweating from exertion. That hideous odor was back, too, in the dark as she ran for her life at full speed to nowhere.

"Lord, why am I running, and who is chasing me?"

God didn't answer. Frustrated, Amethyst reached for her Bible on the nightstand and placed it on her pillow. Closing her eyes, Amethyst drifted off to sleep.

The next morning, Amethyst woke before her alarm. Although her body was rested, her mind was anxious about her present state—no transportation.

She slid out of bed, fell to her knees, and prayed, "Lord, all this is new to me. I don't know what to do."

She thought about calling or texting Reggie.

Call Grayson, God whispered.

Depending on her soon-to-be ex was foreign, but he *had* come to the ER to see about her. She picked up her phone and noted the time. It was seven-seventeen. Was Grayson up? She didn't know his work schedule anymore.

She tapped his number, and he answered as if the phone was in his hand.

"Good morning, Amee. You called." The relief in his voice was endearing.

"Yeah, *ah...*" She paused. Humility had never been her strength with him.

"Ask," he said softly.

Amethyst swallowed. "Can I get a ride to work? I'll get a rental car this weekend, and—"

"What time should I be at your mom's? I don't mind. My life has been boring without..." He stopped. "Do you want me to bring breakfast? I woke wanting some blueberry biscuits, and I just put a dozen in the oven."

Amethyst sucked in her breath and imagined the scent. "I'll take two and make two cups of coffee." She grinned, remembering their breakfast meetups at the beginning of their relationship. Over morning java, they had learned so much about each other that they eventually moved in together against her mother's protest—and probably God's, too.

"Thank you," Grayson said softly.

"For what?" She frowned.

"Letting me be a small part of this journey with you."

Amethyst exhaled. They were on the road to dissolve their marriage, not a journey together—or were they? "Thank you. See you soon."

For some unknown reason, she couldn't wait to see him.

"God, I don't know what You're doing, but thank You. Hallelujah." Grayson worshipped the Lord when he ended the call. He knew without a doubt that his feelings for Amethyst were rekindling, and he had to be at her beck and call so Reggie wouldn't be.

Suddenly, he sniffed the biscuits. He rushed into the kitchen. "Whew." At least he cooked with a timer. They were browner than he preferred, but he hoped Amethyst would overlook his blunder once he sprinkled powdered sugar on top.

He praised God throughout his shower and extra grooming. Ready to impress, Grayson stared at his reflection in the mirror. Last year, he couldn't wait for his divorce to be finalized. "Lord, please change Amethyst's heart so she'll second guess wanting the divorce too."

After dressing, he wrapped the biscuits, grabbed his keys, then headed to Miss Annabelle's apartment. It was opposite the airport, but at least they would be ten minutes from each other's jobs.

When Grayson arrived at Amethyst's place, she was outside in one of the chairs on the front porch of the building. She stood in her heels, fitted khakis, and long, sleeveless white top. Against her brown-tanned arms, she was fashionable for a woman who had to perform safety inspections.

He parked and hurried out of his vehicle to relieve her of the backpack, which probably held tennis shoes, hanging off her shoulder. "Hey, I got this." He took her and the coffee cup.

Grayson studied her face. The bruise was still visible on her upper cheek, along with some thin scratches that marred her forehead. "You probably shouldn't be lifting anything."

"Probably, but I have to work. I'm new on my job."

Right. He nodded. "I got you moneywise, Amee. I mean that."

"O-okay." She stepped into his car after he opened her door. She inhaled, moaned, then giggled. "Biscuits."

Laughing, Grayson shut her door, walked to his side, and tossed her backpack in the backseat.

"Where's my biscuit?" She grinned and danced in her seat until she did too much and yelped from pain. "*Ooh.*" Amethyst huffed, then sat back. "I have to remember my limitations."

Grayson had no right to fuss, so he said nothing and unwrapped the biscuit for her.

"Cheers." Amethyst tapped her coffee cup with Grayson's, then took a sip. "*Oops.* I forgot to bless my biscuit."

"I gotcha. Already done." He grinned.

"Oh," she said, pouting. "I'd love to hear you pray since your salvation experience."

Grayson released a hearty laugh. "It wasn't that type of prayer. I hope the biscuits meet your standards. They may be a little brown."

"I'll be the judge." Amethyst bit into it while he stared, waiting, then she smacked her lips. "Perfect."

"Glad you approve." He started the car and drove off. During the ride, they shared their salvation experiences. Both had been in a spiritual realm and were in awe of how real God is. To Grayson's disappointment, they arrived at her company too soon.

"What time should I pick you up, Amee?"

"Grayson, you don—"

"I don't want to keep having this conversation with me offering and you rejecting me."

"I'm sorry. If there aren't any issues, I'll get off at four-thirty."

He stepped out, grabbed her backpack, then walked to the other side to open her door. "Here you go. Will you pamper yourself for me so you can get better?" *Until you allow me to do it*, he didn't say.

"I will." She smiled, and her face glowed, even with the scars.

Grayson got back into his vehicle and watched until she disappeared from his sight—but not his life. Her perfume lingered in his car as a reminder.

Chapter Twenty-two

O give thanks unto the Lord; call upon His name:
make known His deeds among the people. Sing unto Him,
sing psalms unto Him: talk ye of all His wondrous works.
—Psalm 105:1–2

Amethyst wasn't expecting the attention she received from her new coworkers at work on Thursday.

"I saw your interview," one woman said, stepping off the elevator. "I'm glad you're okay. I hate to hear about the other driver."

"Me too," Amethyst said, then asked God why He didn't save the other woman.

I am the Lord. I make the sun rise on the evil and the good and send rain on the just and on the unjust, God whispered.

Amethyst repented and made a note never to question God again.

She crossed paths with other well-wishers who couldn't believe she wasn't more banged up.

"God protected me."

The more she professed it, the more she realized she was a miracle. She could have died like the other driver.

Some accepted the gospel truth, while others nodded in politeness. When she reached her workspace, her desk was overrun with flowers and cards.

"Lord, You really loved me to spare my life." She sniffed away tears as she made room on the desk for the extra biscuit Grayson had given her to snack on later.

As I have loved you, you must love others, God whispered. *Read John, chapter thirteen.*

Amethyst smiled. She wished she had her Bible from home here, but she made do by downloading a Bible app. It just wasn't the same. She would have to buy a small pocket Bible for her desk. She liked God speaking to her; if the Lord said anything else, she wanted to have the Bible handy.

Minister Morgan might have an extra Bible on hand, she thought. She remembered he was on the fourth floor. Amethyst stepped away from her desk in search of him. He could explain the chapter's highlights to her. Her heart pumped with excitement.

"Welcome back. We're so glad you're okay," another coworker said as Amethyst stepped into the elevator.

"Thank you."

Amethyst reached Minister Morgan's floor. A woman was coming out of the copier room. "Hello, I was looking for Min… I mean Jude."

"Oh, he hasn't made it in yet. Is there something I can help you with?"

No, unless you have a printed Bible. Amethyst shrugged. "I'll talk to him later." She walked away, knowing she had to catch up on her training and inspections. But she also wanted to speak with Minister Morgan about everything that had happened to her.

Jude would be late for work, but he was on a mission from God. He hoped dropping off his three children at summer camp would give him the opportunity to meet Sophia Doyle.

The children were out of their seatbelts and the vehicle, ready to explore the day's activities. Carlton's half-brother, Harry, walked toward them. Sissy and TJ raced to give their bonus brother—as Sinclaire referred to Harry and the younger siblings' relationship—a hug.

Although Harry didn't share a bloodline with the younger two siblings as he did with Carlton, the boy considered and treated them as his siblings, too.

The tragedy of Carlton and Harry losing their biological father in a deranged criminal act brought the half-brothers together as if they were twins separated at birth.

"Sissy! Sissy!" A little black girl with thick braids ran toward his daughter.

Jude watched. Was this Sophia? He trailed her. "Sweetheart, who's your friend?"

The child's mother stepped forward and answered. The girl was her mother's 'mini-me' with the same complexion and facial features. She extended her hand. "Hi. I'm Debra Doyle. This is my daughter, Sophia. These two are inseparable at camp. All Sophia talks about is Sissy."

"I'm Jude Morgan, Sissy's father, and she loves her new friend too."

"Your daughter is delightful and keeps asking Sophia to be her guest at church as if they were giving away a prize or something." Debra smiled.

Jude chuckled. "Well, the Lord does say, *'Behold, I come quickly, and His reward is with Him, to give to each one according to our work,'* so I guess our baby is working for the Lord."

Debra's expression was dismissive, and she twisted her hands before glancing away, searching for a distraction. "Maybe there is another activity the girls can do together."

Not discouraged, Jude nodded with a smile. "Sure. I'll ask my wife."

She fumbled inside her purse and pulled out a business card. She was a real estate agent. "Here's my number. I'd like to chat with her."

"And Sinclaire would love the opportunity to get together with you."

Jude smiled as he returned to his vehicle. Sissy had done her part of inviting her friend to church. Now, it was up to the prayer warriors to get Sophia over the finish line. Whatever God's purpose was for this little one, it was important to His kingdom-building. Jude prayed for guidance as he drove to the office.

Grayson was saved.

Check.

Amethyst surrendered.

Check.

Both were new converts, prepping for their mission to win souls while Hudson was on fire, witnessing to family and friends. Where were the other three?

If the Lord Jesus had a timer set, how much time did the intercessors have left? "God, we know You are soon to come, and it's no time to slack off. Lord, help us stay on guard, in Jesus' name. Amen."

Jude arrived at work and trekked across the parking lot to his building, which was one of a cluster. Walking inside, he stopped by the kitchen for a fresh brew. He overheard coworkers still talking about Amethyst. It was her first day back at work since the accident. Jude planned to see her sometime this morning.

"Have you seen her? It's a miracle. Amethyst looks good," a female employee said.

Yes, Amethyst was God's miracle. Jude smiled as he fastened the plastic lid onto his cup.

"Miracle, huh?" grunted Brody Nelson, a coworker who seemed friendly until he opened his mouth and a bad mood was sure to surface. "A miracle would have been nobody died. What kind of God picks and chooses who lives and dies?"

Jude had to butt in before the devil planted a seed of doubt in the coworker to take away God's glory like the serpent did to Eve.

"Morning. I couldn't help but overhear the good news about Amethyst. Miracles happen when life is spared against the odds. Our Creator, the Lord Jesus Christ, rains on the just and unjust. At His discretion, He extends mercy. The other woman's time was up. Hopefully, she fulfilled everything she was purposed to do in this world."

While the female coworker seemed receptive, Brody wasn't. His spirit became agitated. When he opened his mouth, Jude turned and walked out.

Whew. Demonic spirits were everywhere, from inside the church to the workplace. *We can't let our guards down*, Jude thought. If he didn't have an upcoming conference call in thirty minutes, he would have walked to Amethyst's cubicle to check on her.

Sinclaire called while Jude placed his cup on his desk. He told her about Sophia's mother wanting to get together.

"Yes! All I needed was my charming husband to talk to her." She giggled.

His wife said Jude was a superhero when drawing folks to Christ. It wasn't his powers that drew people to the Lord but the Holy Ghost.

"Have you seen Amethyst yet?"

"I'm getting ready for a meeting but plan to go to her cubicle afterward."

"Okay. I won't hold you, but we should invite Amethyst to our barbecue."

Jude grinned. He loved his wife's generosity. "Sounds good. It will be good for her to know the saints."

"You should have invited Sophia and her mother, too."

"I didn't even think of that." Jude shook his head. "I have her number. You can call her."

"Perfect. I will." Sinclaire ended their call after exchanging endearments of love.

It wasn't until the afternoon that Jude ended all his morning meetings and conference calls. Hungry, he stood and patted his stomach, then headed to the company's lunchroom. Jude spied Amethyst in the corner. He headed her way. As he approached, Jude grinned as her head was buried in a book—the Bible.

"Praise the Lord, Sister Amethyst," he greeted her. "It's good to see you. How are you feeling?"

She looked up. Her face glowed. "Minister Morgan!"

"It's Jude at work." He lowered his voice. "I wanted to speak but don't want to take you from your spiritual lunch. Let me know if you have any questions about God's Word."

"I have so many. I wish I had brought the Bible the church gave me. I downloaded the Bible app, and it's convenient, but I like holding the actual Bible."

"I get it. It's God's Holy Word." Jude understood her sentiments. Even with electronics and the Scriptures flashed on the overhead screen, having it in his hands was different. "It's your personal possession."

"Right, I ordered a Bible online for a two-hour window delivery because I couldn't wait to get home to read something." She paused and pointed to her passage, "Luke 22:31 says, *'And the Lord said, Simon, Simon, behold, Satan hath desired to have you, that he may sift you as wheat.'* She frowned, "Then verse thirty-two says, *'But I have prayed for thee, that thy faith fail not, and when thou art converted, strengthen thy brethren.'* Why wouldn't God stop Satan? I don't know if I have enough faith, and I don't think I'm strong enough to help anybody else." Her questions were earnest.

Slipping his hands into his pants pockets, Jude nodded. "God tells us to pray for His will on earth as is in heaven. Satan is the prince of this earth, and it's our free will that draws people away from Him. The Lord is rooting for us through prayer not to submit to temptation."

Amethyst was quiet as she seemed to consider his answer. "Okay."

"I'll let you read. Oh, before I forget and get in trouble with my wife, you're invited to our house on the Fourth of July if you're not doing anything. There will be plenty of barbecue."

"Will your son be there?" She looked hopeful.

"Yes. Carlton and his siblings will all be home."

She was more than happy to accept. Now only if they could get Grayson there too. The Lord would work out the rest.

Chapter Twenty-three

Not everyone who says unto me, Lord, Lord,
shall enter into the kingdom of heaven; but he that does
the will of my Father which is in heaven.
—Matthew 7:21

Porsha considered her life boring as a single woman. It was Friday night, and Tally was a happily married mom, so their girls' night out ended.

Tonight, she felt restless as she indulged in her favorite pastime—puzzles. It was a solo event until she competed with other jigsaw puzzle enthusiasts for an online or in-person event.

When her phone interrupted her, she was about to open a new puzzle box of African women lugging shopping bags. She didn't recognize the number.

"Porsha?"

"Yes." The voice sounded familiar, but she couldn't place it.

"This is Amethyst Johnson."

"Amethyst! Praise the Lord. I'm so glad you called. How are you feeling after your accident? I'm so glad you surrendered to the Lord." She was more interested in hearing from the new saint than opening a puzzle box. Porsha stood from her table, crossed the room to relax on a chair, and stretched her legs on an ottoman.

"Me too. I believe that made the difference between me being alive or dead."

"Yes. Jesus did."

"Listen, I'm sorry about giving you a hard time at first."

Porsha didn't want her to feel guilty. "Your sins were nailed to the cross. We're good, sis. I'm learning that everyone's salvation journey isn't the same."

"Thank you for saying that." Amethyst was quiet. "I hope we can become friends."

Her request brought mixed emotions. Friendship was all Porsha wanted from the beginning. Was that a possibility for Amethyst if she knew her husband, whom she didn't claim, who said he wasn't married, had been interested in a relationship with Porsha? *She is your assignment*, God whispered.

God had a sense of humor. While Porsha was in the middle of a pity party, lamenting that she didn't have close friends, the Lord reminded her of an assignment with the potential of a friendship. "Sure. What are you doing tonight?"

"Resting after two days of working. I came home tired, but you were on my mind."

"I'm glad." Porsha nodded. "Maybe we can go out to brunch after church on Sunday."

"Perfect."

"Great. See you then." Porsha would casually mention Grayson's temporary attraction to her when she and Amethyst went out. Porsha was about to disconnect when Amethyst asked for prayer.

"I want to make sure I'm praying the right way."

Porsha chuckled. "There is no wrong way to pray if you go to the Lord with a sincere heart. How about we pray together? The Holy Ghost will give us what to pray for."

As the two began to seek God in prayer, Porsha noticed Amethyst's heavenly language was bold, forceful, and full of authority as the Lord spoke. Amethyst's assignment was coming.

Grayson was willing to work on their marriage. Was Amethyst? They had a pleasant conversation over his biscuits on the drive to her job the first day. Yesterday, when he picked her up from work, she agreed to call him for a ride to the rental car place. Maybe the biscuits won her over. Since the other judge hadn't signed off on their divorce, he would call his attorney on Monday and contest it.

Pray for her, God whispered.

He did but felt helpless.

You are more than a conqueror through Me, God thundered.

Grayson shivered as Amethyst called him. He smiled. "Good morning."

"Morning, Grayson. If you're not busy, do you have time to take me to get my rental?"

"There's nothing for me to do on a Saturday morning except to put off house chores." He smiled. "Give me a time, and I'll pick you up."

"Slacker." She laughed. "How about in an hour?"

"Gotcha." They said their goodbyes, then he showered and dressed. Grayson scrutinized his appearance in the mirror. His tiredness seemed to fade from his face after talking to Amethyst. Not one to be late, he grabbed his keys and was out the door, praying on the way to Amethyst's mother's apartment as God had told him.

Amethyst was standing outside when he arrived.

Instead of her signature single long braid, she had brushed it into a fat ponytail. Although they were in their mid-thirties, she retained her youthful appearance.

He stepped out and opened the door. Amethyst's sweet fragrance greeted him with her smile as she climbed in. "Thank you."

"My pleasure. I'm glad to do this."

On the drive to the car agency, which was by the airport, Amethyst looked out the window. She wasn't talkative, so Grayson asked, "Did you ever imagine your life as a divorcee?"

Amethyst turned and faced him. "What do you mean?" She looked clueless.

Grayson shrugged and glanced at her before proceeding as the light turned green. "Where you would live, what you would do, and who you would be with?"

"Honestly, I never thought that far. I just wanted out."

Grayson felt a dagger in his heart. She hated him that much. *And you despised your wife too*, the Lord whispered.

He was guilty. They both were. "Maybe…maybe we can figure this out together."

She said nothing and little else until he drove into the rental company's parking lot. Grayson sighed. "Well, we're here."

Amethyst turned and smiled. "Thanks again."

"I can go in with you to make sure they don't try to sell you something," he said, hopeful for any excuse to spend more time with her.

"The insurance company already paid for ten days."

Grayson tried to hide his disappointment. "I guess I'll see you tomorrow at church?'

"See you tomorrow." She stepped out of his vehicle and disappeared inside.

Grayson planned to spy out a seat where he had seen Amethyst last week.

Bored the rest of the day, he went through the motions as he tidied up his three-bedroom house, which was too big for one person. That evening, Grayson was about to go to a movie—anywhere but be home alone when a phone call interrupted his unexciting plans.

"Praise the Lord, Brother Grayson! How you feel, man?" Minister Morgan asked.

The greeting made him feel like he was part of an exclusive club. "Praise the Lord back. Can't believe God saved me almost a week ago, and in less than a week so much has happened."

"Yes, and it's amazing that God knew all about it. Nothing catches Him by surprise. I called to check up on you, pray, or answer any questions you may have. Also, Christ For All has a men's ministry…" He listed all the auxiliaries he could join if he wanted.

Grayson was slow in responding. "To be honest, right now, Amethyst's on my mind—how to keep her safe. She works at your company, right? Is she okay there? I want to be there for her, but we're barely friends. More like acquaintances."

"Don't worry. I'll watch out for her. Both of you are new saints. Let God strengthen you both, then maybe you two can talk."

"I want more than a surface chatter like we exchanged when I dropped her off at work and earlier today when I took her to get her rental car. She's cordial, but I don't know what she's thinking." Grayson rubbed his forehead. "I just don't want anything to happen to her."

"If the devil couldn't take her out with the car accident, then you have to believe that the Lord has angels assigned to her."

By the time the call ended, Grayson was encouraged, excited about service in the morning, and looking forward to seeing Amethyst at church.

Sunday morning, Grayson dressed with care. The Spirit of God was powerful when he stepped into the sanctuary. He scanned the room for Amethyst, but she wasn't in the same seat. Where was she?

Maybe she was running late, he thought, so he closed his eyes and entered a soulful place of worship.

When Pastor Rodney stepped to the podium to preach, Grayson did another head check for Amethyst. He didn't see her.

"God changed you the day you repented and were baptized in Jesus' name. Jesus has redeemed you—us—from our spiritual and physical sins." Pastor Rodney drew Grayson's attention back to the present. "You received power from His spirit to keep going. Philippians three verse thirteen says, *'Brethren, I count not myself to have apprehended: but this one thing I do, forgetting those things which are behind, and reaching forth unto those things which are before.'* Let it go, release it, shake whatever is distracting you from moving ahead in your salvation."

Grayson repented. He had already failed God. Jesus could take better care of Amethyst than him. He would no longer be distracted by Amethyst's presence in the sanctuary. Grayson needed to learn how to walk as a Christian.

After the pastor gave the benediction, church members approached Grayson like old buddies. They greeted him with handshakes, fist bumps, and pats on the back.

Minister Morgan approached with his family. Their grins were bright. "Praise the Lord, my brother. If you don't have any plans for next weekend, we're having a Fourth of July barbecue. My husband said he spoke with you last night and failed to invite you." Sinclaire shook her head, and her husband looked guilty. "Please come for the fellowship and the food."

"I'd like that." Grayson smiled.

"Good. Amethyst has been invited too." Minister Morgan snickered and walked away with his family in tow. Carlton looked over his shoulder and gave him a thumbs-up.

Grayson grinned. He loved it. He tamed his laughter as he folded his arms with his Bible against his chest. Not only did he have allies, but matchmakers on his side.

All things work together for good for those of you who love Me, God whispered.

"Lord, teach me how to love You." Then maybe everything else in his life would work out.

Chapter Twenty-four

These things I have spoken unto you,
that in me ye might have peace. In the world ye shall
have tribulation: but be of good cheer; I have overcome
the world. —John 16:33

Today was not the day to oversleep when Amethyst couldn't wait to get to Christ For All Church. But she had. It was after noon, and service was probably over.

"Afternoon, Mama." Amethyst stifled a yawn.

Annabelle grunted. "Amee, you've got to stop all this carrying on in the middle of the night," she threatened, lifting a brow. "I will not let you get me evicted from my apartment. I'll put you out first."

"Sorry, I woke you up while praying." Amethyst kissed her cheek and reached for a mug.

God, when I committed to You, I'm not supposed to be homeless or be in a car crash, right? she silently prayed.

All things work together for good for those who love Me, God whispered.

She poured herself a cup of coffee and joined her mother at the table. "Mom, dark spirits keep coming into my room at night, clawing at me. They're as real as you and me," Amethyst explained, "but when I pray, God's angels show up to defend me."

Annabelle tapped her fingernails on the table. "You need to consult a psychic to find out what you've gotten yourself into or check your horoscope. There has to be a reason this is happening."

Amethyst rested her coffee cup on the table, then tilted her head, thinking. "Surprisingly, I kept forgetting to check my daily horoscope a while ago, and it didn't feel like I was missing anything. I crave God's presence, and I'd rather pray for answers."

Her mother squinted. "I'm warning you, Amee, if you keep me up all night again, I will pack your bags the next day, and you can sleep in that rental car out there."

All things work together, God? How? My mother is not working with me on this. If I pray, there's no guarantee I won't wake her. Amethyst waited for guidance from the Lord.

Nothing.

"Mom, did you know I had a gun?"

Annabelle gasped and placed a hand over her mouth. "Why?"

"Reggie gave it to me when I left Grayson. He said I might need it for protection. But knowing I had it made me think about using it when I began to fall into a dark place where there wasn't a blink of light."

"Oh, my God. You were thinking about committing suicide?" Her mother's eyes became teary. "You didn't cause that crash, did you, trying to end your life?"

"Mom, the driver crossed into *my* lane." Amethyst frowned. "But it seemed Jesus kept distracting me from thoughts of death until I forgot I had the gun."

"Why were you in a dark place?" Annabelle frowned, concern masking her face. "Is it about the divorce?"

"Not just that. I struggled in every area of my life—marriage, money, and job—but nothing worked in my favor despite my daily horoscope's positive vibes. Jesus turned me around."

The more Amethyst told her mother about her salvation experience, the more Annabelle pushed back. "I'm not interested in that nonsense." She stood and walked out of the kitchen.

Disappointed, Amethyst sat there, wondering what she could have said to win her mother over. Her day was off to a bad start.

Some come willingly after I draw them, others have a stony heart, God whispered.

Amethyst fixed herself something to eat. Then she realized she and Porsha were supposed to go out to eat after church service. She hurried to her bedroom and grabbed her phone. Porsha had texted her. **I didn't see you at service today, and I wasn't sure if you were resting. Call or text me when you get a chance.**

Porsha, I'm so sorry. I overslept. Maybe we can get together next weekend.

Taking her beloved Bible she had received from church, Amethyst stepped out on the balcony. Tears filled her eyes. "Lord, what am I going to do? I have a rental car for a week and a half, then what? I don't have money for an apartment so I can pray freely. I thought You would make my life better." A plane overhead caught her attention. She hoped God was watching her.

Then there was her divorce. She closed her eyes. The letter from the attorney said another judge needed to sign off on it, which meant, technically, she *was* still married. Amethyst huffed. Once the updated divorce decree arrived, she and Grayson could move on with their lives on friendly terms.

Amethyst read a few chapters in Genesis, then began to doze. Her phone startled her.

"Is everything okay? Do I need to buy you an alarm clock?" Porsha teased when Amethyst answered.

They both chuckled. "No. I don't plan to miss another Sunday."

"Good." They chatted briefly before Amethyst heard a baby's cry in the background.

"Hold on. That's my niece. I offered to babysit when I didn't hear from you after church. I think she's wet. I'll talk later." Then Porsha was gone.

A baby. Did God have another one for her? Did God really show Carlton her baby, who had died before Amethyst could see him—or her?

For the rest of her Sunday, she relaxed, listened to gospel music, and talked to God. That night, under the covers, Amethyst drifted off to sleep, dreaming about her baby, not demons.

Minister Morgan was on a mission Monday morning when he saw Amethyst at work.

The intercessors had become concerned because she had not been to church the day before and weren't sure if her absence was still recovery-related. It was important for new converts to have a support system to encourage them to walk with Christ. He wanted to make sure Satan wasn't testing her faith already.

"Hey. I missed you at church yesterday. Is everything okay?" he asked.

"Yeah." Amethyst seemed frustrated. "I overslept because I was up praying the night before."

He relaxed. "I'm sure your body needed the rest. Is there a specific reason that caused you to petition God that you want to share with me?"

"Well, I might get kicked out of my mother's place because my praying disturbs her sleep." She twisted her lips in sadness.

Interesting. Jude frowned and leaned against the counter in the break room. "I'm sorry to hear that. The devil doesn't want you to pray at all. I'll pray that God will soften your mother's heart to hear God's voice."

"Will you? Thank you." Amethyst's face glowed with happiness, and he noted that the bruise on her face was becoming less noticeable.

He looked around, touched her shoulder, and whispered a prayer. "Lord, in the name of Jesus, encourage my sister, supply her needs, and let her thrive in You. Give her peace in the middle of the chaos, in Jesus' name. Amen."

"Amen. Whew." Amethyst sniffed. "Now, I have the mental strength and clarity to perform my job." She exhaled and seemed to regroup. "I can't be distracted when I inspect departments to determine worker safety violations."

"No, you can't." Jude was glad he prayed for her. The company understood her limitations because of the high-profile crash in which Amethyst was involved—to a certain point. Amethyst was still on probation.

That afternoon, Jude was proud of her for detecting two violations with the improper use of equipment.

"But I had to brace myself from falling on some liquid on the floor." She lowered her voice. "Although I was alone, I heard an echo of snickers. I called on Jesus, then all was quiet."

"Amen," Jude said, then they finished their workday.

The rest of the week was uneventful as Amethyst seemed to be operating at a hundred percent. But more than once, Jude wondered why the devil was on her back.

The three-day Fourth of July holiday arrived on Friday, and Jude was glad to spend the extra day with the children. He woke early on Saturday morning and prayed that Amethyst and Grayson would have some reconciliation at the gathering at his house. He knew it was God's doing to make Amethyst uncomfortable at her mother's place.

Jude's mind went down the list of souls God had assigned Mother Kincaid.

At the breakfast table, the children barely ate, too excited about the fun they would have when their friends came to the barbecue.

Grayson was the first guest to arrive a few hours later, followed by the Addams. While Tally and their baby stayed indoors out of the heat, Randall huddled with the men outside near the grill.

Mother Kincaid showed up with church folks.

Omega opted out of coming because her newborn kept her up all night. Mitchell showed up to take home plates.

Since Sophia was a minor, the intercessors had to speak to her mother to draw the child. That was his wife's mission. Sinclaire waited for Sophia's mother to drop her off at camp after she called Debra Doyle and invited her to the barbecue. His wife didn't want to wait until then to get acquainted.

Sissy has planted a seed, his wife watered it, careful not to drown it so the Lord would allow it to grow. Debra was non-committal about accepting an invitation to church but had no objection to attending the barbecue.

Amethyst arrived after Hudson. Since she missed church last Sunday, members celebrated her salvation there. She welcomed the attention, but Amethyst was more interested in what Carlton knew.

Hudson was testifying and winning souls for Christ, while Grayson and Amethyst seemed eager to grow spiritually but separately. Jude and the other intercessors discreetly watched Grayson's and Amethyst's interaction.

"Where are the others, Lord? Send them our way or to my barbecue," Jude half-joked, but he had learned that God worked in mysterious ways.

Chapter Twenty-five

And said, For this cause shall a man leave
father and mother and shall cleave to his wife: and
they twain shall be one flesh. —Matthew 19:5

Grayson studied Amethyst as she spoke with other sisters from the church. She soaked up the attention. He smiled as she glowed, but Minister Morgan's son Carlton seemed to intrigue her.

The orange in the long sundress, with bold strokes of blue and yellow, complemented her skin. He remembered her buying the dress during happy times. Her long, single braid was neatly styled, and large hoop earrings finished her look. He wondered how many shampoos it took to remove all the glass fragments that had sparkled in her thick mane while she lay in the hospital bed.

"Praise the Lord, saints, and friends." Minister Morgan waved his hands to get everyone's attention. "Everything is ready, so claim a spot around the picnic tables, and I'll bless the food." Then he bowed his head. "Lord, Jesus, thank You for this gathering and the abundance of food for our guests to feast on. Bless those who prepared the food, including me—your griller." He paused and snickered along with others. "Remove the impurities, and Lord, help us do our part to feed the hungry, in Jesus' name. Amen."

Grayson snagged the chair next to Amethyst.

"Hey." He grinned.

She smiled and continued eating.

"Do you think we can talk after this?"

"About what?"

"A lot of things." He stared into her hazel eyes, which seemed to come back to life.

Mother Kincaid approached them. "Do you mind taking your plates inside? Minister Morgan has space. I need this table for the little ones."

Grayson wanted to protest—finally, he had Amethyst to himself, but when she complied, he followed her.

"There's space in here for you two," Sinclaire said, leading them into a home office with unique artwork on the walls. If you need anything, let us know," she said, closing the door.

A setup. Perfect. Grayson hid his smile.

"There's no one else in here but us." She appeared uncomfortable.

"Missed seeing you at church last Sunday, and now that you have the rental car, I haven't seen you at all."

"I overslept," she huffed, "and I was looking forward to hearing the sermon."

"It was good. I enjoyed it." He was quiet, recalling Pastor Rodney preaching press toward the future or something like that. Grayson wondered what a future would look like with Amethyst. At least they were getting along. Leaning forward, he waited for her to meet his eyes. "What can I do to fix us—husband and wife?"

"I don't think we can be fixed. God has already fixed you and me to be at least friends." She twisted her lips and focused on the green beans on her plate.

Grayson covered her hand with his. "Amee, talk to me."

She looked at him with sadness in her eyes. "I've got a lot on my mind. Our divorce is at the bottom of the list."

There will be no divorce. "Like what?" He pushed his plate aside. She was dainty, from her polished nails to the studs in her ears. Her beauty was natural without makeup.

Amethyst scanned the room, stalling to answer him. "I've got three days left before I have to return the rental car. After that, I will need to find permanent transportation. Reggie loaned me money for my sales tax on the other car…"

Right. Grayson hadn't forgotten that as he remained silent at the mention of his half-brother's name. Reggie was a master at sparking an argument between Amethyst and Grayson. She felt Grayson was too hard on his younger brother. He took deep breaths and listened.

"Now, I need to pay Reggie back and save money for a car and new sales tax…" She shook her head as a tear fell.

He touched her cheek and caught it as soon as she blinked. "I offered to pay him back for you." Grayson should have taken care of that debt without waiting for her approval.

She frowned. "I don't think that's a good idea, considering you two don't get along."

"Babe," he said, using the endearment because he still cared, "that was before Christ saved me. Amee, God gave me a new heart to love everyone. I will pay him back and take you car shopping. When you find one you like, I'll put a down payment and pay the sales tax."

"It's fourteen hundred dollars and twelve cents. I'll pay you back."

"There is no need…and I will fight the divorce." Grayson braced himself to prepare for battle. "You're still my wife."

She grunted, and fire blazing in her eyes was ready to shoot darts. Grayson had pushed too hard. "You mentally and emotionally walked out on me when I lost the baby."

"But you physically walked out on me."

"You let me go." Amethyst jutted her chin in a tit-for-tat.

Grayson backed down and sat back. "I was tired of our arguments and the distance between us. I should have fought for our marriage, but I couldn't do that alone."

"Would you have married me if I weren't pregnant?"

"The truth?" He folded his hands and prepared to soften the blow. "I married you because you were pregnant. I welcomed us becoming a family."

"You didn't answer the question."

That's what he tried to avoid. He couldn't lie and stay in God's presence. Didn't he just read about God not suffering fools? "I'm being transparent. Marriage was not on my radar until you told me you were having our baby. That doesn't mean it wouldn't have happened between us."

Amethyst huffed. "I guess you never did love me. Even Reggie saw it. He helped me get out of a loveless marriage."

"I asked you to marry me because I did love you. Some men would have walked away. That was never an option to me." He patted his chest for emphasis. *Help me, Holy Ghost, to tame my emotions for wanting to knock my brother out.*

Reggie always compared their marriages and possessions. When Amethyst lost the baby, it was Reggie's perfect family versus Grayson not having one. "How much did he give you?"

"Loaned me," she corrected and squinted.

"Amee, I'm settling that debt right now." His nostrils flared with attitude as God calmed him down.

"Why all of a sudden are you invested in my life? I don't want to re-live our past. I want a future with Christ."

"Because I'm still your husband, and I may not have shown you the love you deserve, but I will protect you at all costs."

"I believe God orchestrated a new judge for our divorce because Judge Doane signed on the wrong line."

"Estranged, but that will get fixed." She folded her arms and leaned across the table. It was alluring, but Grayson knew that was not Amethyst's intent. "And what do you mean by protecting me? From who or what?"

Grayson wasn't sure. Randall said she was in spiritual danger, and Grayson believed him.

Her soul is important. Pray for her, God whispered.

"I will protect you from any hurt, sadness, or unhappiness. Initially, I was attracted to your beauty when you walked into the movie theater alone."

She smiled, then giggled. "That night became our first date when we sat together."

"Yep, because we watched another movie together after that."

Amethyst chuckled. "Yeah, you bought tickets and treated me to the concession counter as if I didn't have popcorn and a drink in my hands."

Her remembering was a good sign. "Now I want to start over and learn to love you the way you want." He meant every word, even though she didn't look convinced.

"Grayson, you have no idea how much I needed your love, hugs, and kisses after I lost our boy," Amethyst said. "I felt like I lost my mind. I needed hope, comfort, and understanding, which I didn't get from you."

"And I'm sorry I failed, but God gave me and you a second chance. Not only am I fighting for your love, but for your heart and soul."

"What?" She frowned.

Grayson covered her hands with his and began to pray until a tear dropped.

"Are you crying? You never did, even when I lost the baby." She squeezed his hand.

He shook his head. "I didn't want you to see me. I was crushed, wondering if it was a boy or girl."

"It was a boy who probably would have looked like you." Her eyes sparkled.

"Wait." Grayson grinned. A boy. He just realized what she had said. "How do you know our baby was a boy? Are you still visiting those psychics?"

"Of course not. Actually, it was Minister Morgan's son, Carlton, who told me that the first time I met him. Oddly enough, I believed him."

Grayson reached for her hands and squeezed them. They had made a baby. When she tried to pull back, he wouldn't let her. "We had a son." He was in awe.

"I know."

When she sniffed, Grayson looked up. They both needed to heal. He took a deep breath. "What else is bothering you? I can feel it." He rubbed his thumb against her soft hands.

"I'm going to have to find someplace to stay. Mama doesn't like me loudly praying at night and waking her and others who live in the building, but praying has become addictive to me."

A knock came at the door. Tally opened it, then she and Randall walked in and took a seat. "Would you mind if we shared our story?"

No! This was not the time to cue the interruption. Grayson felt he was making progress.

Amethyst was glad for the company because Grayson had her feelings jumbled.

"Sorry to interrupt, but I felt the Holy Ghost wanted me to share my story with you," Tally said. "So I dragged my husband from outside and wanted to give our testimony."

Anyone could see Tally and Randall Addams complemented and loved each other. Like Amethyst, Tally and Porsha possessed hazel-colored eyes. Both sisters had black shoulder-length hair and dimples. Porsha's were faint. Randall was handsome with his dark brown skin and solid build...but Grayson looked better. He was just as tall and solid as Randall, but Grayson wore a trimmed mustache as silky as his long lashes and brows. His faded hair was always trimmed. If there were a bachelor game show, Grayson would take all.

"We lost our baby too," Randall said, jolting Amethyst back to the present. He looked at his wife. "We had broken up, and I didn't know. Now, God has blessed us with a precious baby."

Their look of love made Amethyst catch her breath and her heart race. They looked so happy. What could have caused them to break up?

Carlton's words came back to Amethyst. He had said God had two babies for her but didn't say who was the father. She glanced at Grayson, who was watching her. It couldn't be him because their time was up. That had to mean there was someone else out there for her.

"I understand how you feel, Amethyst." Tally blinked back moisture. "I had gotten saved and refused to walk away from God. True story: Randall died in a car crash—dead in a mortuary—but because of the power of prayer, the Lord raised him and others around the city. It's in the news archives."

Amethyst's jaw dropped in disbelief, then in wonder, scrutinizing Randall. He looked healthy and in love.

"Her prayers saved my soul from hell." Randall squeezed his wife's hand.

"Wow." Amethyst heard what Tally said but couldn't comprehend it. She remembered feeling happy when she and Grayson fell in love three years ago. Marriage was never discussed until after Amethyst learned of her pregnancy. She had been hopeful that Grayson's love for her was the reason, not the baby. After hearing his truth, why stay married?

"I see how much you and Randall love each other. I don't think that was ever Grayson and me." She was being honest despite the wounded expression on his face.

I promise you more babies, God whispered.

"I believe in second chances," Tally said.

"*We* believe in second chances." Randall brought his wife's hand to his lips. "And blessings come with them. A couple that prays together stays together." They stood. "You two need to pray together."

Tally hugged her. "Let's exchange numbers before we leave. You can call me if you ever want to talk or pray."

Pray. Amethyst nodded after they left. She loved the feeling of the presence of God when she prayed. She had to because the demons in her bedroom were real. The first night, her heart pounded with fear. Since receiving the Holy Ghost, God had sent angels to fight her battles as long as she prayed.

"Hey, what are you thinking?" Grayson asked softly.

"How much I love to pray, but doing so will get me kicked out of Mom's apartment." She sighed.

"You can always move back home," he offered.

"And be roommates?" She shook her head. "I don't think so. Honestly, we don't know each other anymore." He had hurt her to the core, and she had walked away numb from emotion. "Grayson Tate, I forgive you, but I can't forget how rejected I felt."

Grayson folded his hands. He was thinking, and she was always drawn to his intense expression. "I'll take the house off the market. You can pick any three bedrooms and claim whatever space you need. I promise to keep my distance." He paused. "All I ask is that you allow us a second chance to start over whenever you're ready."

Never was on the tip of her tongue, but God restrained her mouth, so she couldn't turn him down like she wanted.

An hour later, Amethyst said goodbye to her hosts. *Lord, help me to stick it out with my mom and get another vehicle.*

God didn't answer.

Chapter Twenty-six

And it shall come to pass in the last days, saith God,
I will pour out of my Spirit upon all flesh: and your sons
and your daughters shall prophesy, and your young men shall
see visions, and your old men shall dream dreams.
—Acts 2:17

Mother Kincaid prayed for reconciliation while Grayson and Amethyst were inside the house. God's purpose for them was to work together.

She turned her attention to the little people playing in Jude's backyard, including Sophia Doyle, who had arrived with her parents, Debra and Quinton. Sissy was ecstatic to see her friend.

Three activities were going on simultaneously among the age groups, with the younger children setting up chairs to play church. Pew babies liked mimicking their parents and other behavior they were exposed to at church.

Right or wrong, it was entertaining.

To Mother Kincaid's surprise, the small ones begged Hudson Lane to pretend to be their preacher. A Holy Ghost powerhouse, Hudson didn't have to act. Sissy used a plastic red firefighter's hat the small children were given at church on Sunday and passed it around like an offering plate. The children ran to their parents for change.

Carlton and his brother Harry acted as ushers, seating members. Their mini-production got the adults' attention as they watched from afar.

Matthew 18:4 came to Mother Kincaid's mind: *Whosoever, therefore, shall humble himself as this little child, the same is greatest in the kingdom of heaven.*

Minister Morgan's youngest son, TJ, ran into the house and grabbed his child-size tambourine. The children sang "What A Mighty God We Serve," and Hudson stood up and cleared his throat.

"Praise the Lord, Church!"

The children responded with, "Praise the Lord." Some adults, too.

"I stand before you today to remind you that the kingdom of heaven belongs to us—the children—and we have to stay pure in heart. We have special assignments from God to bring our friends and family to Jesus..."

Mother Kincaid listened with interest. The teenager's message was timely, bold, and filled with the Holy Ghost's anointing, and she imagined stirring in the spiritual realm.

Suddenly, God's presence appeared in a strong wind that encircled the children. The trees, the umbrellas erected over the tables, and the tablecloths remained still.

Tall angels stood at attention, making the children appear as ants. Mother Kincaid wondered if all the other guests could see the vision. God's breath seemed to blow on each child—about nine of them—and they began to praise God and speak in heavenly language, even little Sophia, who began to prophesy to the children and adults boldly. She spoke to conditions in some people's bodies, then laid her hands on them, and God delivered them of their ailments.

Sophia hurried to Mother Kincaid and rested her hands on her knees. "You are healed of arthritis in your right knee. Instantly, her pain ceased to throb, and she praised God.

Not one person was unaffected by the impromptu service. Sophia's parents' interest seemed piqued.

"I can't believe my backache is gone." Debra Doyle rubbed her back in disbelief. "I almost didn't come because of it."

Jude walked into the midst of his guests and offered baptism in water, in Jesus' name, then faced Mother Kincaid. "This is a backyard Azusa Street."

"Yes." Mother Kincaid nodded. "Wouldn't that be something?" She wondered if God was turning the Fourth of July holiday into backyard revivals like Azusa Street in Los Angeles, where people were filled with the Holy Ghost in record numbers for almost ten years in the early 1900s.

"Hudson's pretend sermon was real, and it appears Sophia received two gifts today—the Holy Ghost and healing hands."

"Maybe Amethyst and Grayson should have been outside for the Lord to heal their broken hearts." Mother Kincaid sighed. "I've been praying for their marriage."

"Me too," Minister Morgan said, "God's timing is perfect, and His anointing is not limited to outside my house. Grayson and Amethyst haven't missed anything that God has for them."

Porsha wasn't expecting Amethyst's call Saturday night, and it came at the same time as Tally's, who was giving her an update about the barbecue.

"I missed seeing you at Minister Morgan's house," Amethyst said. "I spoke with your sister and brother-in-law."

I know, Porsha wanted to say. That's why Tally and Randall had skipped the Gilbert family gathering, hoping to minister to Grayson and Amethyst if they both showed up at the barbecue. Porsha had been waiting for the scoop. Plus, she wanted to keep her distance so not to distract Grayson. He belonged to someone else.

"Did you have a good time?"

"Yes," Amethyst said. "I want to ask your opinion about reconciling with Grayson since you're a neutral party. You might not know he was baptized the same day as me."

Porsha swallowed. "I did know that."

"Well, my thoughts are all over the place, and I need a listening ear. Are you available for brunch after church tomorrow?"

"Of course." It was becoming a tag team effort to bring these two together. Tally had mentioned that Amethyst seemed receptive to what Randall and she had to say.

Sunday morning, Porsha walked into the sanctuary as the praise team began their rendition of "Nobody Greater." She looked around for Amethyst, who still preferred the east section but not as far back. Praise God, Grayson was there, too, sitting not far from her.

Well, at least he had changed locations.

When the music quieted, Pastor Rodney took his spot on the pulpit. "Praise the Lord, saints, guests, and friends. Not long ago, God sent a message to the church that He's coming for the children."

He paused. "He's still coming for them to do His mighty works. Yesterday, Minister Morgan told me the power of the Holy Ghost fell on his house after one of our fairly new saints preached a mock sermon. Today, I have asked Brother Hudson Lane to give us a message God has for His people. Before he comes, let me remind you of what Paul said to Timothy, 'Let no man despise your youth.'"

He motioned for Hudson to approach, and he was received with a roar of applause. Porsha smiled to herself. She had effectively won a soul for Christ.

"Praise the Lord, everyone," Hudson said nervously. "I'm as shocked as you that God picked me to speak. I'm only sixteen." He inhaled and shrugged as saints in the congregation shouted, "Let God use you," "It's alright, son," "Bless him, Jesus," and other encouraging words.

Hudson nodded as if giving himself a pep talk, then flipped through his Bible, searching for a passage. "*Whew*. I found it.

Luke, chapter fourteen, beginning at verse twenty-one." He grinned, then read, "*'And the Lord said unto the servant, Go out into the highways and hedges, and compel them to come in, that my house may be filled.'* People gave him excuses," he said, repeating the word, "excuses on why they couldn't come to his party, a free party. Who passes up free? I think the feast means the Word of God being served at churches that believe in the Bible." The teenager stood tall and confident. He angled his head as if listening to the Lord's whispers.

Porsha smiled with godly pride. God had put her in Hudson's path to draw him to Christ, and she had seen the transformation.

"It's important that we do what God says. The next verse, *'Go out quickly into the streets and lanes of the city and bring in the poor, the crippled, the blind, and the lame.'* That is our assignment. Go tell the world about Jesus and pull them from hell, which burns day and night."

Hudson laid the microphone on the podium and pushed both hands toward the crowd, and the Power of God fell across the sanctuary. "We don't have much time. Go tell the world about Jesus." As he returned to his seat, he began to jump in place, lifting his hands and worshipping God.

Tears streamed down Porsha's cheeks. Now, she understood why God had Hudson on the salvation list. Jesus' special gifts for Grayson and Amethyst hadn't been revealed to anyone. "Lord, help me stay on full alert for the others we haven't found yet but have a purpose in Your kingdom building."

The service ended with many baptisms in Jesus' name.

Moments before the benediction, another move of God stirred those with physical disabilities—in wheelchairs, on canes, and blind—to gravitate toward Sophia, who was speaking in a heavenly language.

With her eyes closed, the girl began to lay hands on them, and many were healed on the spot, according to their faith. That prompted Sophia's parents to seek salvation for themselves. They came to the altar, repented, and were added to the baptism candidates.

The service left Porsha breathless. She couldn't imagine the miracles that happened at Minister Morgan's house yesterday, but she had just witnessed a small sampling.

Once they were dismissed, she turned to find Amethyst so they could go out to brunch. She spied Grayson nearby, waiting patiently for Amethyst as she chatted with other church members.

Porsha felt sorry for him. "Lord, whatever is keeping them apart, please mend it so they can do Your will." She paused to add, "God, remember me with a special someone, in Jesus' name. Amen."

Chapter Twenty-seven

*For God is not the author of confusion but of
peace, as in all churches of the saints.*
—1 Corinthians 14:33

After service, Amethyst continued to be bombarded with well-wishers. She had never met so many people at one time who were ready to become friends.

One friend at a time, she thought as she craned her neck, searching for Porsha. She made eye contact with Grayson more than once.

Their conversation at the barbecue yesterday left Amethyst confused about what to do. Maybe Porsha could advise her since she no longer consulted psychics or horoscopes.

Seek Me, God whispered, *and I will guide your path.*

The Lord was right, of course. She saw Porsha patiently waiting for her.

Amethyst excused herself from the group and walked toward her new friend, who was always a polished dresser, even when they'd crossed paths in the Cortex at work. They did have three things in common: she and Porsha were around the same age, had hazel-colored eyes, and seemed to like tied-dyed fabrics. Did the men at this church not want companionship? She was attractive and genuine.

"Hi. Sorry to keep you waiting."

Porsha shrugged. "You seemed occupied, and it looked like Grayson had other plans for you to consider."

Glancing over her shoulder, Amethyst saw Grayson standing patiently, waiting to speak to her. She shook her head and faced Porsha again. "I'm not sure what to do about that man. That's why I need a friend to help."

"Okay." Porsha's smile was slow in coming. "I'm honored to be called your friend, but can you speak to him or tell him goodbye? As Christians, we're not to purposely hurt one another."

Slumping her shoulder, Amethyst sighed. "Yeah, you're right." She gripped the strap on her purse, swallowed, and slowly walked toward Grayson.

She didn't hold any malice against him. They no longer argued when in each other's presence. Amethyst thought the Holy Ghost had a lot to do with that. But he made her nervous. Grayson wanted something that Amethyst was unsure about. He didn't want a divorce, and she hadn't changed her mind about whether or not it was the best thing for them. Right?

His eyes locked with hers with each step. Now, she wasn't sure if she was right about their marriage.

From his handsome features to his body language, Amethyst could tell Grayson had put aside his overbearing personality, which she initially considered sexy, then annoying.

"Praise the Lord, Amee." His brown eyes sparkled, and his voice was gentle. He seemed so unsure of himself too. That mannerism was foreign to her.

"Hi, Grayson. Praise the Lord." Amethyst didn't know what else to say, so they stared at each other.

Grayson cleared his throat. "Are you hungry? I'll treat."

"Sorry," Amethyst said, watching the disappointment flash on his face. "I already have plans. Rain check?" Why did she say that? She couldn't promise him anything in the future.

"Sure. Any time." Grayson picked up his Bible, nodded at a few lingering church members, and strolled out of the sanctuary as if he hadn't a care in the world.

Mama Lou's Soul Food Kitchen was the hotspot as Amethyst and Porsha entered the spacious storefront business. Amethyst's mouth salivated for the smothered pork chops, candied yams, and collard greens. They ordered the same sides, while Porsha opted for the fried chicken wings.

"Let me treat," Amethyst insisted. Although she watched her spending, Porsha was special because she was persistent about Amethyst's salvation. "It's been a while since I've eaten out."

"Me too," Porsha acted as excited as Amethyst for company. "Next time, I'll treat," she said.

They found booth seating and then slid inside. "You say grace." Amethyst grinned.

Porsha reached for Amethyst's hand and bowed her head. "Oh, Lord, I thank You for this fellowship and for drawing Amethyst into Your kingdom. Bless her and sanctify our food and the hands who prepared it. Remind us to feed the hungry, in Jesus' name. Amen."

Amethyst sampled the yams, which liberated her taste buds. "Wow. I taste a hint of vanilla. These are so good." She grinned.

"I know, right?" Porsha smiled. "My sister and I would come here often after church until she married." She paused to take another bite of her pork chop, then swallowed. "So tell me, what's your hesitation with Grayson."

"You know how to spoil the mood." Amethyst pouted and gave her a bittersweet smile.

"In what way?" Porsha took a sip of her soda and waited for Amethyst to answer.

"Well," she said, shrugging, "we don't love each other like that anymore."

"Who says? Number one, you need to repent. From how he looks at you, I see love waiting for the green light. I wish I had someone to love me," Porsha said whimsically.

"Yeah, but you don't know Grayson. We once were in love, and we married when I became pregnant, but it went downhill after I lost the baby—when I needed him most. Even his younger brother called out his behavior." She frowned, remembering how calm Grayson was when she told him about Reggie loaning her money for the sales tax. Any other time, he would have exploded.

"You are important to God and your husband," Porsha said.

Husband? She hadn't thought of him that way since she'd left him. He was her ex in her mind. Amethyst said nothing as she cut off a piece of pork chop.

"There's something you need to know…" Porsha reached into her purse, pulled out her phone, and then showed Amethyst a text message forwarded from the older woman at church named Mother Kincaid. "It's God's will that you and Grayson reconcile."

Amethyst read it twice, blinked in disbelief, and then looked to Porsha for an explanation. "Why am I on this list?" she asked, pointing to Porsha's phone, "and why do I feel like I was singled out? What does it mean 'Grayson Tate and his wife,' then 'especially Amethyst Johnson?'"

"God singled you out. If we're to be friends, I'm being honest with you: God loved you so much that He put out a search team to find you. That's how important you are to Him." Porsha's eyes were filled with sincerity.

Amethyst was quiet as she processed this information, then frowned. "Grayson and his wife? Especially Amethyst?" she repeated. "That's odd the way it's worded. It's Grayson and his wife, which was me—or I guess still is, and then I'm listed separately."

What I have joined together, let no man separate, God whispered.

"You're a team. When we met, you didn't mention you were married. In full disclosure, I randomly met Grayson one evening at the airport. We chatted for a while. He never mentioned he was married, and I was interested in him without realizing he was on God's list until Mother Kincaid and my brother-in-law Randall stepped in before we went out on a date. I felt sorry for him because he seemed to think you two were divorced when he asked me out." Porsha exhaled.

Amethyst didn't know how she felt with this confession. So, Grayson was ready to move on with the woman she had just treated to a meal. With mixed emotions, Amethyst was ready to walk away again until the Lord spoke.

I used her to bring you two together, God whispered.

Amethyst grunted. "Sounds like a setup."

"It was, and Jesus is the mastermind behind it," Porsha said. She had no way of knowing God had said that to Amethyst.

Picking at her meal, Amethyst sighed. "I guess it was an honest mistake between you and him. Minister Morgan's son Carlton said God showed him another baby. Two of them. One was a girl. I asked him who was the father."

"And?" Porsha seemed amused.

"Carlton told me I know… How? I'm supposed to be divorced, so I don't know."

"Give Grayson a chance." Porsha reached across the table and squeezed Amethyst's hand like Grayson had done the day before at the barbecue. "You're both different people in Christ, and you've lived apart for a while. Grayson longs for the other half God gave him, no matter the circumstances, how you two met, and what broke you up. When I looked at Grayson today, watching you, I saw love. I saw regret."

"How could you see this when you don't have a boyfriend?" Amethyst challenged her, then took a sip of her iced tea.

Don't you dare judge her! God thundered.

Amethyst exhaled. "I'm sorry. That was rude. I shouldn't have said that."

Porsha smiled. "You're forgiven. I'm forgiven. I have a brother-in-law, and I saw the same expression when he and Tally broke up."

Amethyst recalled the love between Tally and Randall yesterday. It was very tangible. "I can't imagine them apart. They seem really happy."

"They are, and I'm holding out for that type of love, and yours is waiting for you. Talk to God about your marriage. Now," Porsha said, resting her fork on her plate, "that's enough of my free, unqualified marriage counseling."

They both laughed, then Amethyst became quiet. "I don't know where to go from here."

"Come to our all-night prayer shut-in next Friday. God reveals a lot during those shut-ins."

Lord, is it wrong not to love Grayson anymore? she wondered because she felt like an invisible line was preventing her from crossing over.

Fight, Amethyst, for what I've given you, God whispered.

Grayson arrived home after church, frustrated and hungry. He and Amethyst could have enjoyed lunch, a snack, or shared dinner. After their talk the previous day at the barbecue, Grayson thought they had made some progress.

Amethyst had purposely ignored him at church while he admired her from afar. Instead of her trademark single braid, she wore her hair past her shoulders. The tan dress showed off her figure, but not in a seductive way. He approved of her attire as if he had a say. At one time, she wanted to know his thoughts about what she was wearing.

In all honesty, Amethyst soaked up the attention she received from the sisters at Christ For All Church. Good for her. She never had many close female friends, even Reggie's wife, Jessica. They were cordial but not best friends.

Pray for Amethyst, God's voice thundered, interrupting his wandering thoughts. *Danger is stalking her.*

Danger? He shivered as fear overcame him. Grayson had to act fast if this had to do with Jessica's threat to her husband.

Grayson couldn't be still as he walked through his house, room after room, pleading for mercy and Amethyst's protection. God's presence surrounded him.

The heavenly tongues became more forceful and commanding. Authority demanded obedience in a spiritual realm, which Grayson couldn't see but of which he was aware.

After a while, Grayson became weakened from the prayer, so he sat quietly in his living room, recalling God's list with his name on it. Reggie came to mind, as did the money he lent his wife. Grayson stood and freshened up, then took money from his home safe and headed to his brother's house.

Walking up the stairs to a ridiculously large home with six bedrooms, Grayson rang the doorbell as he heard his niece and nephew's voices outside in the back. He'd started to walk around there when Jessica opened the door.

"Grayson?" She didn't hide the surprise in her voice as he watched her children barge through the kitchen patio door, hearing the ring that chimed throughout the house.

"Uncle Grayson!" Victor, who had just had a sixth birthday, yelled and headed straight to him as he stepped into the foyer.

"Uncle Grayson!" three-year-old Kiya said, mimicking her older brother.

Squatting, he received their affection and, in turn, smothered them with love. He longed for the baby he and Amethyst lost. He stood. "Where's your daddy?"

"In the back." Kiya pointed, grabbed his hand, and led the way.

Jessica closed the door and followed.

His brother was stretched out on a patio lounger, watching a Cardinals baseball game on his device. Reggie looked over his shoulder at Grayson and grunted before he faked a smile.

Lord, I know we haven't had the best sibling relationship, but help me be the light, in Jesus' name. Amen.

"Haven't seen you in a while. How's the bachelor life treating you?" Reggie sat up.

"Well." Grayson sat nearby, resting his hands on his knees. "I have news."

"Yeah?" Reggie tilted his head, ready to take the bait. "I'm listening."

"I'm fighting the divorce, which isn't final, and I've asked Amee to work things out."

Victor yelled from inside the house, and Jessica left them to investigate. Once alone, Grayson reached into his back pocket, pulled out an envelope, and tossed it to Reggie. He caught it with ease.

"I brought you one thousand, four hundred dollars and a quarter—keep the change. It's the money you gave—or loaned—Amee. She owes you nothing now."

The expression that flashed across Reggie's face was disconcerting. Why was he mad that Grayson was settling her debt? In a blink, his brother displayed a smile. "Is Amethyst considering going back to you?"

"I hope so. We're both saved now. We have repented, and God washed our sins away." A blurry, dark image slowly distorted Reggie's face. It was ugly, not human, but a demon.

You'll never get her back. The voice coming out of Reggie's mouth was eerie. It wasn't human.

Grayson feared the worst. Did they have an affair, as Jessica suspected?

I will possess her soul. The voice sounded scratchy.

No! When Grayson demanded, *Who are you?* Heavenly tongues filled his mouth.

Destroyer.

Then, Grayson saw the landscape change from the colorful, meticulous patio and backyard to an open field in gray. Lifeless bodies were littered around him, including women, children, and even animals, thrown around the ground like garbage. Blood covered them. He was no longer in this world. This had to be the spiritual realm.

Suddenly, a forceful wind circled his waist and pushed him back for safety. An angel matched Destroyer's height, which had swelled to ten feet, taller than Reggie's six-four height.

The angel had its massive sword drawn. Scriptures were engraved on it. Grayson began to pray for the Lord to remove whatever strongholds Reggie had allowed in his life.

The atmosphere shifted, and Reggie—the old Reggie—stood before him as if there had been no skirmish between them.

Grayson knew what had just happened. Was Reggie clueless when he said, "Thanks for stopping by. I'll walk you to the door."

Were Jessica and the children privy to what had just happened? Grayson couldn't tell from their expressions as he hugged his niece and nephew, then Jessica goodbye.

When the front door closed behind Grayson, he sensed the battle was beginning. More was at stake than just his and Amethyst's physical lives but their eternity too.

Chapter Twenty-eight

*Praying always with all prayer and supplication in
the Spirit, and watching thereunto with all perseverance
and supplication for all saints.*
—Ephesians 6:18

Monday morning, Porsha sat at her desk, already bored with the tasks on her calendar for the week. This was when she missed traveling from client to client performing audits. Despite the move, she was glad to be closer to family and to spoil her niece.

Her supervisor's voice interrupted her musings.

"Porsha, I want you to meet the newest member to join our team," Doug said as she turned around and smiled at a pretty Black woman who seemed to be the same age as her. The woman's smile was her best feature. Joyce was petite and wore her neat braids in an eye-catching updo.

"This is Joyce Clark. She'll be working in IT."

Porsha stared. Was God assigning her to another candidate on His list? "Hi. Welcome to StartUP."

"Thanks," Joyce tilted her head. "You look so familiar."

"Really?" That could be an open door for Porsha.

Doug guided Joyce to the next office for introductions.

Porsha was so excited that she could barely see the numbers on her spreadsheet for the rest of the morning. She silently praised God before she texted Mother Kincaid.

**I got another one! Joi Clark is a new hire in my building.
:)**

Mother Kincaid responded moments later. **Your witnessing will earn you great rewards in heaven. God bless you, Sister Porsha.**

Porsha had to admit that working for the Lord had a true purpose in a person's life and death.

At 12:30, Porsha shut down her computer for lunch, grabbed her purse, and headed to the company's bougie cafe instead of going outside in the Cortex. With fewer than seventy employees, salaries weren't the only thing the company splurged on. The décor and perks are what enticed Porsha to accept the job.

Joyce happened to enter the café about ten minutes later, and Porsha waved her over to the window wall overlooking the courtyard.

Okay," she mouthed, placing an order at the lunch counter, waiting for it, and then joined Porsha. Once she was comfortable and Joyce said grace over her hamburger and seasoned crinkled fries, Porsha asked, "So, how was your morning?"

"Boring as most first days are. I can't wait. I'm excited to jump in."

"I get it. I've been here for almost a month. I was a traveling auditor for years and loved it. I took the position here to be close to family." Porsha crunched on her salad, waiting to start her interruption.

Joyce took a bite. "This is good." She swallowed and squinted. "I know you from somewhere, or maybe you have a twin."

"I have a sister, Tally."

"No, I would have remembered that name." She leaned closer as if she was about to divulge a secret." Okay, let's start with what St. Louisans are known for when meeting someone."

"Where did you go to high school?" they said at the same time and laughed.

It was a trivia question between locales but held discriminatory information. A person would be profiled with assumptions if they attended an affluent private, predominantly white suburban high school or a historically black urban school in a depressed neighborhood. It was a judgment call on a person's character and qualifications.

They both had resided in St. Louis County and attended public schools.

The questions were back and forth until the woman frowned. "It doesn't appear that we could have crossed paths anywhere."

Suddenly, Porsha noticed the ring on Joyce's finger.

"Is Clark your married name?"

"Yep."

Porsha gnawed on her lips. Maybe it was similar to Amethyst using Johnson when she was legally a Tate. "Do people call you Joi?"

"Nope. I've always been Joyce since the day I was born. My mother didn't believe in nicknames or nontraditional spellings, so mine is J-O-Y-C-E."

Bummer. Porsha didn't have the right Joi. "We covered everything, but we didn't discuss church."

"I'm a member at Mt. Bethel—whenever I go." The confident woman avoided eye contact.

"Nope, never been there. Currently, I'm a member of Christ For All Church."

"I've seen that building. I'll admit I don't feel connected to God at Mt. Bethel. Odd, huh?"

Porsha didn't want to come across as judgmental about Mt. Bethel, but she had to be truthful. "A person should always feel God's presence whenever they walk through the church doors."

Joyce switched subjects as they finished their lunch, and when Porsha returned to her office, she texted Mother Kincaid. **False alarm. Wrong Joi Clark, but I did invite Joyce to our church anyway.**

Saints are to witness to all men and exclude no one, Sister Porsha. God will bless you. Mother Kincaid's text lifted her spirit.

Porsha learned a valuable lesson: The world was filled with many Joi, Joy, and Joyce Clarks.

The two became lunch buddies for the rest of the week, and Porsha liked her. The downside lately was Porsha's new friends were married. Where were the single ladies?

On Friday, while the coworkers enjoyed lunch in the courtyard, Joyce laughed hysterically at Porsha. "Girl, I haven't seen you eat with this much gusto all week."

Porsha blushed with embarrassment, then laughed. "Sorry. I'm trying to make every sandwich crumb count."

Folding her arms, Joyce stifled a chuckle. "Why? Do you need money for groceries?"

"Save your money, girl. Tonight is my church's prayer and shut-in service. After we eat lunch, we skip dinner to start fasting in preparation for spiritual dominance during prayer."

"What and what?" Joyce frowned.

"Remember you said you didn't feel God's presence at your church?" She nodded, and Porsha said, "You definitely would feel the Lord's presence during the prayer shut-in service."

"Is it mandatory for members?" The frown hadn't vanished from Joyce's forehead.

"Oh no. Our pastor calls for the saints who can come to church for overnight prayer. Some miss because they may have to work early the next day, have babies at home, or have other reasons. After midnight, you are committed to praying until seven the next morning because the doors are locked for our safety. When I traveled a lot, I would attend when I was home. The signs are everywhere that we are nearing the End Times, and God doesn't want any soul to burn in hell."

"That's deep." Joyce nodded. "I wasn't expecting anything close to that explanation. So you believe there is a hell, even though I believe we're living in it already?"

"Don't be deceived, Joyce. Our body belongs to the dust in the ground, but our soul belongs to God. The wicked will perish in hell and burn forever in torment while those who live holy will see God."

Joyce was quiet, then exhaled. "But I never turn down prayer. If you can, include me and my husband and my sister, too, in your prayers."

Porsha didn't mean to have a deep heaven-and-hell conversation with Joyce because most people didn't want to talk about death, but it was a reality. She was a witness to that with her brother-in-law. Randall Addams was as dead as Lazarus, but God raised him up.

Amethyst didn't know what to expect when she walked into Christ For All Church at nine p.m. for the shut-in prayer service. She was excited about the liberty to pray without disturbing her mother, but she worried whether she couldn't pray until seven a.m.

Dressed for comfort, she left the apartment under her mother's scrutiny. "Get a good night's sleep." Amethyst kissed her cheek and left.

Mother Kincaid smiled and greeted her in the church foyer, hugging two decorative blue pillows. If she dressed for comfort, the older woman was fashionable in her long denim dress. She handed one to Amethyst. "It's for your knees. If you need another one, there is a pile of them at the altar."

Although Amethyst's knees weren't old, she accepted it.

"Are you ready?"

"Excited. I can't wait." She danced in place. "No restrictions."

As she was about to follow Mother Kincaid, she saw Grayson walking in with Randall and Mitchell from the corner of her eye. While Amethyst had become friends with Porsha, the two new dads had befriended Grayson. Did they know Grayson had almost become a father?

She dismissed the memory, entering the sanctuary where many were spread out. Amethyst picked a secluded spot near a corner.

Randall, Grayson, and Mitchell must have tracked her because all three headed her way.

"It's good to see you again, Amethyst. Tonight will change your prayer life for the better." Randall grinned.

His brother-in-law agreed. "We're only staying until midnight—before the doors are locked and you are shut in," Mitchell said.

"We've got to get some prayer in," Randall added, then the two walked away, leaving her alone with Grayson.

"I'm staying all night," he said.

"Me too, since that's when I wake up Mama praying."

She and Grayson seemed to be growing in their faith. He didn't hide his feelings for her, but what kept her from moving forward emotionally?

"Did you drive Miss Annabelle's car? I could have picked you up if you had told me."

"Thanks, but I got an extension to finish the work week," Amethyst said as the pastor led a congregational song, "Jesus Is On the Main Line," to signal the start of prayer. Afterward, he asked everyone to turn off their phones and resist the temptation to watch the wall clock over the main door to the sanctuary.

She got into position on her side of the pew, then a couple entered her row but stayed at the other end. Couples.

Families that pray together grow stronger in me, God whispered.

You promised me babies, Lord, Amethyst thought as Pastor Rodney instructed the congregation.

"Saints, we have a lot to pray for. We praise God for the souls that have been redeemed, but remember there are others on the list."

Amethyst waved her hand in the air and grinned. "I was on the list, and God saved me."

The saints applauded.

"Yes, Sister Amethyst, Brother Grayson, Brother Hudson, Sister Sophia…" He finished the list. "Now, remember, we want to thank God before petitioning Him. This service is praying to set the captives free from sin. If you can't stay all night, you have until midnight before the doors are locked. With that said, let's begin."

Amethyst positioned her pillow and knelt on the floor. Bowing her head, she closed her eyes and felt God's presence as she prayed. His army fought back animal-looking figures. Angels quoted the Word, and it caused the enemy to retreat, but with a lot of resistance. The angels held up shields that seemed to absorb fireballs from the beasts.

"Jesus, save us. Fight our battles…" She prayed until she was exhausted. A roar of praise filled the sanctuary as heavenly tongues exploded around her. Amethyst heard cheers, moans, groans, cries, and more, but she knew she was in a safe place.

When Amethyst dozed, she felt like angels were lifting her up. She opened her eyes and saw nothing, but she was recharged to continue praying.

Amethyst didn't know the time, but she could see splinters of light through the hall's stained glass windows.

She made one last effort in prayer, petitioning God for her mother and those at her new job. She felt hands on both shoulders, which seemed to give her strength. The angels must have returned, so she kept praying as she sobbed, the tears flowing as she surrendered more and more to His will.

"Saints, we have petitioned God. Let's praise Him for answered prayers," Pastor Rodney said.

When Amethyst opened her eyes, she was surprised to see Grayson on one side of her and Mother Kincaid on the other. They removed their hands from her shoulders.

Grayson helped her and then Mother Kincaid to stand.

"You're going to be alright, Sister Amethyst. The Lord isn't sending you to the battlefield alone. Through your heavenly tongues, I heard the Lord say from Psalm ninety-one and seven: *'A thousand shall fall at thy side, and ten thousand at thy right hand, but it shall not come nigh thee.'* He's calling you to intercede for others' souls."

"And I'm here to fight with you," Grayson said with dark circles under his eyes. He wasn't a night hawk. Yet, he had survived the overnight prayer.

Amethyst admired him. She had no idea what they were referring to, but she thanked them.

Instead of returning to his seat like Mother Kincaid had done, Grayson hesitated. "Is it okay if I sit here next to you?"

She nodded. "Yes."

Pastor Rodney asked everyone to stand. "Saints, be careful going home and then get some rest. The devil is mad, but stay alert; God is with us. Now, may the words of our mouths and the meditation of our hearts be acceptable to You, O Lord, our Redeemer, in Jesus' name. Amen. See you back on Sunday."

"Amen," the congregation said as many yawned and stretched.

"Do you mind if I trail you back to your mom's place to make sure you get there safe?" He looked so hopeful.

Besides their apologies, what else was there between them? No love or babies. But there was a spark of attraction when Grayson reached for her hand to lead her out of the pew. Amethyst couldn't believe she blushed.

❦

Grayson had prayed for many things during the shut-in, especially for Amethyst, as God had said on the list. He hadn't expected the intensity of the prayer service, but he was thankful for the experience.

He escorted Amethyst to the rental car and waited as she strapped in and started the engine, then he jogged to his car.

When he'd arrived at church, Grayson had shared with Randall and his brother-in-law, Mitchell, the unbelievable and scary demonic spirit he'd encountered at his brother's house. Grayson was concerned about the devil's goal of destroying Amethyst's soul.

"We're praying for Sister Amethyst. Trust that God has dispatched angels to be her bodyguards. We won't stop praying as she grows stronger in the Lord," Randall had said.

"No weapon formed against us will prosper," Mitchell added. "Memorize Isaiah fifty-four verse seventeen."

"I will," Grayson said. He yawned. How did people stay up all night? he wondered.

Grayson called Amethyst through his Bluetooth. "I'm going to make a quick stop at the store near the apartment, so I'll be five minutes behind you."

"Okay, but you know I'm a big girl and know my way home." She chuckled.

"But you're *my* girl." They ended the call, and minutes later, he detoured for one thing. Grayson parked, perused the store's floral section, and purchased a red rose.

When Amethyst opened the door, Grayson noticed she had changed in record time from her wrinkled clothes to a simple dress. She saw the rose, and her face glowed. "Thank you." She sniffed. "I can't remember the last time I got one."

Whatever expression crossed Grayson's face caused Amethyst to apologize quickly. "I didn't mean that to start an argument."

"No offense taken," he said as Miss Annabelle approached the door, and Grayson spoke to her mother.

"Good morning. I hope staying at church all night helped you and your wife figure out your lives." She *hmmph*ed and walked away.

It didn't go unnoticed that was the first time she'd referred to Amethyst as his wife instead of ex-wife—whether it was intentional or a slip of the tongue—and Amethyst didn't fuss about it. Grayson was glad.

"Before we return the car, do you want to eat first?"

She sniffed the rose again. "I'd rather turn in the car."

The impromptu romantic gesture had been a big hit. Grayson thanked God for dropping the thought in his mind at the last minute. "Okay. I'll trail you."

Amethyst's phone alerted her of a text. She read it, frowned without responding, and slipped it into her purse.

"Is everything okay?"

"Yeah. Reggie wants to make sure I don't need a ride after I drop off my car."

Hold your temper. This is bigger than sibling rivalry, God whispered.

"Oh?" They continued the walk to her car. He tried to sound casual. "I didn't know he was keeping track of the rental car. Also, I took care of the debt."

"Thank you. Reggie couldn't believe you would do that for me. He's been making sure I was taken care of. I spoke to him the other evening and told him you and I were talking."

His heart swelled that she acknowledged his efforts, but he needed to warn her subtly about Reggie. "Stop playing with the devil," Grayson said, jokingly but meant it.

She tilted her head and studied him as he opened her door. "Funny to hear you say that because I've always been at ease around him, but lately, I feel uncomfortable. It's odd."

"It's not." Grayson tucked one strand that had escaped from her braid. We both have the Holy Ghost, and He gives us discernment about people and situations. We have to pray for him."

"You're right." She nodded and slid behind the wheel.

Grayson took off and trailed her to the car rental place.

Satan wants her dead, but she belongs to Me to do My will, God whispered.

What mission did God have for her? The devil seemed to have a target on her back. Grayson wasn't a night owl like Amethyst, but he planned to stay close.

Once she turned in the car, Amethyst walked outside with her purse, sniffing the rose with a smile. The wind teased her hair and the hem of her short dress, and his mind captured the photo for safekeeping.

Grayson opened the passenger door, walked around, and slid back under the wheel. Spending the day with Amethyst gave him contentment. "Ready?" She nodded. "What do you have a taste for?"

She scrunched her nose. "Guess?" She grinned.

"Waffles?" He chuckled. "And chicken."

"Yep."

He drove away, enjoying the floral scent that mingled with her perfume. They arrived at Bagels & Breakfast. When he and Amethyst were happy and on good terms, this was their hangout on most Saturday mornings.

As they walked in, Grayson kept his hand on her back as the host led them to the table and handed them menus.

"I already know what I want. Waffles and crispy fried chicken wings. To drink, I want a cup of half coffee and hot chocolate," Amethyst said and handed the menu back.

"I'll have the same." He grinned at Amethyst and wiggled his brows, a flirt that often made her blush. She did.

When was the last time he had that effect on her? *Thank You, Jesus, for softening her heart.*

"What?" She blinked.

"I've missed you, and I'm happy to have this time with you, Amee."

She shook her head. "You said you were going to fight the divorce. No need. I see the effort you're putting in. You must really love me."

"I do," he said softly, staring into her hazel eyes.

"Well, I've decided to withdraw my petition before a new judge signs off. I want to be Amethyst Tate."

"Yes!" Grayson shouted, then composed himself after the outburst and pumped his fist.

Amethyst shrugged. "I'm going to be honest. I'm not sure how to pick up the pieces. We have a lot of them, and I've spent the time apart building a wall around my heart, never to be hurt again."

Grayson reached across the table and took her hands. "Amee, I suppressed those feelings for you when you walked out the door, but seeing those couples at Christ For All Church makes me want to be one of them with you."

She was quiet as emotions played on her face. "What if…what if we can't make it and end up hurting each other and ourselves more?"

He smiled. "I don't want to look back but press toward a future. We didn't have the tools to build a solid house…" He paused and swallowed. "We do now, so…will you be my girlfriend as of today?"

"You haven't had a girlfriend since we split?"

Grayson squirmed and looked away, then exhaled. "This is going to be embarrassing, but almost."

Tilting her head, Amethyst studied him with a blank expression.

"Ah, I didn't know we were still married when I approached this woman. I also didn't know we would go to the same church."

The waitress reappeared, buying Grayson time to craft his confession. They thanked her, then Grayson squeezed Amethyst's hands and bowed his head. "Lord, I thank You for this moment, this woman, and our salvation. Sanctify our food."

"And bless the hands that prepared it," Amethyst added, and they both said, "In Jesus' name. Amen."

Grayson had to finish his confession. "I was interested in Sister Porsha Gilbert, but the Lord intervened, and I'm thankful."

He patted his chest. "I don't want that to affect your friendship with her."

Amethyst grinned. That's when Grayson saw it in her eyes—she still loved him. "Porsha told me. Yes, you can take me off the market as of today as your girlfriend." She batted her long lashes.

"*Whew*. Woman, you're a tease. Thank you for a second chance." It was the best breakfast ever. He took her hand and led her back to the car once he paid their tab. "After we get some rest, maybe we can spend the day together and do whatever you want."

"I want to move my things back to the house." Her voice was shaky. The expression on her beautiful, tired face asked for permission.

Grayson's heart stumbled as he leaned forward, wanting to seal her declaration with a kiss.

"That doesn't mean I'm ready to share a bed. You just asked me to be your girlfriend, and I don't think we should sleep together on the first date."

Grayson backed up and laughed, releasing all the emotions that had clogged the arteries to his heart. He kissed her head. "You can sleep in any room you want, and I think we need to get some counseling."

Back at her mother's apartment, Amethyst informed her mother as they were about to pack up her things.

"Now I can get some sleep, and make sure you take that gun with you."

"Gun? What? Why?" Oh, yeah, he was taking that away from her.

Amethyst looked nonchalant. "Reggie gave it to me for protection."

Humph. Grayson grunted. "From now on, the Lord and I are your protection." Their first stop would be to the pawn shop to sell the weapon. No way was he giving Reggie back that gun.

Chapter Twenty-nine

But sanctify the Lord God in your hearts: and
be ready always to give an answer to every man that asks
you a reason for the hope that is in you with meekness
and fear. —1 Peter 3:15

Porsha was never the first to leave church after a shut-in service. She stayed behind to collect floor pillows and tidy the ladies' restroom. When she stepped outside, Porsha yawned and slipped on her sunglasses.

"It's going to be another hot, humid July day." Porsha walked to her car and drove off. While waiting for a streetlight to change, she noted The Brew Shoppe at the corner and surprisingly craved a hot brew to help her sleep. She detoured as her mouth watered for white chocolate cocoa with whipped cream.

A crowded lobby meant it wouldn't be an in-and-out stop. Porsha prided herself on looking her best whenever she left the house, but a wrinkled yellow T-shirt and long denim flare skirt with sunglasses to hide her tired eyes was how she would greet the clerk. To her delight, the staff was fast and efficient. Porsha didn't have to wait as long as she had thought.

"Your name?" the teenager asked, taking her order, poised to scribble on the cup.

"Gilbert," Porsha said, stepping aside, then found a chair out of sight in a corner and began to scan social media on her phone.

Talk to him, God whispered.

Who? On alert, Porsha jerked her head up. The door opened, and a tall man walked inside. Judging from his neon orange vest, he was a construction worker. He removed his sunglasses, looked around, and briefly made eye contact with Porsha.

Wow. Handsome was too simplistic to describe him. His black hair was cut into a fade, and his mustache was trimmed. From a distance, she guessed he was inches over six feet tall. Porsha greeted him with a smile but couldn't look away.

Could he be Wyatt Sheppard from the salvation list? If so, Porsha prayed for a conversation starter. She stood and walked back to the counter to wait for her drink, overhearing him order the same as hers but iced.

As she debated what she could say that wouldn't come across as flirting, the barista called, "Gilbert," and placed her covered cup on the ledge.

Another barista called, "Clark." The man reached for the cup.

Clark. So he wasn't Wyatt. "Excuse me, do you have a sister named Joi, spelled J-o-i?'

He frowned. "How do you know that?" his deep voice was guarded.

Porsha removed her sunglasses. She didn't care how tired she looked.

She reached for her cocoa as the man waited for her answer. "It would be easy to say a lucky guess, but it was God."

He relaxed and seemed curious. "Really? Do you have a few minutes to talk?"

Now, Porsha was caught off guard. She wasn't expecting an easy opening as she stifled a yawn. "A few minutes. I've been in prayer all night, and sleep is calling me. Can we exchange numbers?"

Talk to him! God thundered.

"You know what, sure." Porsha turned around and led him to the table she had vacated.

Once they were seated, she introduced herself. "My name is Porsha—"

"Gilbert, I got that," he said. "I'm Kwame Clark, and Joi is my sister. She's in jail."

"Jail," she repeated, trying to keep her voice low.

"I've been praying for her too."

A praying man. She loved it, and he wasn't wearing a ring. But this wasn't a romantic meetup. It was God's spiritual setup to do His bidding.

"I'm sorry to hear that. God heard your request before you asked. His will for Joi is to save her soul. My entire congregation has been praying for her, especially last night. We had a shut-in service from nine last night to seven this morning."

Bowing his head, he gripped his cup with both hands. Relief relaxed his broad shoulders. "Thank You, Jesus," he mumbled. When he glanced up, his eyes were watery.

"Joi is my younger sister. She struggles with drug addiction. She'll get clean in a program, then something sets her off, and she'll start using again. My parents and I have been praying that God intervene because nothing is helping her." He squinted, and Porsha hoped she didn't have sleep in her eyes or worse. "How does your church know about my sister?"

"Our church believes in adding fasting to our prayers, and God speaks." Porsha pulled out her phone and showed him the text from Mother Kincaid. "Recognize a name on this list that came from God to a church mother who is an intercessor?"

A tear fell from this intimidating man with his muscular build and shamelessly commanding looks. Kwame had a tender spot for his sister.

Without thinking, Porsha patted his hand. Realizing her mistake, she quickly withdrew. She had no liberties with this man, not knowing his marital status—he could be another Grayson Tate despite no sign of a ring. She wasn't going to make that mistake again. "Sorry."

"It's alright. My mother has soft hands, and your touch is comforting." Kwame smiled.

"I didn't want to send the wrong message." Porsha turned away to hide her embarrassment, then covered another yawn. "God wants to save your sister to do His work."

"Well, she's in jail right now."

"Christ For All Church has a prison ministry. Minister Jude Morgan is one of our intercessors who God has empowered to cause demons to tremble while in prayer and rescue God's people."

He exhaled. "Thank you for praying. You look tired—that's not an insult. I'll let you get home."

Porsha nodded. "It's okay. I am, and I know I look bad, and you stated the obvious." They stood. Her drink had cooled, and his was melting.

He nodded. "Can we still exchange numbers?" His eyes sparkled.

"Of course, and I'll pass it on to Minister Morgan to reach out to you."

"It's okay for you to call me too." He flashed a slow grin, then walked out, leaving Porsha suddenly fully awake.

Tuesday morning, Joyce was waiting near Porsha's office with expectancy on her face. "Morning. Missed you yesterday."

"I took off for a doctor's appointment. So, how did your shut-in go? I've been wondering about that all weekend." Her eyes were wide with curiosity as Porsha unlocked her office door in the finance department.

"It was powerful." Porsha rested her purse on the desk and flopped in her chair, facing Joyce. "Souls were delivered. Through heavenly tongues, God told me to command the scales to fall from backsliders' eyes, and I did."

Porsha couldn't believe how empowered she felt, knowing God was fighting her battles.

"Wow." Joyce grabbed a nearby chair from Porsha's colleague's desk and scooted in front of her like an eager student. "Did you pray for me, my sister, and my husband?"

"Yep." Porsha nodded. "Our church takes prayer requests seriously. I prayed you would have a stronger salvation walk with the Lord."

"Thank you." Joyce looked over her shoulder toward the hall and lowered her voice. "Do you think I can go to the next shut-in with you, or is it just for your church members?"

Porsha blinked. "You can." The surprises since the shut-in were catching her off guard. "It's ten hours before God's presence."

"Alright. When's the next one?"

"It could be a month or a couple of months. It all depends on what our pastor feels the Lord is directing him to do."

"That long, huh?" She twisted her lips in disappointment.

Leaning closer, Porsha said, "Joyce, if you have a prayer request, you can go to God anytime with it, and I'll be your prayer partner."

"Really?" Her coworker and new friend looked relieved. "Thank you because I don't think God hears my prayers." Joyce shrugged. "Maybe it's because I don't know how to pray."

Porsha explained God's formula. "Jesus told His disciples in the books of Matthew and Luke to first acknowledge that God is in heaven and to praise His name. We are to pray His will on this wicked earth as it is in His heaven."

Joyce's serious expression hinted she was taking mental notes as Porsha continued.

"We must believe God will provide our food, clothing, and shelter. The big one is asking God to help us forgive whoever wronged us so that when we need forgiveness, the Lord will grant it. An unforgiving heart will hinder our prayer life. Then we need God's help to deliver us from yielding to the devil's temptation to sin."

"*Hmmm*. I never looked at it like that, but I want to go with you next time you have a shut-in."

"Girl, you are welcome to attend Christ For All Church any time."

"Okay." She stood and rolled the chair back to the desk. "See you at lunch. Maybe we can practice praying in the courtyard."

Her coworker was serious, and Porsha couldn't ignore her spiritual hunger for God. "I gotcha." Moments later, Minister Morgan texted her.

I made contact with Kwame Clark. The ministry team is on it!

Amen! Porsha texted back and pumped her fist in the air.

What wasn't there to like about being Christ's disciple when missions were accomplished?

Chapter Thirty

You will keep him in perfect peace,
whose mind is stayed on thee because
he trusts in You. —Isaiah 26:3

The following Friday, Amethyst planned to schedule inspections at three plant locations next week. When she stood and turned around, her coworker, Brody Nelson, was there. She patted her chest. "You startled me."

He was Reggie's contact for helping Amethyst get this position at the aerospace company. If she had any issues, Reggie said to go to Brody. So far, so good. Amethyst loved her job, the people, and the salary. It was a bonus to have a minister nearby as her go-to for prayer.

"Oh, sorry. I'm checking up on you—for Reggie. He's been trying to reach you," he said accusingly.

"I know. I haven't had a chance to call him back, but I will." She smiled and stepped around him, but he blocked her path.

Her Holy Spirit sent out warning signals. What did this man want?

"I've been watching you from afar for the past few weeks." He folded his arms behind his back as if he was hiding something or had a gift for her. Suddenly, a dark spirit flashed on his face. She blinked to see if it was real. It was quick, but she saw it—the thing resembled the haunting figures she'd wrestled with in her sleep.

Had they followed her to work?

"Wait." He showed his hands. Nothing was in them. "You seem happy and content. I heard you're doing a good job and recovered from that bad accident."

Yet, you haven't come to check on me like others have. Hmmm. Amethyst kept that thought to herself. "Yes, it was fatal for the other driver, but my life was spared. The joy of the Lord is my strength." Amethyst beamed. "I have no complaints. If you want to tell Reggie something, tell him everything is alright in my world. Everything." She gave him a pointed look.

"Okay, well, good." Brody bobbed his head as if he was thinking of something else. "Because of your divorce, he was concerned about you."

Indignant, Amethyst fumed. How dare Reggie put her business out there like that? Amethyst used a slight force to get away from Brody. "I'm not divorced, and I'm not getting one," she tossed over her shoulder.

Amethyst had been replaying Grayson's heartfelt apology. His words, as well as his gentleness and kindness, helped her overcome the imaginary barrier that kept her from him.

During her break, she stopped by Jude's office and told him what she'd noticed around Brody. She shivered, remembering the ugliness.

"Yeah, he definitely has a spirit on him."

He can't touch you because you are under My protection, God whispered.

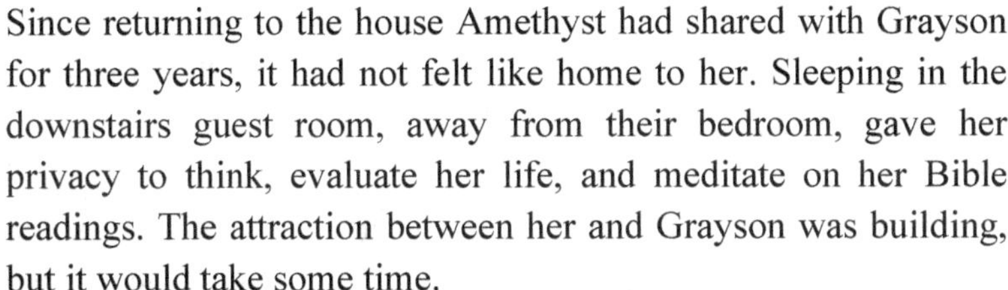

Since returning to the house Amethyst had shared with Grayson for three years, it had not felt like home to her. Sleeping in the downstairs guest room, away from their bedroom, gave her privacy to think, evaluate her life, and meditate on her Bible readings. The attraction between her and Grayson was building, but it would take some time.

Her phone buzzed, alerting her of a text from Reggie.

Hey. I feel neglected. Want to grab a bite and catch up?

She needed to give her brother-in-law an update on her new living arrangements.

After she'd separated from Grayson, Amethyst and Reggie had grown closer. Now, her spirit flashed, *BEWARE* at the mention or thoughts of him. She prayed silently, then paused to listen to the Lord before responding.

Hey, brother-in-law. I'm exhausted. Grayson helped me move back home, so I'm resting. Grayson told me he paid you back the money I borrowed. Thank you for loaning it to me. Grayson and I will work out our differences.

What? After all he did to you???? Reggie's attitude screamed through the text.

Grayson's crime was he ignored me. He didn't cheat *or assault me.* Amethyst surprised herself that she was ready to defend Grayson.

Reggie continued his tirade. **I was the one who stood by you.**

And I thank you. Grayson and I can get together with you, Jessica, and the children.

Silence. Amethyst shrugged and stood to finish hanging clothes in the closet. After two weeks, she was slowly unpacking more of her things.

Fight, Amethyst. Fight, God whispered.

Moments later, Reggie called. He released curses and profanities like a madman before she could say hello. His behavior caught her off guard.

"Reggie, what is wrong with you?" Jamming a fist on her hip, she lifted her voice. "Don't you ever call and disrespect me again. I pick God over Satan." She began to feel dizzy, so she ended the call as a piercing pain attacked her head. She hurried across the room for her purse as her heart raced and she panted for breath. During one church service, Mother Kincaid had given her a prayer cloth—a square patch that had been anointed and prayed over. She found it and placed it over her head. "Jesus, help me."

Her discomfort dissipated. Amethyst's irrational breathing calmed, and her heart regulated. For the first time, Amethyst saw that the divide between the two brothers was real and not imagined, as Reggie had brainwashed her to believe.

She didn't have time for Reggie or any distractions, spying the time. Tomorrow was church, and Amethyst wanted to look her best. She showered and performed her nightly regimen, including reading a few chapters to wind down, then she would have to pray to shake the fallout she'd just had with her trusted brother-in-law.

Amethyst thought she heard noises outside the bedroom door, as if a pet or animal were clawing to get inside. She ignored the noise and kept reading.

When she crawled into bed and closed her eyes, Amethyst smelled something. A subtle, sweet scent tickled her nose. It seemed familiar, but she couldn't remember when and from where. Images suddenly appeared and surrounded her in the room.

Reggie was there, but he had two faces. So was Brody from her job. There were other people from her past, and they all had two faces. Their eyes were red like balls of fire. The psychic she had visited a few times had a wand and commanded them to get her.

"No! Jesus, send help. Don't let them hurt me. The scent grew stronger and began to form a mist as if it were an air bomb. Amethyst began to choke for air, but she kept calling on Jesus. She tried to open her eyes. A burning sensation caused her to blink.

"Come to me," the voices chanted.

"Jesus!" Amethyst screamed at the top of her lungs. She might be outnumbered until the Lord sent help, but she would fight until the end with the Word of God.

Amethyst quoted a handful of Scriptures she had memorized, including 2 Corinthians 10:4—5: *"The weapons of our warfare are not carnal but mighty through God to the pulling down of strongholds. Casting down imaginations and every high thing that exalts itself against God's knowledge and bringing every thought into captivity to the obedience of Christ."*

"You have no authority, demons. In the name of Jesus, I banish you back to darkness."

She opened her eyes, and they didn't sting. Angels stood at attention with their swords drawn as Grayson burst into her bedroom.

Tears were streaming down Amethyst's cheeks. "Sorry to wake you. I've been in a battle against demons for souls. When this happens, I wake up Mama."

I can see that. Grayson now understood what Miss Annabelle meant about getting some sleep. "Are you okay?" He cupped her face and wiped the moisture from her cheeks with his thumbs.

Grayson had heard the ruckus and sat up in bed. Voices were coming from the guest bedroom. He grabbed his robe and headed downstairs to investigate. With each step, his spirit was on heightened alert. Grayson was still trying to process what had happened. "You were in a spiritual realm. I came to back you up. Two is better than one."

Search her things for symbols of darkness, God whispered.

Frowning, Grayson released her and walked into her closet. "Do you have any beads, tarot cards, zodiac symbols, or anything you brought that might be demonic?"

She shrugged. "I haven't unpacked everything. Plus, I stopped reading horoscopes a while back." While he opened her boxes, Amethyst searched the pockets of her handbags.

Grayson couldn't believe the stockpile of items connected to witchcraft and dark powers she had in her possession. "When did you get mixed up in this stuff?" He measured his words so as not to spark an argument.

"Checking horoscopes has been a part of my daily routine since I was a teenager. Mom named me after my February birthstone. You know that."

"Right." He nodded.

"After I left you." She bowed her head, but Grayson lifted her chin with his finger to look into her eyes.

"It's okay to talk about our past if it will strengthen our future. Tell me." Grayson squeezed her hands and sat on the end of the bed.

Amethyst exhaled and continued. "Well, I was searching for peace and trying to make sense of my life's purpose. I desperately needed someone to hear me, and I gave credence to the psychic and believed those trinkets were harmless." She pointed to the pouch of crystals. "Whenever I had a headache or pain, I'd grab a crystal and apply it to the area because I foolishly believed in its power to release or amplify positive energy."

Grayson had no idea the extent of her unhappiness and mental torment. He took his share of the blame for her suffering. "What's in that freezer-size plastic bag?"

"Those are miniature scented candles I purchased from a street vendor. He told me burning them at night would reduce my agitation. I never did." She paused. "At the time of our separation, I was moody. Nothing I tried gave me peace."

He gritted his teeth. "*Whew*. Babe, I'm so sorry I wasn't there for you."

Amethyst hugged him and snuggled closer. "But you're here now." They fell asleep in each other's arms.

Grayson woke first and gathered all the demonic items. He threw them in the trash outside.

Enjoying breakfast before church, they grinned at each other over sausage, eggs, and toast.

"About last night, what started the…" He didn't know what to call it. "I guess the spiritual battle?"

Amethyst sipped on her juice, then shrugged. "I'm not sure. One minute, I was on the phone with Reggie, and he sounded out of control, spewing curses at me. I ended the call, and the next thing I knew, I was attacked with this piercing headache."

Grayson listened without interrupting but silently fumed. When she finished, he measured his response. "Babe," he said, grinning at the endearment, which made her blush, "when I visited my brother to give him back the money…" Grayson paused and shook his head. "I can't even describe the darkness I saw that seemed to possess him, but that spirit through Reggie was coming for you."

She shivered. "That could explain why he wasn't the same sweet and kind Reggie. I guess a vicious beast-acting creature possessed him."

"I want us to stay away from him and pray for him and his family from afar," Grayson said, and she didn't protest, a change from the past where his comment regarding Reggie would have sparked an argument. He was glad. "Maybe when we get to church, we can ask Randall—"

"Or Minister Morgan," Amethyst said, "what we should do."

***

Mother Kincaid smiled when she saw Amethyst and Grayson walk into the sanctuary together, holding hands. She patted her chest in thanksgiving. Her job was done with those two.

There's more, God whispered.

After service, when she planned to greet the couple, Mother observed Minister Morgan speaking with them and then directing Grayson and Amethyst to her. That's when she saw an angel with wings spread as if shielding them while the Lord spoke.

She will lead the intercessors.

"Praise the Lord, Mother Kincaid," the pair greeted her in unison and smiled at each other.

Yes, their love was coming back. She hugged them, then listened as Amethyst replayed what had happened the night before.

Recalling God's words, she sat and invited them to join her. "Amethyst, God has called you to become an intercessor. Because He has delivered you from witchcraft and other demonic spirits, you can recognize them and now have the power to rebuke them in Jesus' name and deliver others."

Amethyst looked at her husband, and he squeezed her hand.

"God is going to strengthen you spiritually to fight, and you will never fight alone," Mother Kincaid said.

"I'll be with her." Grayson had a set determination.

"And that is well, but God is sending you an innumerable company of angels before you to be victorious. Whenever God shows you a face or a name, pray like they were your sister or brother. Welcome to the elite group of intercessors. Prayer is our war cry. I'll send you the conference call number. Be prepared to pray thirty minutes every morning at five-thirty. We will go into battle behind you and fight the same enemy."

"I'll be on the line," Amethyst said and stood.

"We'll be on the line." Grayson helped Mother Kincaid to her feet. She walked out of church rejoicing. God was assembling His team of fighters for the last days.

Chapter Thirty-one

But I would have you without carefulness.
He who is unmarried cares for the things that belong to
the Lord, how he may please the Lord: But he who is married
cares for the things that are of the world, how
he may please his wife. —1 Corinthians 7:32–33

Jude was exhausted. It was the end of August already. Where did the summer go? He wanted to spend more time with the children before school started. Jude juggled being "on-call" for the Lord and his role as a husband and father.

Sinclaire deserved to have the best of him as a husband, and Jude doted on her every day to remind her that he loved her. She sometimes rolled out of bed with him in the early morning when he prayed.

Now that Joi Clark had been located, he had to become more involved in the church's prison ministry. Counseling Joi's brother, Kwame, was easy. He didn't fight God on anything—the perfect candidate for salvation.

"We haven't been married long, and I already feel that I've been ignoring you as your husband," Jude told Sinclaire as they prepared for bed one night.

Wrapping her arms around his neck, she looked into his eyes. "Babe, God had you before me. I knew your commitments when I said yes. I love you, and I don't feel slighted. I've got to get in wherever I fit in, and I'll be blessed."

"You'll always fit." Jude choked on emotion as his heart swelled with love for his wife. "He that finds a wife finds the best thing." He kissed her passionately.

The next day was Jude's second trip with Kwame to jail to see Joi. This also was her second stint in jail because she hadn't completed the community service agreement extended to her. With each repeated offense, Joi was running out of options when it came to her drug recovery. Fines and community service hadn't been an effective "punishment" for her.

Despite the glass barrier between them, Jude could see how the devil used drugs to beat her up. She had aging skin, dark circles under her brown eyes, and hair that needed attention; even her frame was thin as if she was starving.

Yet, there was a hidden beauty that God would reveal once she surrendered to Him. She wouldn't need makeup. Joi could shine by being the person God created her to be.

"Joi, drugs are controlling you. Your brother tells me you've always been a go-getter. What's triggering you to give up on life?"

"I like the taste and the feel of not thinking, caring, or worrying whether someone loves me." Joi hugged herself.

Gritting his teeth, Kwame balled his fist. "Joi..." He sounded like he wanted to explode.

Jude squeezed his shoulder. "Hear her out."

Kwame relaxed, following Jude's suggestion. His voice cracked, "If you die, sis, I'll die too."

His statement seemed to jolt Joi's attention. "No. You can't die!" She became frazzled.

"Neither can you. I need you to fight like the tomboy within you. Will you try to get better? Fight the urge. Fight for your life."

Joi shook her head and fumbled with her fingers. "I don't know how to do that."

"Because the weapons of our warfare are of this world, if you surrender to God, Jesus will pull down the satanic drugs that have a stronghold on your spirit," Jude said. "The devil is controlling you like a puppeteer. That's the simple truth."

The horror on Joi's face meant Jude had hit home. "I'm demon possessed? Oh no. I don't want demons to possess me. I'm scared of spooky movies."

"Then let's see if we can get you to church so you'll be set free."

"Okay." Joi gnawed on her lips.

Jude prayed, repeating what God told him to say. Although Jude could feel a demonic presence surrounding Joi, an army of angels held them back. Yes, his job was done—for today—but her salvation journey was beginning.

As he and Kwame walked out, Kwame thanked him. "I felt something when you prayed. This time might be different for my sister."

"It will be. She's on God's list, and Jesus has a special assignment for her." The two shook hands and parted ways.

At home, Jude emptied his spirit of the day's burdens to relax and enjoy his family.

During dinner, Carlton blurted out, "Dad, you think Sophia can pray for Miss Joi when she comes to church? Maybe God will heal her of the bad stuff she's doing."

"Sure, son." Although Carlton had memorized the names on the list, Jude was careful not to go into details that would expose their privacy and shame the candidate for salvation. But as a child intercessor, Carlton understood more about life at eleven than Jude did as a teenager. He was very astute.

Jude chewed on his brisket and glanced at Sinclaire, who shrugged. "Son, I think that's a good idea. We have been working with the administrators so she can have a pass to come to church next Sunday."

"Yay!" Carlton whooped, and his siblings mimicked their brother.

Laughing, Jude rubbed his oldest son's head, thankful that God had protected him during a tragedy and gifted the child with a desire to pray.

"But we have to keep praying for Miss Joi and not wait for her or someone to come to church," Sinclaire said.

"Yes, ma'am." Carlton grinned.

Happy chatter filled the room around the dinner table as Jude thought about the addictive drugs that were controlling Joi's mind and ravaging her body. God had already timed out the second He would redeem her soul from that stronghold.

Jude admired Kwame's relationship with his younger sister. Although their resemblance was hidden at times, it peeked out at others, and their love was unmistakable.

Kwame called Jude later that evening and emotionally broke down. The anguish in his voice caused Jude to signal to Sinclaire that he had to take the call.

She smiled, blowing him a kiss.

Once Jude was in his home office, he gave Kwame his full attention.

"Thank you for today at the jail. I saw a glimmer of hope because of what you said to Joi. You have no idea how my family and I watched for signs of suicide because she didn't seem to fight to live, and her caseworker signed off on a day pass when she learned it was to attend church, so I'll pick her up in the morning. But if she tests positive for drugs when she returns, Joi will go before a judge for prosecution for drug possession and be sentenced. That's not going to happen on my watch."

"No, it won't. Praise God," Jude said. Each candidate brought a set of challenges to their deliverance. Kwame sounded hopeful, in contrast to the helplessness that filled his voice when they first talked.

"My family has prayed for intervention and asked for resources," Kwame had said.

Jude had told him. "Sometimes that works, but in other cases, God is the only answer for deliverance."

Kwame said he didn't think God heard them. "A few days later, Porsha caught my eye when I entered that coffee shop. She was breathtaking."

Coming from a prayer shut-in, Porsha may argue with that assumption. She and Sinclaire were polished when it came to their appearance. All-night prayer required comfort over beauty. *"Well, the Lord had her there for a reason."*

"I guess so," Kwame had said. *"Porsha said your church has been praying for Joi, and my life seemed to change at that moment. When I told my parents, they broke down and cried."*

"The other reason I called is…" Kwame interrupted Jude's musing. "I've tried to call Porsha a few times, but they go to voicemail, and my texts are unread."

After the confusion with Grayson, Porsha wasn't about to mix God's business with personal attraction and be caught in the devil's snare again. "She doesn't want to get in the way of what God is doing for the Clark family."

"I admire that about her, and I understand. I'm thankful my sister's recovery is a priority." He hesitated. "Can you confirm whether she is seeing anyone?"

"Bro, I'm a newlywed. My interest is solely in one woman, my wife. When you come to church, you can talk to her yourself."

"You're right. I guess I'll have something else to pray for." Kwame chuckled, and they ended the call.

Jude respected a man willing to pray for the woman he wanted. In his opinion, Kwame was a good candidate for his sister-in-Christ. But where was he on his salvation journey? Jude wondered, recalling Acts 19:2: *He said unto them, Have ye received the Holy Ghost since ye believed? And they said unto him, We have not so much as heard whether there be any Holy Ghost.* Tough situations required prayer, fasting, and spiritual warfare led by the Holy Ghost.

Jude knew people prayed in desperate situations but forgot their promises to the Lord once God delivered them. With Kwame and his family, Jude hoped they would continue to worship God after He saved Joi for His purposes.

And we know that all things work together for good to them that love God, to them who are the called according to His purpose.

Porsha reflected on Romans 8:28 as she dressed for church. Last night, Minister Morgan called and said Joi was approved for a one-day pass to attend church.

Porsha had shouted and praised God when she'd heard the news. She wished her friend and coworker Joyce Clark would come. Despite her curiosity about the prayer shut-in service, Joyce made no commitments to visit Christ For All Church soon but said, "But the idea isn't off the table."

An hour later, Porsha stepped into the church foyer and greeted members. Glancing over her shoulder, she almost stumbled. Kwame was also there. It made sense if the woman beside him was his sister, Joi, who had the same skin color and similar features. The man had been eye-catching in a T-shirt and jeans, but he turned heads in a suit and tie—a male specimen to be studied.

Perfection.

Wow.

She looked in the opposite direction to avoid staring and to recalibrate her breathing. Then Porsha chided herself. She should at least speak. She approached the group, talking with Sinclaire.

"It's good to see you again, Porsha." Kwame's voice was heavy, and his eyes smiled with his lips.

Not a shy person by nature, Porsha was tongue-tied. "Hi. Same here."

"This is my sister, Joi." Kwame's voice showed relief as he put his arm over her shoulders. "And my parents."

Porsha greeted them. Joi was quiet and observant. She barely acknowledged her with a nod. That didn't stop Porsha from hugging Joi as if welcoming her home from a long trip. "I've been praying for you—the entire congregation has. It's good to meet you."

"Thank you so much. I've felt strength I didn't know I possessed." She sniffed as Porsha released her. Life had worn Joi down. She looked like Kwame's older rather than younger sister. But God could restore whatever damage drugs had done to her body.

Kwame didn't say anything else as Porsha sensed him watching her, teasing her to sneak a peek at him.

Nope. Porsha stayed focused on God's agenda. The Clark siblings were at Christ For All Church for His purpose— redemption.

"I hear the praise team singing," Sinclaire said. "Let's go in. Jude told me to save seats so there is plenty of room for you, your sister, and your parents."

"Thank you." Kwame nodded and turned to Porsha. "Aren't you sitting with us?"

"I usually sit with my parents, brother-in-law, and sister to hold my niece." Why was she rambling? But Porsha recovered. "I know God will have a message for all of us today."

Once Kwame and Joi trailed Sinclaire into the sanctuary, Porsha exhaled and walked to a door on the other side where Amethyst and Grayson sat close together. She felt her mission was accomplished. Porsha greeted her family, knelt to pray, then sat beside her sister and reached for her beautiful niece.

"I am so praying for you to get a husband. Then you'll have a baby of your own." Tally giggled.

Randall leaned over his wife and whispered, "It's coming. I've been looking out for you."

Porsha playfully scrunched her nose at them, then admired the sleeping baby she cuddled in her arms. Rocking in her seat, Porsha worshipped along with the praise team. She hoped the Clark siblings were enjoying the service too.

When Pastor Rodney stood at the podium, he welcomed their guests, then led the congregation with an old hymn, "At the Cross." On the last note, he shouted, "Hallelujah. This is more than a song. We don't reflect on the cross enough. It was more than two thick pieces of wood put together to kill someone as capital punishment. When Jesus was nailed to the cross, He nailed my sins and yours with Him." He paused. "I wonder how many sins each of us had a piece. *Hmmm?*"

Pastor started a running list: "Unforgiveness, murder, lying, boasting, cheating, sexual immorality…" He opened his Bible and found more passages listing God's condemnation. "Any sin imaginable was hung on that cross with Him. My question is, why do you keep taking them down and wearing your sins over and over, which are meant to torment you? Why?"

The sanctuary was quiet. "God is ready to forgive you of your sins if you repent. His spiritual gift will strengthen your resistance against the temptations of alcohol, drugs, lust, or whatever is leading you down a dark path. Come get delivered today!"

A roar of praise erupted throughout the sanctuary. Some were on their feet.

"God is not a man that He should lie. He's coming back. As sure as this world is real, so is heaven and hell. To get into heaven, the road is narrow because it's not a path for everyone. All are welcome, but the temptation to detour is great. Won't you come today and start a new life with Christ?"

When Pastor Rodney extended the call for salvation, Porsha noted that Kwame turned to his sister. The two walked down the aisle to the altar.

Then something happened. Joi became violently sick and began to empty her stomach. The nurses rushed to assist as his mother raced to Joi at the same time. She didn't appear sick despite throwing up.

"I'm fine," Joi said more than once and began to repent. I want to get baptized. I want my sins gone from me forever.

So she was led to the dressing room to prep for the baptism as Kwame watched, then he and his mother returned to their seats and briefed his dad who looked concerned and eager for an update.

Whatever was going on with Joi, Porsha was confident that Jesus was about to fix it.

The pastor announced a dozen souls had repented and requested the baptism in Jesus' name. "Hallelujah! The promise of His Spirit is fulfilled with the initial evidence of speaking in a heavenly language. This gift is for you, your children, and all who are afar off, *even* as many as the Lord our God shall call," he said, quoting Acts 2:39. Then Kwame stood and walked back to the altar and requested the baptism too.

When Porsha saw Kwame's action, she whispered, "Thank You, Jesus." Soon, she enthusiastically witnessed each candidate's baptism. Usually, the women were baptized together, followed by the men. Sometimes, husbands and wives were baptized together in Jesus' name. Today, Joi stepped into the water from one end, and Kwame joined her from the other side.

Once in the pool, Joi nodded at her brother with determination. Crossing their arms over their chests, the siblings bowed their heads as Minister Morgan raised one hand, gripping the back of Kwame's white T-shirt. Another minister held the back of Joi's white gown.

"My dear brother and sister, Kwame and Joi Clark, it is a privilege and honor to baptize both of you in the name of our Lord and Savior Jesus Christ—the only name under heaven given to us to be saved—for the remission of your sins, and God promises you the gift of the Holy Ghost in the Book of Acts, chapter two. In Jesus' name. Amen."

They were submerged, then resurfaced. Joi jumped up, screaming thanks to God, while Kwame clapped and encouraged his sister to praise the Lord.

The scene was touching, and Porsha sniffed. She understood the bond between siblings because she and Talley were also close.

Waves of celebration and rejoicing raced across the sanctuary. Members rejoiced that another soul from God's list had been snatched from the devil's clutches and redeemed.

Soon, the offering was taken, and the service was dismissed. Porsha was not in a rush to leave without congratulating the new converts. Sinclaire and her family spoke to the Clarks.

It wasn't long before Mother Kincaid and Minister Morgan opened the side door, praising God and motioning them to the prayer chapel where church mothers encouraged the new saints to worship Jesus while they waited for God to fill them with His Holy Ghost.

Joi was on her knees as if she was going to vomit again, but this time, it was the Lord speaking to her through heavenly tongues.

Kwame was nearby, seemingly in his own world, praising God in a heavenly language with his hands lifted.

It was a beautiful sight to see someone surrender. Who would come next from God's list?

Chapter Thirty-two

*And we know that all things work together for good
to them that love God, to them who are the called
according to His purpose.* —Romans 8:28

On Labor Day weekend, Mother Kincaid stood proudly in the church's small garden courtyard, decorated for a special occasion. She was among many well-wishers who showed up to pray for Grayson and Amethyst's big day.

Pastor Rodney was satisfied with the couple's commitment to each other, prayed for them, and encouraged them to renew their vows sooner than later. Amethyst and Grayson agreed to attend monthly marriage counseling sessions until the pastor felt they were no longer needed.

Mother Kincaid was in awe of the gifts God had bestowed on each person on His salvation list. Amethyst was becoming fearless in her discernment of demons. Her spiritual gift would embolden the intercessors.

With little guidance, Hudson Lane had become the Lord's teenage prodigy and a powerful witness of Jesus' salvation. Although she didn't see him there today, Mother Kincaid knew he was about the Lord's business. When Hudson spoke, people were amazed at his knowledge of God.

Little Sophia was also a shining star in God's kingdom. When the Lord opened her mouth to talk about Jesus and their faith, God's healing usually followed once she laid hands on them. The healings came instantly or within days. By the time the summer camp had ended, she and Minister Morgan's daughter, Sissy, had become the best of friends.

When Sophia witnessed Joi getting sick the Sunday Kwame and his sister repented and were baptized, she wanted to pray for Joi, and she did. Her healing couldn't be seen, but Mother Kincaid was confident it was mental and spiritual.

Joi, who had been given another chance at probation, had spoken at a community forum and testified about her miraculous recovery at the altar, where the taste of the drugs in her system was expelled from her body, giving hope to many in the audience. Mother Kincaid and others from Christ For All Church had attended to support her. "Lord, thank You for entrusting me with that list." She was humbled.

A church member sang a rendition of "A Ribbon in the Sky." Kwame was nearby, and she watched his handsome face admire Porsha, who seemed to ignore him purposely. When Joi joined Porsha, Kwame followed. Mother Kincaid inched closer to them.

"Porsha, get to know me and allow me to get to know you." Kwame's whisper reached Mother Kincaid's ears.

Porsha didn't answer. The Lord had placed people on her path, and she had accepted her role as an intercessor. Mother Kincaid admired Porsha's maturity in the matter of the heart but silently prayed she wouldn't miss her blessing if Kwame were the one God sent. If the woman gave him the time of day, those two would make a cute couple. She chuckled.

Pastor Rodney began the ceremony. "Brother Grayson and Sister Amethyst, you stand before God and these witnesses today as proof that God still mends broken marriages."

"Amen," Amethyst and Grayson both said as they held hands. Curls replaced Amethyst's single braid; she wore a cream sleeveless after-five dress, and Grayson wore a cream-colored suit. They looked excited to be husband and wife again.

"Amethyst, do you take Grayson to be your lawfully wedded husband in sickness and in health…"

"I do."

Annabelle Johnson dabbed at her eyes. Amethyst hadn't been able to convince her mother to visit Christ For All Church, but the intercessors were already petitioning God on her behalf.

Pastor Rodney turned to the groom. "Grayson, do you promise to love Amethyst, cherish her until death, do you part?"

"Absolutely." He didn't break eye contact as the guests cheered.

"By the powers invested in me by the Almighty God and the State of Missouri, I renew your vows before God, and let no man, woman, or demon ever separate you again, in the name of Jesus Christ, our Lord. Amen."

Grayson gathered his wife in his arms, kissed her, and then the two hugged for the longest time.

Mother Kincaid nodded, knowing they would be alright because God had called Amethyst to be fearless in spiritual warfare, and her husband would fight beside her.

***

"That's beautiful." Joi sighed and hurried to congratulate the newlyweds again, leaving Porsha alone with her brother.

Kwame leaned over and whispered, "If I'm this passionate about my love for my sibling, can you imagine the love and commitment I can give my future wife?"

Porsha turned slowly and saw the sincerity in his eyes. "No, Kwame, I can't imagine the love and commitment you would give your wife. Have you ever had one?" Initially, she had suppressed her attraction, so opening up to him wasn't easy. Although he said no, Porsha excused herself and walked away on shaky legs to congratulate Grayson and Amethyst. They would be in good hands if they fellowshipped with other married couples who would act as godly role models. Porsha knew that couples in the church provided a support system to encourage husbands and wives to love each other and resist temptation on all fronts.

She had avoided him for weeks after his sexy statement at the renewal ceremony. She refused to take the bait. It was hard for Porsha to avoid Kwame at church when she'd hit it off with Joi.

One morning, she arrived at Tally and Randall's house for babysitting duty so Randall could treat his wife to a day of pampering.

While Porsha sat in the baby's room, cooing to Valeria, Randall walked in and lovingly took his daughter out of Porsha's arm and cuddled her.

"Now, remember, be a good little girl for Auntie, and Mommy and Daddy will bring you back a toy."

Porsha snickered. "Ah, bro, she's too small for a toy."

Randall handed the baby back and sat on the window seat while waiting for Tally to finish dressing. "So what's the deal with Brother Kwame Clark?"

"What do you mean?" She avoided his eyes as she smiled at the baby.

"He likes you. I see him watching you, even when the other sisters are trying to talk to him.

Lowering her head, Porsha blushed but didn't answer.

"Do you like him?" Randall cut to the chase.

"I guess I could." Porsha shrugged.

"You could, huh?" He laughed. "Then I'm going to feel him out. If he passes my inspection, I'll give him my okay to proceed." Randall liked playing the older brother role.

"Sounds like a plan. But he better bring his A-game because I'm not settling."

"That's my little sister." Randall grinned, then suddenly became distracted. He whistled and stood when Tally entered the room. "Wow. My wife is gorgeous, sexy, and belongs to me."

Tally glowed and spun around, showcasing her figure after losing her baby weight.

Randall did a slow appraisal and then escorted Tally out of the baby's bedroom.

"We'll be back soon," Tally yelled.

"No, we won't," Randall overruled to Tally's giggles.

To Porsha's surprise, Randall reported back within days. Randall didn't waste time vetting Kwame Clark and gave her a character sketch.

Kwame worked in construction, was single, and had no wife or children. His relationship with God was growing because of Joi's troubles. He appreciated Christ For All Church for teaching him that although his salvation journey had begun with his belief, he had to grow in Christ with the gifts God had for those who received the Holy Ghost. Finally, Kwame's interest in Porsha was genuine.

That last tidbit scared and excited her.

"Sis, what you do with this information is up to you," Randall said.

"Right." Porsha picked up her fork and enjoyed the dinner her sister had prepared. The food became tasteless as her mind jumbled with emotions. She wasn't good at making first moves when it came to relationships.

By the last Sunday in September, Porsha had done nothing but avoid Kwame at church.

After the benediction, she chatted with friends and then left. She had caught a glimpse of Kwame with his parents and sister. He always seemed to know when she stole a glance at him and was ready with a smile and an intense stare.

Porsha had rooted for every couple in their church. *God, is it really my turn?* Kwame had made known his interest, but that didn't mean he was the one God had sent for her. Back home, she petitioned God to show her His choice.

I have, God whispered.

You have? Porsha scanned her memory for all the eligible bachelors she had met in and outside the church. The answer came when she finished praying.

You have ministered to him and his sister, God whispered.

Joi and Kwame. Porsha swallowed. Kwame was on another list from God—for her. "Lord, thank You, in Jesus' name. Amen." Her phone rang, and Porsha frowned at the unexpected caller.

"Porsha, this is Kwame."

She could recognize his voice in a crowd. "Well, thanks for answering because I can't stalk you forever. I've been praying to God for help to get your attention."

Lifting her brow, Porsha twisted her lips. "And what did God say?" It better be in line with what God had just told her, or she would consider him a decoy from the devil.

"God saved Joi for His purpose and saved me for you."

Whew. Whew. Yes, Porsha's heart filled with happiness. The confirmation she needed. "Dinner would be nice."

"How about next Friday? A movie or play and dinner."

"I would like that." Porsha grinned.

"One last thing. You haven't given me your address."

And she wasn't about to just yet. "I'll meet you there."

Chapter Thirty-three

Be sober, be vigilant; because your adversary
the devil, as a roaring lion, walks about, seeking
whom he may devour. —1 Peter 5:8

Being newlyweds a second time was better than the first time. Amethyst knew that Grayson loved her, and she loved him.

Blueberry biscuits and morning carpools to work made Amethyst and Grayson in no rush to get another car. Amethyst suspected a new car would be her Christmas gift based on Grayson's sly questions during their commute, like interior preferences, car styles, and crossover versus a sedan.

It was apparent he wasn't good at planning surprises.

She and Grayson had matured and changed. Pastor Rodney told them their love was worth fighting for, and they agreed.

The day they said "I do" for the second time, they officially became a Holy Ghost power couple at the church, and a party was held in their honor. Amethyst grinned every time she thought about it.

"You know, babe," Amethyst said one evening as they prepared dinner together, "now that I walk in the light, I can't believe I was drowning in the darkness of Satan's underworld."

"Thank God our names were on the Lord's salvation list, and the intercessors prayed to rescue us from a spiritual battlefield." Grayson kissed her cheek and continued stirring spaghetti.

"Yes. Mother Kincaid said that God had appointed me to lead the intercessors at Christ For All Church in the battle against the world of darkness and witchcraft. I can't believe some of the items I had at home and in my possession were used in witchcraft and spells that seem harmless to me." Amethyst was careful when she admired beads and steered away from crystals.

"I'm so glad the Lord saved us and restored our marriage."

Amethyst stopped chopping the ingredients for the sauce, wrapped her arms around Grayson's waist, and rested her head on his back. "I love you," she whispered.

"I know." He kissed her forehead. "But not as much as I love you."

"That's debatable," she challenged him.

"We have a lifetime to decide the winner." This time, she kissed his lips.

On a Friday date night, Amethyst saw figures hovering over unsuspecting victims or entrenched in their being as they were on their way to a movie. As they neared an intersection, a beggar handed out little stickers in exchange for donations.

The light turned red, so Grayson rolled down his window. "Hungry, brother?"

The man was dirty with matted hair and a few missing teeth. His eyes were glossy as he shook his head. "I'm passing out these stickers for food or a few dollars. It's all I have to give."

A dark mist seemed to tie the beggar up to strangle the man.

Amethyst felt the Holy Ghost speak through her and call the man by name. "In the Mighty Name of Jesus, release Lemar now!"

The beggar began to convulse until he fell back, shaking as if he were experiencing a seizure. "I will not let him go," a growling voice said.

"The Lord rebuke you, in Jesus' name. Jesus is the Master, and you have to obey." Amethyst continued to call on Jesus, as did Grayson.

The beggar yelled in agony before his body calmed. He then sat up, crossing his legs. He looked peaceful and innocent, like a kindergartener.

Someone honked behind them, and Grayson waved them forward. "I'm going to get you a meal and bring it back."

"Thank you." His voice was hoarse.

When they returned fifteen minutes later, the man was still there, waiting patiently. Grayson parked across the street. "You stay here, babe. I'll take him the ribs and potato salad. Why don't you make calls so someone can find him a shelter?"

Since her salvation, Amethyst had come to discern dark spirits to rebuke, and the name of Jesus had power over them. She hadn't realized that so many people had demonic spirits attached to them or that the spirit of witchcraft was controlling them like it had her. She whispered her thanks, and then Amethyst smiled when her husband returned. "What?"

"I love you so much for your kindness. You're the type of man that I would marry again."

Grayson grinned. "You already did."

Rolling over, Grayson snuggled beside his wife as a ringing sound echoed in his head. He ignored anything that would disrupt his slumber.

Amethyst elbowed him in the stomach. "Grayson, Grayson," she said softly. "The doorbell. Wake up."

"Huh?" He groaned and rubbed his face, then Grayson heard the doorbell and scooted up. He and Amethyst threw the cover back at the same time.

"It's four in the morning." Amethyst reached for her robe.

"You stay here." He hurried downstairs. Grayson glanced through the peephole, and a police officer stared back at him. He opened the door. "Are you Grayson Tate?"

"I am." Grayson folded his arms as Amethyst joined him. "What's going on?"

"I'm Officer Dawson, and we have you down as the next of kin for Reggie Hart."

"That's my brother." Since Grayson's salvation, he no longer referred to Reggie as his half-brother, but Reggie no longer kept a line of communication with them.

Amethyst was aware of Jessica's threat to Reggie and Amethyst if she thought they were having an affair, which Amethyst denied, and Grayson believed her. Reggie's behavior had been suspicious to Grayson and Amethyst for different reasons—demonic from what Grayson had witnessed the day he paid Amethyst's loan and the way he spoke to Amethyst the night she fought a spiritual battle, and Grayson had come to assist.

They both agreed to stay away and pray for them from afar. "But his wife, Jessica, would be the next of kin." He slipped his arm around Amethyst's waist. "Is something wrong?"

"Reggie has been shot with life-threatening injuries, and his wife is in custody."

Amethyst gasped. Speechless, Grayson felt the strength leave his body. As his mind replayed "life-threatening" and "wife in custody." He recovered quickly because his wife couldn't bear his weight.

"Can you take temporary custody of his children?" the officer asked.

For the first time, Grayson thought about his niece and nephew in this tragedy.

"Of course," Amethyst answered for him. "Where are they?"

"In our patrol car."

Despite the cool October night, Amethyst slipped on her shoes and ran outside in her pajamas. The children opened the door and screamed, "Auntie, Auntie!" She showered them with hugs and then led Kiya and Victor into the house.

Fear and confusion gripped their faces. "It's going to be okay," Grayson said, not knowing if it would be. He stepped outside on the porch to learn what happened.

Officer Dawson explained. "We responded to calls of shots fired coming from the Hart residence. One neighbor said she heard loud voices when she let her dog out. Upon arrival, we found Reggie Hart lying in the living room with a gunshot wound to the neck and stomach. CPR was administered, and he was transferred to the hospital in critical condition."

Grayson swallowed the lump in his throat. His brother. Despite their differences, they had the same mother. "Thank you, Officer." He noted which hospital and stepped inside the house to check on his niece and nephew.

"God forgive me for not trying harder to talk to Reggie about Your salvation." Grayson sniffed as he walked toward the kitchen. "Lord, please spare his life on my behalf so he can repent and serve You."

I will have mercy on whom I will have mercy, and I will have compassion on whom I will have compassion, God whispered.

Does that mean You're not accepting favors tonight, Lord?"

The Lord was quiet about His will.

Chapter Thirty-four

*And the people shall be oppressed, everyone by another,
and everyone by his neighbor: the child shall behave
himself proudly against the ancient, and the base against
the honorable.* —Isaiah 5:3

Mother Kincaid sat in her living room, watching the late-night news before she retired to bed. "Senseless, just senseless," she called the steady stream of news stories that broadcasted one violent act after another, "and so close to Thanksgiving too."

She *tsk*ed and shook her head in disgust. The End Times were near. The saints had been praying non-stop once Brother Grayson told them about his brother's injuries and Reggie's prognosis.

It had been a month since Reggie's wife had shot her husband. Grayson said his brother was paralyzed from the neck down and needed wheelchair assistance. He would be released soon to enter a rehab facility for an unspecified length of time. God knew how to get Reggie's attention. Hopefully, he would repent and ask the Lord for a full recovery as the church ministries visited him.

Mother Kincaid chuckled. "Wouldn't that be something for him to stand up, walk again, and testify of God's mercy and second chances?"

Reggie's wife, Jessica's fate wasn't any better. Prosecutors had stacked so many charges against her, including endangering the welfare of a child and attempted murder, that her children might be adults by the time she would be released. The prison ministry had visited her too.

"Those poor children." At least they were in the loving care of Grayson and Amethyst. Despite the circumstances, they were adjusting. Amethyst had confided in her that the Lord had said two more babies for her through Carlton, and she assumed Kiya and Victor were fulfilling the promise.

While most people would have turned off the news by now, Mother Kincaid watched until the end. She had to know who and what to pray for, hoping the devil hadn't gotten to Olivia and Wyatt before the intercessors. Another news story caught her attention.

"People have charged a man who purposely rammed his vehicle into a duplex in the Metro East, sparking a blaze that killed a young mother and her four-year-old daughter," the female newscaster said.

Mother Kincaid's heart bled at the senseless crime.

"Witnesses say it was intentional. Authorities will only say he was a neighbor," another newscaster added.

"Lord, please hurry and come before Satan kills us all."

Souls remain unclaimed, God thundered through the wind.

Yes, two more. No one had met Olivia Baker or Wyatt Sheppard, and the intercessors had been fasting and praying. A few weeks after Thanksgiving, another shut-in prayer service was scheduled.

Behold, a knock comes at your door. Do not be afraid, for I am with you.

The knock turned into a frantic pounding. Mother Kincaid stood to answer the door. She checked the peephole. A young woman stood, looking over her shoulder. "May I help you, honey?" she said without opening it.

"Yes, please help. Someone is following me." Her voice shook. "May I come in and call the police?"

Mother Kincaid's heart pumped with fear for the girl, even though the Lord told her not to be afraid. She hurried back to her chair, grabbed her phone, and called 911 as she fumbled with the door lock and cracked it.

"Nine-one-one. What's your emergency?" the dispatcher answered and asked.

Before Mother Kincaid could say anything, her door crashed open, causing the phone to fly out of her hand as she lost her footing. A young man who barely looked old enough to drive pointed a gun at Mother Kincaid, not the woman supposedly in danger. They were accomplices.

Be not afraid. This is Olivia Baker and Mark White.

But where is Wyatt Sheppard? she wondered as she stared at danger.

"Give me your money," Mark said with a steady hand on the trigger.

Mother Kincaid ignored him and addressed the woman. "Olivia Baker, I've been expecting you."

That caught the pretty young woman by surprise. The hard attitude she displayed was an act. "You know me?"

"Shut up." The teenager snarled at her.

"Mark White, the devil has been waiting for you, too, and he's at the door to take you to hell unless you repent."

"Ain't happening." Mark looked at Olivia. "Search her bedroom for jewelry."

Olivia seemed hesitant about whether she should finish the crime she'd come to commit. The other teenager shoved Mother Kincaid and began to tie her arms behind her back with a belt. Suddenly, Mother Kincaid heard footsteps, a lot of them, like marching. She remembered reading when the Lord sent an army for David, and the sound of footsteps in the mulberry trees was a signal. Was God sending her a signal now?

She hoped so because she was being held captive with a gun pointed at her head and the belt pinching her skin. Mother

Kincaid squinted at the doorway. Angels of God constrained a beast-like figure shouting to Mark to pull the trigger.

The angels, clothed in full army gear, dragged the beast out of the house at the same time the police appeared.

"Drop your weapon," an officer said with his gun drawn. "I said drop your weapon!"

He's going to die tonight, God whispered, and a tear fell down Mother Kincaid's cheek. She would see and hear about Mark White's crime and death on tomorrow's news. Unfortunately, her name would be linked to the home invasion.

Olivia appeared with some of Mother Kincaid's things in her arms.

"Drop it," the officer shouted. "Let me see your hands."

"Run, Olivia!" Mark scrambled out the front door with an officer running behind him. Mark had left his accomplice behind to take the blame.

Then, they all heard yelling and gunshots. Tears sprang in Olivia's eyes as she looked from Mother Kincaid to the officer.

"I will shoot you if you don't obey my command," the officer said, getting irritated.

"Oh, no, don't do that. God has an assignment for Olivia," Mother Kincaid told the officer, then turned to the young woman. "Baby, do what he says."

Immediately, Olivia complied, and within minutes, she was in handcuffs.

"Mrs. Kincaid, are you okay?" her next-door neighbor asked, hurrying through the door and helping her sit up.

"Yes," she said as she pushed herself off the floor. "With the help of the Lord. I need to speak to those young people."

Minutes later, one officer returned. "Unfortunately, you won't be able to. The male is deceased after failing to drop the gun and firing at an officer. We returned fire. The female is in custody."

A male paramedic entered and squatted to examine the bump on her head. Mother Kincaid grimaced. "Is your name Wyatt?"

"No, ma'am."

The officer took her name and statement. "Do you feel up to pressing charges?"

"Absolutely. They held a gun to my head and came into my house with their shoes on." They helped her stand, and Mother Kincaid walked to the police car with some assistance.

A female officer opened the door, and Mother Kincaid looked at Olivia. "God's been calling you, Olivia, but so has the devil, and you took the bait. Many church members have prayed for you to come to the Lord before this happened."

Olivia rolled her eyes. "You don't know anything about me!"

"But God knows everything about you. See you at the jail."

Mother Kincaid walked back into the house and phoned Pastor Rodney, despite the time.

He answered on the second ring.

"We found Olivia, Pastor."

"Praise the Lord! Thank You, Jesus." He rejoiced. "Where?"

"She broke into my house. The young man she was with was shot and killed. The police have arrested her and are taking her to be processed at the jail. It may be a long night for me because I'm not leaving that jail without me witnessing to that young lady."

"Whether she can get an attorney or not, The Bible says we have an advocate with the Father. Praise God, He spared her life. Whether incarcerated or not, God's will will be done."

Epilogue

Three months later…

Five-thirty morning prayer had been more powerful since Amethyst and Grayson joined them. Mother Kincaid could feel a double portion of spiritual boldness on the intercessors.

"Let's continue to pray for Olivia—that her attorney will represent her well. Until then, I can see using her within the jail when the prison ministry goes to have a service with her every other Saturday. She brings another inmate to the group prayer every time."

"Amen," the intercessors rejoiced.

Mother Kincaid asked if there were any prayer requests.

"Can I give a praise report first?" Amethyst asked, and Mother Kincaid agreed. "Before God saved me, Brother Carlton said God would bless me with two more children. When Grayson and I took custody of our niece and nephew because their dad can't care for himself—oh, don't stop praying for Reggie—I thought Jesus meant those would be our two children. Well…Grayson and I are expecting a baby!"

Amens, hallelujahs, and congratulations floated among the dozens of intercessors on the call, including Porsha and Kwame, who had begun to date.

"But I have a prayer request for my mom, Annabelle Johnson." Amethyst sighed. "Grayson and I see demons altering her mind whenever we talk to her about the Bible, church, or the Lord.

"Also, my coworker Joyce Clark," Porsha added. "She's hungry for the move of God, but something is holding her back."

"Will do, Sister Porsha." Mother Kincaid paused. "I do have some sad news to report. We lost one on the list. Wyatt Sheppard is dead. God revealed to me that he died in a house fire last week."

Everyone on the call was quiet.

Despite their best efforts to witness to people and evangelize through community service, Mother Kincaid knew some people refused to accept Christ. "Everybody doesn't want Jesus—that's a fact—and nobody can go to heaven without Him," she said.

Book club discussion

1. What was the source of Amethyst's troubles?

2. What was the purpose of God separating Grayson and Amethyst on His list?

3. Discuss a time when God had you pray for a person, and you didn't know why.

4. What do you think was Amethyst's path if she didn't come to the Lord?

5. Discuss whether you felt Porsha was an effective witness.

About the Author

Pat Simmons is a multi-published Christian romance author of forty-plus titles. She is a self-proclaimed genealogy sleuth passionate about researching her ancestors and casting them in starring roles in her novels. She is a five-time recipient of the RSJ Emma Rodgers Award for Best Inspirational Romance: *Still Guilty, Crowning Glory, The Confession, Christmas Dinner*, and *Queen's Surrender (To A Higher Calling)*. Pat's first inspirational women's fiction, *Lean On Me*, with Sourcebooks, was the national library system's February/March Together We Read Digital Book Club pick. *Here for You* and *Stand by Me* are also part of the Family is Forever series. Her holiday indie release, *Christmas Dinner*, and traditionally published, *Here for You*, were featured in *Woman's World*, a national magazine. *Here for You* was also listed in the "7 Great Reads That Help to Keep the Faith" by Sisters From AARP. She contributed an article, "I'm Listening," in the *Chicken Soup for the Soul: I'm Speaking Now* (2021). Pat is the recipient of the 2022 Leslie Esdaile "Trailblazer" Award given by Building Relationships Around Books Readers' Choice for her work in the Christian fiction genre.

As a Christian, Pat describes the evidence of the gift of the Holy Ghost as a life-altering experience. She has been a featured speaker and workshop presenter at various venues nationwide. Pat has converted her sofa-strapped sports fanatical husband into an amateur travel agent, untrained bodyguard, GPS-guided chauffeur, and administrative assistant who is constantly on probation. They have a son and a daughter. Pat holds a B.S. in mass communications from Emerson College in Boston,

Massachusetts, and has worked in radio, television, and print media for over twenty years. She oversaw the media publicity for the annual RT Booklovers Conventions for fourteen years. Visit her at www.patsimmons.net.

Other Christian Titles

The Jamieson Legacy
Book 1: Guilty of Love
Book 2: Not Guilty of Love
Book 3: Still Guilty
Book 4: The Acquittal
Book 5: Guilty by Association
Book 6: The Guilt Trip
Book 7: Free from Guilt
Book 8: Sandra Nicholson's Backstory
Book 9: The Confession
Book 10: The Guilty Generation
Book 11: Queen's Surrender (To a Higher Calling)
Book 12: Contempt: Grandma BB's Shenanigans
Book 13: Christmas Takeover (The Next Generation)
Book 14: Accomplices in Love (The Next Generation)

The Intercessors
Book 1: Day Not Promised
Book 2: Day She Prayed
Book 3: Days Are Coming
Book 4: Day of Salvation

The Carmen Sisters
Book 1: No Easy Catch
Book 2: In Defense of Love
Book 3: Driven to Be Loved
Book 4: Redeeming Heart

Love at the Crossroads
Book 1: Stopping Traffic
Book 2: A Baby for Christmas

Book 3: The Keepsake
Book 4: What God Has for Me
Book 5: Every Woman Needs a Praying Man

Restore My Soul
Book 1: Crowning Glory
Book 2: Jet: The Back Story
Book 3: Love Led by the Spirit

Family is Forever
Book 1: Lean on Me
Book 2: Here For You
Book 3: Stand by Me

Making Love Work Anthology
Book 1: Love at Work
Book 2: Words of Love
Book 3: A Mother's Love

God's Gifts
Book 1: Couple by Christmas
Book 2: Prayers Answered by Christmas

Perfect Chance at Love series
Book 1: Love by Delivery
Book 2: Late Summer Love

Single titles
Talk to Me
Her Dress
House Calls for the Holidays (short story)
Christmas Dinner
Christmas Greetings
Taye's Gift
Waiting for Christmas

House Calls for the Holidays
Anderson Brothers
Book 1: Love for the Holidays (Three novellas):
A Christian Christmas
A Christian Easter
A Christian Father's Day
Book 2: A Woman After David's Heart (A Valentine's Day Story)
Book 3: A Noelle for Nathan

In *Crowning Glory*, Cinderella had a prince; Karyn Wallace has a King. While Karyn served four years in prison for an unthinkable crime, she embraced salvation through the Crowns for Christ outreach ministry. After her release, Karyn remains strong and confident, despite society's stigma against ex-offenders. Since Christ strengthens the underdog, Karyn refuses to stray from the scripture, "He whom the Son has set free is free indeed." Levi Tolliver, for the most part, is a practicing Christian. One contradiction is that he doesn't believe in turning the other cheek. He's steadfast in his belief that there is a price to pay for every sin committed, especially after the untimely death of his wife during a robbery. Then Karyn enters Levi's life. He is enthralled by her beauty and sweet spirit until he learns about her incarceration. If Levi can accept that Christ paid Karyn's debt in full, then a treasure awaits him. This is a powerful tale that reminds readers of the permanence of redemption.

Jet: The Back Story to Love Led By the Spirit, to say Jesetta "Jet" Hutchens issues is an understatement. In Crowning Glory, Book 1 of the Restoring My Soul series, she releases a firestorm of anger with an unforgiving heart. But every hurting soul has a history. In Jet: The Back Story to Love Led by the Spirit, Jet doesn't know how to cope with losing her younger sister, Diane. But God sets her on the road to a spiritual recovery. Jesus sends the handsome and single Minister Rossi Tolliver to guide her to ensure she doesn't get lost. Psalm 147:3 says Jesus can heal the brokenhearted and bind up their wounds. That sets the stage for Love Led by the Spirit.

In *Love Led By the Spirit*, Minister Rossi Tolliver is ready to settle down. Besides the outward attraction, he desires a sweet, humble woman who loves church folks. It sounds simple enough on paper, but when he gets off his knees, praying for that special someone to come into his life, God opens his eyes to the woman who has been there all along. There is only a slight problem. Love is the farthest thing from Jesetta "Jet" Hutchens' mind. But Rossi, the man and the minister, is hard to resist. Is Jet ready to allow the Holy Spirit to lead her to love?

In *Stopping Traffic*, Book 1, Candace Clark has a phobia about crossing the street, and for a good reason. As fate would have it, her daughter's principal assigns her to crossing guard duties as part of the school's Parent Participation program. With no choice in the matter, Candace begrudgingly accepts her stop sign and safety vest, then reports to her designated crosswalk. Once Candace is determined to overcome her fears, God opens the door for a blessing, and Royce Kavanaugh enters her life, a firefighter built to rescue any damsel in distress. When a spark of attraction ignites, Candace and Royce soon discover more than one way to stop traffic.

In *A Baby For Christmas*, Book 2, yes, diamonds are a girl's best friend, but in Solae Wyatt-Palmer's case, she desires something more valuable. Captain Hershel Kavanaugh is a divorcee and the father of two adorable little boys. Solae has never been married and longs to be a mother. Although Hershel showers her with expensive gifts, his hesitation about proposing causes Solae to walk and never look back. As the holidays approach, Hershel must convince Solae she has everything he could ever want for Christmas.

In *The Keepsake*, Book 3, Until Death Us Do Part…or until Desiree walks away. Desiree "Desi" Bishop is devastated when she finds evidence of her husband's affair. God knew she didn't get married to one day have to stand before a judge and file for a divorce. But Desi wants out no matter how much her heart says to forgive Michael. That isn't easier said than done. She sees

God's one acceptable reason for a divorce as the only opt-out clause in her marriage. Michael Bishop is a repenting man who loves his wife of three years. If only…he had paid attention to the red flags God sent to keep him from falling into the devil's snares. But Michael didn't and fell. Although God forgives him instantly when he repents, Desi's forgiveness moves at a snail's pace. After all the tears have been shed and forgiveness granted and received, the couple learns that some marriages are worth keeping.

In *What God Has For Me*, Book 4, pregnant or not, Halcyon Holland is leaving her boyfriend. When her ex makes no attempts to reconcile their relationship, Halcyon begins to second-guess whether or not she compromised her chance for a happily ever after. But Zachary Bishop has had his eye on Halcyon since he first saw her. What one man doesn't cherish, Zach is ready to treasure. He's on a mission to offer her a second chance at love that she can't refuse: unconditional love for a ready-made family. Halcyon will soon learn that her past circumstances won't hinder the Lord's blessings for them.

In *Every Woman Needs A Praying Man*, Book 5, first impressions can make or break a business deal, and they definitely could be a relationship buster, but an ill-timed panic attack draws two strangers together. Unlike firefighters who run into danger, instincts tell businessman Tyson Graham to be weary of a certain damsel in distress and run. Days later, the same woman struts through his door for a job interview. Monica Wyatt might possess the outward beauty and the brains on paper, but Tyson doesn't trust her to work for his firm, or maybe he doesn't trust his heart around her.

In *Guilty of Love*, when do you know the most important decision of your life is the right one? Reaping the seeds from what she's sown, Cheney Reynolds moves into a historic neighborhood in Ferguson, Missouri, and becomes a reclusive. Her first neighbor, the incomparable Mrs. Beatrice Tilley Beacon aka Grandma BB, is an opinionated childless widow. Grandma BB is a self-proclaimed expert on topics Cheney isn't seeking advice—everything from landscaping to hip-hop dancing to romance. Then there is Parke Kokumuo Jamison VI, a direct descendant of a royal African tribe. He learned his family ancestry, African history, and lineage preservation before he could count. Unwittingly, they are drawn to each other, but it takes Christ to weave their lives into a spiritual bliss while He exonerates their past indiscretions.

In *Not Guilty*, one man, one woman, one God, and one big problem. Malcolm Jamieson wasn't the man who got away, but the man God instructed Hallison Dinkins to set free. Instead of their explosive love affair leading them to the wedding altar, God diverted Hallison to the prayer altar during her first visit back to church in years. Malcolm was convinced his woman had lost her mind to break off their engagement. Didn't Hallison know that Malcolm, a tenth-generation descendant of a royal African tribe, couldn't be replaced? Once Malcolm concedes that their relationship can't be savaged, he issues Hallison his edict, "If we're meant to be with each other, we'll find our way back. If not, that means there's a love stronger than we had." His words haunt Hallison until she begins to regret their breakup, and that's where their story begins. Someone has to retreat, and God never loses a battle.

In *Still Guilty*, Cheney Reynolds Jamieson made a choice years ago that is shaping her future and the future of the men she loves. A botched abortion prevented her from carrying a baby to term, and her husband, Parke K. Jamison VI, is expected to produce heirs. With a wife who cannot give him a child, Parke vows to find and get custody of his illegitimate son by any means necessary. Meanwhile, Cheney's twin brother, Rainey, struggles with his anger over his ex-girlfriend's actions that haunt him, and their father, Dr. Roland Reynolds, fights to keep an old secret in the past.

In *The Acquittal*, two worlds apart, but their hearts dance to the same African drum beat. On a professional level, Dr. Rainey Reynolds is a competent, highly sought-after orthodontist. Inwardly, he needs to be set free from the chaos of revelations that make him question if happiness is obtainable. To escape the drama, Rainey is willing to leave the country under the guise of a mission trip with Dentist Without Borders. Will changing his surroundings change him? If one woman can heal his wounds, then he will believe that there is really peace after the storm.

Ghanaian beauty Josephine Abena Yaa Amoah returns to Africa after completing her studies as an exchange student in St. Louis, Missouri. Although her heart bleeds for his peace, she knows she must step back and pray for Rainey's surrender to Christ so God can acquit him of his self-inflicted mental torture. In the Motherland of Ghana, Africa, Rainey not only visits the places of his ancestors but also embraces the liberty that Christ's Blood does to set every man free.

In *Guilty By Association*, how important is a name? To the St. Louis Jamiesons, tenth-generation descendants of a royal African tribe—everything. To the Boston Jamiesons, whose father never married their mother, there is no loyalty or legacy. Kidd Jamieson suffers from the "angry" male syndrome because his father was absent in the home but insisted his two sons carry his last name. It takes an old woman who mingles genealogy truths and Bible verses together for Kidd to realize his worth as a strong black man. He learns it's not his association with the name that identifies him, but the man he becomes that defines him.

In *The Guilt Trip*, Aaron "Ace" Jamieson lives carefree. He's good-looking and respectable when in the mood, but his weakness is women. If a woman tries to ambush him with a pregnancy, he takes off in the other direction. It's a lesson learned from his absentee father that responsibility is optional. Talise Rogers has a bright future ahead of her. She's pretty and has no problem catching a man's eye, which is exactly what she does with Ace. Trapping Ace Jamieson is the furthest thing from Talise's mind when she learns she is pregnant, and Ace rejects her. "I want nothing from you Ace, not even your name." And Talise meant it.

In *Free From Guilt*, it's salvation round-up time, and Cameron Jamieson's name is on God's hit list. Although his brothers and cousins embraced God—thanks to the women in their lives—the two-degreed MIT graduate isn't letting any woman take him down that path without a fight. He's satisfied with his career, social calendar, and good genes. But God uses a beautiful messenger, Gabrielle Dupree, to show him that he's in a spiritual deficit. Cameron learns that man's wisdom is like foolishness to God. For every philosophical argument he throws her way, Gabrielle exposes him to Scriptures that make him question his worldly knowledge.

In *Sandra Nicholson's Backstory*, Sandra has made good and bad choices throughout the years, but the best one was to give her life to Christ when her sons were small and to rear them up in the best Christian way she knew how. That was thirty-something years ago and Sandra has evolved from a young single mother of two rambunctious boys: Kidd and Ace Jamieson, to a godly woman seasoned with wisdom. Despite the challenges and trials of rearing two strong-willed personalities, Sandra maintained her sanity through the grace of God, which kept gray strands at bay. But there is something to be said about a woman's first love. Kidd and Ace Jamieson's father, Samuel Jamieson, broke their mother's heart. Can Sandra recover? Her sons don't believe any man is good enough for her, especially their absent father. Kidd doesn't deny his mother should find love again since she never married Samuel. But will she fall for a carbon copy of his father? God's love gives second chances.

In *The Confession*, Sandra Nicholson had made good and bad choices throughout the years, but the best one was to give her life to Christ when her sons were small and to rear them up in the best Christian way she knew how. That was thirty-something years ago and Sandra has evolved from a young single mother of two rambunctious boys, Kidd and Ace Jamieson to a godly woman seasoned with wisdom. Despite the challenges and trials of rearing two strong-willed personalities, Sandra maintained her sanity through the grace of God, which kept gray strands at bay.

Now, Sandra Nicholson is on the threshold of happiness, but Kidd believes no man is good enough for his mother, especially if her love interest could be a man just like his absentee father.

In *The Guilty Generation*, seventeen-year-old Kami Jamieson is so over being daddy's little girl. Now that she has captured the attention of Tango, the bad boy from her school, Kami's love for her family and God have taken a backseat to her teen crush.

Although the Jamiesons have instilled godly principles in Kami since she was young, they will stop at nothing, including prayer and fasting, to protect her from falling prey to society's peer pressure. Can Kami survive her teen rebellion, or will she be guilty of dividing the next generation?

In *Queen's Surrender (To a Higher Calling)*, Opposites attract...or clash. The Jamieson saga continues with the Queen of the family in this inspirational romance. She's the mistress of flirtation, but Philip is unaffected by her charm. The two enjoy a harmless banter about God's will versus Queen's, who prefers her own free-will lifestyle. Philip doesn't judge her choices—most of the time—and Queen respects his opinions—most of the time. It's perfect harmony sometimes. Queen, the youngest sister of the Jamieson clan, wears her name as if it's a crown. She's single, sassy, and most of the time, loving her status, but she's about to strut down an unexpected spiritual path. Evangelist Philip Dupree is on the hot seat as the trial pastor at Total Surrender Church. The stalemate: They want a family man to lead their flock. The board's ultimatum is enough to make him quit the ministry. But can a man of God walk away from his calling? Can two people with different lifestyles and priorities cross paths and continue the journey as one? Who is going to be the first to surrender?

In *Contempt (Grandma BB's Shenanigans)*, Grandma BB, the unofficial matriarch of the Jamieson clan, is getting her house for the perfect homegoing celebration. After all, she's eighty-something. She summons Parke Jamieson VI, his brothers, cousins, and their families to participate in the practice funeral program—only if they follow her instructions. Since the Jamiesons are at her house with bodyguards Chip and Dale, they might have an impromptu family game night. The evening is full of surprises, especially when an unexpected visitor shows up to steal the show. With more work that needs to be done, Grandma

BB plans to put her funeral on hold and stick around for a couple more generations.

In *Accomplices in Love*, Parke "Pace" Jamieson VIII knows something is special about Harmony Reed, his sister's college friend who was almost stranded in St. Louis for Christmas. She checks all his compatibility boxes: looks, charm, a great sense of humor, and intense attraction. Plus, the Jamiesons love her.

When not at school, Harmony lives in Chicago with her three overprotective brothers. She is not interested in a relationship with her best friend's brother.

Pace, who lives in St. Louis, is not deterred by the distance, her objections, or her brothers. He's a Jamieson, and they play to win.

In *Fun and Games with the Jamieson Men*, The Jamieson Legacy series inspired this game book of fun activities:• Brain Teasers• Crossword Puzzles• Word Searches •Sudoku •Mazes •Coloring Pages. The Jamiesons are fictional characters that emphasize Black Heritage, including Black American History tidbits, African American genealogy, and strong Black families. Relax, grab a pencil and play along.

THE CARMEN SISTERS SERIES

In *No Easy Catch*, Book 1, Shae Carmen hasn't lost her faith in God, only the men she's come across. Shae's recent heartbreak was discovering that her boyfriend was not only married, but on the verge of reconciling with his estranged wife. Humiliated, Shae begins to second guess herself as why she didn't see the signs that he was nothing more than a devil's decoy masquerading as a devout Christian man. St. Louis Outfielder Rahn Maxwell finds himself a victim of an attempted carjacking. The Lord guides him out of harms' way by opening the gunmen's eyes to Rahn's identity. The crook instead becomes an infatuated fan and asks for Rahn's autograph, and as a goodwill gesture, directs Rahn out of the ambush! When the news media gets wind of what happened with the baseball player, Shae's television station lands an exclusive interview. Shae and Rahn's chance meeting sets in motion a relationship where Rahn not only surrenders to Christ, but pursues Shae with a purpose to prove that good men are still out there. After letting her guard down, Shae faces another scandal that rocks her world. This time the stakes are higher. Not only is her heart on the line, so is her professional credibility. She and Rahn are at odds as how to handle it and friction erupts between them. Will she strike out at love again? The Lord shows Rahn that nothing happens by chance and everything is done for Him to get the glory.

In *Defense of Love*, Book 2, nothing in Garrett Nash's life has made sense lately. When two people close to the U.S. Marshal wrong him deeply, Garrett expects God to remove them from his life. Instead, the Lord relocates Garrett to another city to start over, as if he were the offender instead of the victim. Criminal attorney Shari Carmen is comfortable in her own skin—most of the time. Being a "dark and lovely" African-American sister has its challenges, especially when it comes to relationships. Although she's a fireball in the courtroom, she knows how to fade into the background and keep the proverbial spotlight off her personal life. But literal spotlights are a different matter altogether. While playing tenor saxophone at an anniversary party, she grabs the attention of Garrett Nash. And as God draws them closer together, He makes another request of Garrett, one to which it will prove far more difficult to say "Yes, Lord."

In *Redeeming Heart*, Book 3, Landon Thomas (In Defense of Love) brings a new definition to the word "prodigal," as in prodigal son, brother or anything else imaginable. It's good that God's love covers a multitude of sins, but He isn't letting Landon off easy. His journey from riches to rags proves to be humbling and a lesson well learned. Real Estate Agent Octavia Winston is a woman on a mission, whether it's God's or hers professionally. One thing is for certain, she's not about to compromise when it comes to a Christian mate, so why did God send a homeless man to steal her heart? Minister Rossi Tolliver (Crowning Glory) knows how to minister to God's lost sheep and through God's redemption, the game changes for Landon and Octavia.

In *Driven to Be Loved*, Book 4, on the surface, Brecee Carmen has nothing in common with Adrian Cole. She is a pediatrician certified in trauma care; he is a transportation problem solver for a luxury car dealership (a.k.a., a car salesman). Despite their slow but steady attraction to each other, neither one of them are sure that they're compatible. To complicate matters, Brecee is the sole unattached Carmen when it seems as though everyone else around her—family and friends—are finding love, except her. Through a series of discoveries, Adrian and Brecee learn that things don't happen by coincidence. Generational forces are at work, keeping promises, protecting family members, and perhaps even drawing Adrian back to the church. For Brecee and Adrian, God has been hard at work, playing matchmaker all along the way for their paths cross at the right time and the right place.

Lean on Me, Book 1. No one should have to go it alone... Caregivers sometimes need a little TLC too.

Tabitha Knicely believes in putting family before everything. She may be overwhelmed caring for her beloved great-aunt, but she would never turn her back on the woman who raised her, even if Aunt Tweet's dementia is getting worse. Tabitha is sure she can do this on her own. But when Aunt Tweet ends up on her neighbor's front porch, and the man has the audacity to accuse Tabitha of elder abuse, things go from bad to awful. Marcus Whittington feels a mountain of regret at causing problems for Tabitha and her great-aunt. How was he to know the frail older woman's niece was doing her best? As Marcus gets to know Aunt Tweet and sees how hard Tabitha is fighting to keep everything together, he can't walk away from the pair. Particularly when helping Tabitha care for her great-aunt leads them on a spiritual journey of faith and surrender.

Here For You, Book 2. Rachel Knicely's life has been on hold for six months while she takes care of her great aunt, who has Alzheimer's. Putting her aunt first was an easy decision— accepting that Aunt Tweet is nearing the end of her battle is far more difficult. Nicholas Adams's ministry is comforting those who are sick and homebound. He responds to a request for help for an ailing woman, but when he meets the Knicelys, he realizes Rachel needs the most support. Nicholas is charmed by and attracted to Rachel, but then devastating news brings both a crisis of faith and roadblocks to their budding relationship that neither could have anticipated. This beautifully emotional and clean story contains a hero and heroine who are better at caring for other people than themselves, a dark moment that shakes their faith, and a well-earned happily ever after.

Stand by Me, Book 3. An uplifting story about embracing love and giving others—and yourself—one more chance. When it comes to being a caregiver, Kym Knicely has been there and done that. Then she meets Charles "Chaz" Banks and soon learns that every caregiving situation is different. Chaz takes care of his seven-year-old autistic granddaughter, Chauncy. Although Kym's attraction to Chaz is strong, she has to decide whether a romantic relationship can survive and thrive between two people at different stages in life. It's a journey with a different set of rules that Kym has to play by if she and Chaz are to have their happily ever after and the faith and family they envision.

About *Waiting for Christmas*,

A chance meeting. An undeniable attraction.

And a first date that starts with a stakeout that leads to a winner-takes-all shopping spree. It's the making of a holiday romance. While philanthropist Sterling Price believes in charitable causes, he and licensed social worker Ciara Summers have a difference of opinion on how to bless others. Ciara is a rebel with a cause and a hundred reasons why helping those less fortunate is important. Sterling is a man of means who believes a financial responsibility comes with giving.

The Lord will make sure everyone's needs are met, and He has something extra for Sterling and Ciara that can't wait until Christmas.

About *Christmas Dinner*,

How do you celebrate the holidays after losing a loved one? Take the journey, beginning with Christmas Dinner. For months, Darcelle Price has suffered depression in silence. But things are about to change as she plans to celebrate Christmas Eve with family and share her journey. Darcelle invites them via group text, not knowing she had included her ex. Evanston Giles is surprised to hear from the woman he loved after months following their breakup. Seeking closure, he shows up on her doorstep for answers. A lot can happen on Christmas Eve. Restoring family ties, building her faith in God, and falling in love again is just the beginning of the night of miracles.

About *Taye's Gift*,

Welcome to Snowflake, Colorado—a small town where wishes come true! When six old high school friends receive a letter that their fellow friend, Charity Hart, wrote before she passed away, their lives take an unexpected turn. She leaves them each a check for $1,500 and asks them to grant a wish—a secret wish—for someone else by Christmas. Who lays off someone before the holidays? Taye Thomas' employer did, so instead of Christmas shopping, she's job hunting. More devastating news comes when an old high school friend passes away. Could God be answering her prayers for help when she learns that Charity Hart left a $1500 check? No, the caveat is it's more blessed to give than receive. Taye has 30 days to find someone else in need to bless. To complicate matters, she's lives in Kansas City, which is more than eight hours away from Snowflake and she can't do it alone. Keeping a secret has never been so much work.

About *Couple by Christmas*,

Holidays haven't been the same for Derek Washington since his divorce. He and his ex-wife, Robyn, go out of their way to avoid each other. This Christmas may be different when he decides to give his son, Tyler, the family he once had before they split. Derek's going to need the Lord's intervention to soften her heart to agree to some outings. God's help doesn't come in the way he expected, but it's all good because everything falls in place for them to be a couple by Christmas.

About *Prayers Answered By Christmas*,

Christmas is coming. While other children are compiling their lists for a fictional Santa, eight-year-old Mikaela Washington is kneeling, making her requests known to the Lord: One mommy for Christmas, please. Portia Hunter refuses to let her ex-husband cheat her out of the family she wants. Her prayer is for God to send the right man into her life. Marlon

Washington will do anything for his two little girls, but can he find a mommy for them and a love for himself? Since Christmas is the time of year to remember the many gifts God has given men, maybe these three souls will get their heart s desire.

About *A Noelle for Nathan*,

A Noelle for Nathan is a story of kindness, selflessness, and falling in love during the Christmas season. Andersen Investors & Consultants, LLC, CFO Nathan Andersen (A Christian Christmas) isn't looking for attention when he buys a homeless man a meal, but grade school teacher Noelle Foster is watching his every move with admiration. His generosity makes him a man after her own heart. While donors give more to children and families in need around the holiday season, Noelle Foster believes in giving year-round after seeing many of her students struggle with hunger and finding a warm bed at night. At a second-chance meeting, sparks fly when Noelle and Nathan share a kindred spirit with their passion to help those less fortunate. Whether they're doing charity work or attending Christmas parties, the couple becomes inseparable. Although Noelle and Nathan exchange gifts, the biggest present is the one from Christ.

One reader says, "A Noelle for Nathan makes you fall in love with love…the love of mankind and the love of God. You cannot read this without wanting to give and do more, all while being appreciative of what you have."

About *Christmas Greetings*,

Saige Carter loves everything about Christmas: the shopping, the food, the lights, and of course, Christmas wouldn't be complete without family and friends to share in the traditions they've created together. Plus, Saige is extra excited about her line of Christmas greeting cards hitting store shelves, but when she gets devastating news around the holidays, she wonders if she'll ever look at Christmas the same again. Daniel Washington is no Scrooge, but he'd rather skip the holidays altogether than spend them with his estranged family. After one too many arguments around the dinner table one year, Daniel had enough and walked away from the drama. As one year has turned into many, no one seems willing to take the first step toward reconciliation. When Daniel reads one of Saige's greeting cards, he's unsure if the words inside are enough to erase the pain and bring about forgiveness. Once God reveals His purpose for their lives to them, they will have a reason to rejoice. *Come unto me, all ye that labor and are heavily laden, and I will give you rest. Take my yoke upon you, and learn of me; for I am meek and lowly in heart: and ye shall find rest unto your souls.* Matthew 11:28-29

About *A Baby for Christmas,*

Yes, diamonds are a girl's best friend, but unless the jewel is going on Solae Wyatt-Palmer's ring finger, they hold little value to her. When she meets Fire Captain Hershel Kavanaugh, their magnetism is undeniable and there's no doubt that it's love at first sight. Since Solae adores Hershel's two boys from his failed marriage, she wouldn't blink at the chance to become a mother to them. But when it seems as if Hershel doesn't have a proposal on his agenda, she has no choice but to cut her losses and move on. But Christmas is coming. And in order to win Solae back, Hershel must resolve some past issues before convincing her that she possesses everything he wants.

About *A Christian Christmas,*

Christmas will never be the same for Joy Knight if Christian Andersen has his way. Not to be confused with a secret Santa, Christian and his family are busier than Santa's elves making sure the Lord's blessings are distributed to those less fortunate by Christmas day. Joy is playing the hand that life dealt her, rearing four children in a home that is on the brink of foreclosure. She's not looking for a handout, but when Christian rescues her in the checkout line; her niece thinks Christian is an angel. Joy thinks he's just another man who will eventually leave, disappointing her and the children. Although Christian is a servant of the Lord, he is a flesh and blood man and all he wants for Christmas is Joy Knight. Can time spent with Christian turn Joy's attention from her financial woes to the real meaning of Christmas—and true love? A Christian Christmas is a holiday novella to be enjoyed at any time of the year.

In *Every Day is Christmas*, A Christmas ornament

A Christmas ornament, an ailing grandmother, and a matchmaking sister are all ingredients for a holiday romance.

Landon Michaels is on a mission to fulfill this grandmother's request for a one-of-a-kind Black angel ornament. With dementia setting in, this might be the last Christmas she remembers.

Gina Christmas is the gatekeeper of unique handcrafted ornaments. It's tax season, and the accountant is too busy crunching numbers to track down an ornament, especially since the holiday is months away.

When Granny Lonna wants something, Landon, her favorite and only grandson, is determined to make it happen. But what she wants for Christmas is for Landon to find the perfect love.

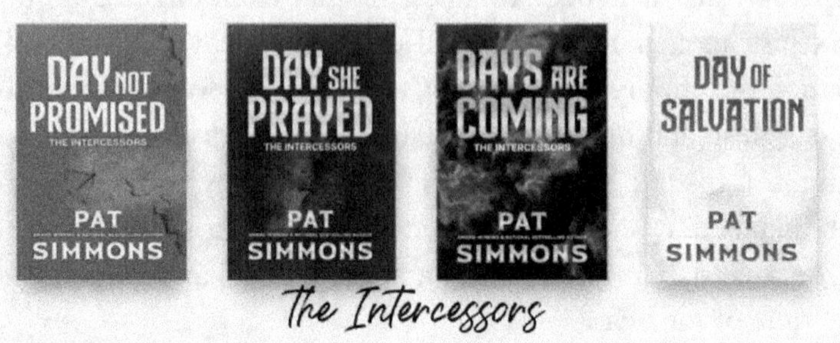

Pat Simmons introduces a new Christian fiction series that reminds readers that the bad guys don't always win, especially when the Lord fights our battles.

In *Day Not Promised*, Omega Addams thought it was a typical workday until a detour on the way home changes everything. She's almost killed, but an innocent bystander, Mitchell Franklin, takes a bullet for Omega during a gas station robbery. In the aftermath, Omega has no idea that God expects her to "pray it forward" until a spiritual battle unfolds before her eyes. Another innocent bystander is in trouble; unless Omega gets her prayer life together, others will die without Christ. It's a chain reaction that highlights the responsibility of a Christian--hot, cold, or lukewarm. It's time to get our acts together. We are our brother's keeper.

In *Day She Prayed*, New Christian convert Tally Gilbert knows the power of prayer and the pain of walking away. She's witnessed family and friends' healing, salvation, and deliverance. There's one holdout, and he's at the top of her prayer list. The love of her life, Randall Addams, won't surrender to the Lord, so Tally ends the relationship. What will it take for Randall to turn to God? Will Tally's prayers be answered, or will Randall—and their love—be lost forever?

Don't underestimate a woman who knows how to pray, has backup, and believes "The Word of God is quick, and powerful, and sharper than any two-edged sword, piercing even to the dividing the soul from the spirit, and of the joints and marrow, and is a discerner of the thoughts and intents of the heart." Hebrews 4:12.

If the devil wants a battle, he picks the wrong woman to fight.

In *Days Are Coming, I'm coming for the children.*

Minister Jude Morgan has a strong relationship with the Lord but doesn't know what the latest message means. He is determined to intercede for his young mentee, Carlton Oliver, and children worldwide.

Nine-year-old Carlton wants to get to know his estranged dad, but at what cost? He's about to discover many things he doesn't know about the man who fathered him, and he's on a mission to worship the Lord.

Sinclaire Oliver regrets getting her ex, Harrison Wakefield, involved in her life and that of his son Carlton. He's more trouble than the monthly child support payments she had to sue for. She knows he's angry but never expects it to take a dark turn. Sinclaire learns that God makes no mistakes, even when things don't make sense.

As God sends His judgment on the earth, the devil plants decoys to distract the saints from their mission to be on guard. Is the world doomed, or is there room for redemption?

In *Day of Salvation*, Mother Kincaid, from Christ Is For All Church, has been fervently praying, along with other prayer warriors around the world, for Jesus to return and rescue His saints from this wicked world.

One day, God answers her with a list of unknown individuals who need salvation and a commission for the intercessors and prayer warriors to find and draw them to Christ. Then He will come to redeem His saints, and judgment will begin on the earth.

The caveat to the Lord God's edict: the timer has been set, and if the intercessors don't witness to them, those people will be lost forever.

God thunders, "Get set, get ready, GO!!!!!"

www.ingramcontent.com/pod-product-compliance
Lightning Source LLC
Chambersburg PA
CBHW060300310726
48976CB00007B/2147